THE BRINK

JAMIE FEWERY

Legend Press Ltd, 51 Gower Street, London, WC1E 6HJ
info@legendpress.co.uk | www.legendpress.co.uk

Contents ©Jamie Fewery 2023
The right of the above author to be identified as the author of this work has
been asserted in accordance with the Copyright, Designs and Patents Act
1988. British Library Cataloguing in Publication Data available.

Print ISBN 9781915643872
Ebook ISBN 9781915643889
Set in Times.
Cover design by Rose Cooper | www.rosecooper.com

Jamie Fewery's first two books – *Our Life In A Day* and *The Way Back* – were published by Orion. He is an author, journalist and copywriter. He has written for the *Daily Telegraph*, *Five Dials* and *Wired*, and works for a London-based marketing and creative agency.

He lives in Berkhamsted, Hertfordshire with his wife and son.

Follow Jamie on Twitter
@jamiefewery

and Instagram
@jamiefeweryauthor

For Alice, Rufus and Wilf

DAY ONE

NOW

The office looked exactly as Dan had thought it might. All glass panels, metal beams and revolving doors swallowing up and spitting out a parade of professional-looking types. Most of them staring at their phones instead of their feet. Inside, people milled around a reception area that was decorated with books no one would ever read, flowers that were ignored rather than enjoyed and stylish chairs that looked far too uncomfortable to sit in.

Melrose and White took up four floors of a seven-storey block on New Fetter Lane. Two serious-looking women sat behind the austere beige stone reception desk, wearing formal black suits that made them look like funereal air stewards. Beside them was a burly bloke in a dark suit and with an earpiece that felt more necessary for a presidential bodyguard than a man checking passes in an office building.

All of them regarded Dan with suspicion as he pushed through the revolving door, looked around for a brief few seconds, then left again like a lost tourist. Perhaps they thought he was up to something. He wasn't; it was simply the supreme discomfort of a man who was just not used to being in their sort of environment.

By virtue of the fact that he couldn't see Anya anywhere, Dan assumed that he was the first to arrive. He'd got there ten minutes early, determined not to be late. Although if you counted the twenty minutes he spent camped out in a branch of Leon around the corner, it was actually half an hour. He went to check his phone, if only for something to do, but couldn't find it inside his left trouser pocket, where it always was. Then he remembered that he was wearing a jacket – tired and slightly damp-smelling from months spent at the back of the wardrobe – and felt inside the breast pocket, finding it sat alongside his credit card and a receipt from the restaurant he'd eaten in the last time the blazer had been displayed to the public.

No messages, of course. He opened a flight simulation app to drain some time and had only just begun taxiing an Airbus A380 towards the runway when he heard a voice call 'Daniel?' from the entrance to the building. He looked up from the plane that was now ready for take-off, and over at a tall, pale woman with short hair, dressed in a pair of tight black trousers, a light blue jacket over a white shirt and small heels. She was carrying an overstuffed black backpack, which seemed incongruous set against the formal outfit.

'Charlotte,' she said cheerfully, waving. 'You are Daniel?'

'Yeah. Sorry. Yeah. Well, Dan.'

'Of course,' Charlotte said, offering her hand. 'I thought it must be,' she continued. 'Think we're the first ones here. I'm just having a coffee. Do you want to come inside? It's free. The coffee, I mean.'

Dan nodded and followed her, immediately worrying that her cheerful disposition, the sunny-side-up attitude, might not be right for this sort of thing. Would she not need a bit more steel and rigour? Too late now, he supposed.

'Urgh. This bloody thing,' Charlotte said, dropping her rucksack before they sat down on the chairs that Dan had been right to think were too uncomfortable to sit in (too low down, too hard, not enough back support). 'Weighs a ton.'

'Paperwork?' Dan said.

'And the rest,' Charlotte said with another laugh. 'I'm

staying for a couple of days. I don't get up here much, so I thought I'd make a weekend of it.'

'Right.'

'The plan is *Aladdin* tonight, Tate Modern Saturday. And the Natural History Museum on Sunday. I want to see the dinosaurs.'

'Sounds fun. Didn't you say you live near Norwich?'

'Ipswich.'

'Of course.'

'Yeah. So, you know, a bit of an event,' she said, unclipping her water bottle from where it was attached by karabiner to her bag. 'We were a bit surprised you asked us, really. Most of our cases are local.'

'Yes. Well… your firm did such a good job with the… the…'

'Conveyancing?'

'Yeah.'

'Well, it's a different division entirely, really. Property's a world away from family. Although, we do meet in the middle, I suppose,' she said. 'Ha!'

'Right. Of course.'

Dan and Charlotte both looked on as a tall man Dan was half sure he knew from the telly sat down opposite them. He could almost sense her need to ask him who he was and where she might recognise him from. And in fairness, he was a little curious himself.

'It's not there, by the way,' Dan said. 'The dinosaur.'

'Sorry?' Charlotte said, wrong-footed.

'The dinosaur. The big one. Dippy or whatever his name is. He's on tour.'

'Oh. Okay. Well maybe I'll do the Science Museum instead…' she said. But Dan had stopped listening, seeing that Anya had arrived in reception and was standing at the desk to sign in.

She looked well, wearing the dark blue jacquard patterned trousers she put on whenever there was a big meeting at work, and a white shirt under the beige trench coat that he'd once compared to Inspector Gadget's. She'd straightened her shoulder-length brown hair and had the fringe trimmed recently so that it sat just above her eyebrows, bringing out her dark eyes. He also noticed the maroon lipstick she'd worn on a thousand date nights and dinners with friends.

Matt – now her solicitor, previously their friend (ish) – was suited, clean-shaven and well-turned-out. Though Dan was pleased to see his belly straining slightly against his white shirt. A sign of his recent drift towards middle-aged comfort and the sale of his racing bicycle.

'That's her,' he said to Charlotte. 'Anya.'

'Well, let's go and say hello then, shall we?' she said, walking over to meet Dan's wife.

* * *

For a second, Anya felt exposed. Matt was signing her in with one of the stern-looking receptionists, and here was Dan's solicitor, marching over with her hand held out to shake while Dan lurked behind, hands in his trouser pockets and staring at the space between his unpolished, scuffed black brogues, dusty with the months they'd spent undisturbed on a shoe rack.

'Matthew Barnaby,' Anya heard, as Matt quickly stepped forward – the first line of defence between her and her husband's legal representative.

Matt shook his opposite number's hand. Then Dan's. It was strange to watch. They had been friends for years. Well, sort of. Things had always been a little fraught between them. Either way, she was sure Matt wouldn't treat Dan like an adversary, as if he was any other divorce case. Dan was Dan. And at that moment, he was standing around and looking for all the world like a teenage boy picking his date up for a secondary school prom – visibly uncomfortable and out of place in his (relatively) formalwear, vaguely threatened by the adults in the room.

It almost made her sad, seeing how hard he had tried to dress for this sort of thing. How he'd missed the mark with the dark blue chino trousers she had only ever seen him put on for funerals or meetings with the bank, along with the least weathered and worn of his checked shirts (yellow, blue and white) and the light grey tweed jacket he'd found in a thrift shop. His hair was messy but short – he'd cut it back since Anya had last seen him. The recent addition of a beard (a similar grey-brown blend) added weight to his thin face.

The last time she and Dan had been together with Matt and his wife Emma was a few months ago, at a barbecue round a mutual friend's house in Balham. Everyone knew that they were 'working through some things'. No one knew that the work was about to stop.

Now, Anya wondered if she'd made the right decision appointing Matt. He was good and reliable and doing it all for mates' rates with a promise of no judgment. And yet here she was, opening the door to the most vulnerable hours of her life and giving him unprecedented access to the interior, domestic details of her marriage, her family and the fractures, cracks and dents across it all.

'Charlotte,' the woman in front of Anya said, pulling her back into the present.

'Anya.'

She tried to smile. But inwardly, she was wondering what kind of person Charlotte was. All that she knew was that Dan had hired her from the same firm that once did their conveyancing. No doubt he had panicked and not known where to turn, then called the only law firm he knew of.

Then Charlotte turned away. And she made eye contact with Dan for the first time that day.

'Hi,' she said.

'Hey,' he replied, timid and hesitant.

'Find it all right?'

'Yeah. Just about.'

Anya smiled and Dan smiled back. There was a *so we're really doing it, are we?* energy about it.

'Right,' Matt said, stepping between them. 'Shall we, then? Lifts are over here. We're on the third floor. Not much of a view from there, I'm afraid. The family division tends to get the cheap seats here.'

The four of them fell into pairs, as if they were walking to a table in a restaurant. But instead of staying beside Dan, as she almost always would have, Anya had Matt next to her. He was her partner for now. Another little Rubicon crossed in a process that seemed to involve constantly crossing thousands of the buggers.

The ride up took around fifteen seconds before the soft voice of the lift announced 'Floor three', and Matt led them down a short corridor to a meeting room called Serenity. Glass-walled, but with blinds pulled down to protect the privacy of those inside.

'And this is us,' Matt said, opening the door to usher them all inside. 'Home for the next couple of days.'

There already was a woman of about forty-five, with a close-cropped afro and big, pink-framed glasses. She was sitting on one of five armchairs arranged around a low glass coffee table that was decorated with a terrarium housing some gravel and a cactus.

The woman stood up and shook hands with Dan and Anya. 'Margot,' she said. 'We spoke on the phone.' But neither of them offered more than a vague, mumbled greeting that roughly approached 'Hi' in return.

* * *

For some reason, Dan had pictured Margot completely differently from their fifteen-minute call the previous week. In his head, she was kind-looking, more maternal, with soft features. Not so severe as she turned out to be. When they shook hands, he noticed bony fingers and a loose, gentle grip.

'Help yourself to drinks,' Matt said, bustling around the room, laying out coasters on the coffee table and adjusting the lights. Dan wondered if it was a power play. Changing the conditions to suit him, like a home team might in a football match. 'Coffee, tea, water. All here,' Matt continued, gesturing to a unit that ran down the side of the room, which housed four glass jars full of those expensive teabags that come in some sort of fancy netting rather than paper, and a Nespresso machine with a choice of four different coloured pods. Dan regretted parting with almost three quid for a flat white not half an hour ago.

'Thanks,' Anya said, arranging her coat over the back of one of the armchairs and settling down as Matt delivered a coffee to her.

'I'll make sure we have some snacks for later. A little pick-me-up for the afternoon. Cakes or something.'

She, Dan and Margot all muttered their gratitude and assent.

'There'll be a mix. We always order too much.'

Dan sat down directly across from Anya, as though they were about to arm-wrestle, not settle the finer details of the rest of their lives. Charlotte was next to him, sipping from a machine-made espresso. And Matt, opposite her, arranging papers and documents in plastic binders.

A moment of silence fell on the room. Just for a second or two before Margot checked her watch, referee-like, and smiled.

'Shall we begin, then?'

THREE MONTHS AGO

Westleton, Suffolk

Anya stared into her wine glass – half-full of a white she'd been working her way through since they sat down an hour ago – as Dan did the same with a red. She picked it up, took a long drink and replaced it on the blue and white patterned ceramic coaster, the last of the set she'd bought back from Seville and had seen periodically chipped, cracked and smashed over the years. Next to it, her phone was face down on the chunky, solid oak dining table, itself decorated with cup rings, food and drink stains and the occasional line of felt-tip pen from when one of the kids had gone off the page with a drawing.

She looked at Dan. In his regular chair at the nominal head of the table, in front of the big, brushed chrome cooker that acted as the centrepiece of the kitchen.

'So we'll do it, then?' he said. 'You know… it.'

'I think so. It seems… I don't know. It seems best, I suppose. For the best, I mean.'

'Yeah,' he said, quietly, then exhaled heavily through his mouth to steady his voice and shaking lower jaw.

Neither of them had been able to say the word yet. Even though they'd both thrown it around liberally during their last few months of arguments, accusations and attributions of blame.

Maybe we should just get a fucking...
If you're not careful, this'll end up in...
I swear we'd be better off if we got a...

But now, with the process green-lit, the project signed off, actually uttering it felt impossible. So much easier to say as a threat or an idea than a confirmed plan. Like grounding a child or starting a war.

'Fuck,' Dan said. 'I never thought.'

'You never do. Do you?' Anya said, trying not to look at the photos they kept on the windowsill that looked out on to the garden. One each of Martha and Edie. One of the four of them against the front door, taken at their house-warming party, a few weeks after they'd swapped their small house in Queen's Park for this much bigger one in Suffolk. And one of their wedding day, just over a decade ago. Anya was wearing a dress she now thought looked dated (too low-cut across the front, no sleeves), he was in a rented suit, under which he wore one of his band T-shirts – The Wedding Present, naturally. Both of them smiling in a way that betrayed a certain confidence about how they'd weather the coming years.

'Suppose not,' Dan said, taking a sip. 'Stupid question. But what happens now, then?'

'I don't know. Can't say I've done it before.'

'No. But, like, what do other people do? What did Carl and Tania do?'

'Lawyers. Court. The lot. It wasn't friendly.'

'Oh yeah,' Dan said, remembering that they were still some way from speaking terms. Two years on from their split and still transferring their kids in dead drops and conducting all conversations through testy WhatsApp conversations. 'Peter and Gemma?'

'It was nicer. Well, she says that anyway. No big day in court arguing every little thing. There was a lot of politics, though.'

'Politics?

'Kids. I mean, it's probably impossible to do it and not fuck them up a bit. I think Barney's in therapy.'

'Seriously? What the fuck can a seven-year-old get out of therapy?'

'Dan,' she said, in that *don't judge someone until you've walked in their shoes* way.

'What about Luke and Nila?' he said.

'Mediation.'

Dan let this one sit for a while. Mediation *sounded* kinder, less stressful than a full-blown, acrimonious courtroom battle of lawyers. In his head, couples who went through mediation were the kind who could still spend Christmas together or meet for coffee, and their new partners wouldn't think it weird.

But was mediation the right path for him and Anya? Or did he just want to think of them as the type of people who did that sort of thing? Well meaning. Ethical. Holistic, whatever that meant. Like part-time vegetarians, oat milk drinkers and hipsters who shop at farmers' markets.

'What do you think about that?'

'Mediation?' Anya said.

'Yeah.'

'Well, it sounds nice. Nic*er*, I mean.'

'I know.'

'Maybe,' she said, not sure if he really meant that he wanted to try mediation, or if he was just saying it because she might like the idea. Which she did, actually. From what Nila said, it was a difficult process, but the steadying force in the room had at least kept her and Luke from hating each other in the end.

True enough, the calm, centred way they were talking now suggested that mediation might work. That they could become the grey-haired couple who, thirty years ago, had traded in their marriage for friendship. But now wasn't representative of who they had been over the last few months, with all the irretrievable insults thrown back and forth, along with a few plates.

Was it common for mediating couples to have spent an evening feeling wretchedly guilty after their kids had presented them with a piece of paper reading *please stop fighting* – decorated with a crayon-drawn sun, moon, family portrait and a dog they had never owned?

Did mediating couples have text message arguments that lasted upwards of three days because they couldn't stand verbal communication with each other?

Did mediating couples surreptitiously record conversations on their phones, just in case evidence might be needed during a subsequent row?

The theoretical appeal of mediation aside, Anya couldn't escape the sense that she and Dan were too far gone for all that. The wounds could be stitched up, but the scars would always be too painful to ignore.

'We don't have to decide now,' she said, draining her wine glass and refilling it, enjoying this moment of calm acceptance so much that it felt worth extending.

'No. Of course,' Dan said, leaning back in his chair so that his belly just protruded from the tight grey T-shirt he was wearing beneath a tatty old cardigan he'd bought five years ago in order that it could become a tatty old cardigan. 'But, like, what do we do now?' he said, refilling his glass. 'Now that it's, like, decided, I mean.'

'You mean telling people?'

'Yeah.'

'Well, I thought a Facebook announcement.'

Dan laughed. '"It's complicated",' he said, miming the scare quotes with his fingers.

The laughter died quickly, both of them acutely aware that tomorrow would bring some of the worst and hardest conversations they would ever have.

'I suppose the kids first,' Dan said.

'Of course. Then families.'

'How do you think they'll take it?'

'Who?'

'All of them, I suppose.'

'God,' Anya said, struggling to envisage the conversations she would have with Martha and Edie, then her mum and dad. Her mum would inevitably be angry and defensive, her dad understanding and kind.

'Kids confused. Parents cross. What about your nan?'

'Don't know. I doubt she'll be all that surprised. I didn't have the best example, did I?'

'Come on,' she said. 'You can't blame that.'

'I'm not,' Dan said. She was right. The fact that he didn't come from a nuclear family was no excuse for the fact that he'd blown up his own.

'What about friends?' Anya asked. 'I was thinking not right away.'

'No. Maybe tell a couple. Then let word, like, get around,' he said. That was how these things worked, wasn't it? Bad news was pinged from one friendship pod to another via shared connections and gossipmongers who 'really ought to tell' other people.

'Sure,' Anya said, envisaging the well-wishing, commiserating texts and calls she'd get.

Then came the silence again, both of them sipping at their wine, looking at the flagstone floor, the big butler sink, the wooden kitchen cupboards. All those things that had enticed them into buying the house less than a year ago. Part of a new start that turned out to be more of a last hurrah.

The way they were sat together reminded Dan of evenings they might spend playing cards or Scrabble. Occasionally chatting, mostly quiet but comfortable with it. This evening had a very different tenor to it. They were resigned rather than satisfied. Defeated rather than easy. But then at least it was peaceful. For a second, he even wondered if they were doing the right thing – was this a reminder that they *could* talk and laugh and be normal?

Or was it that the pressure had been relieved?

The admission that all had gone wrong – that the marriage was finally over – was a leveller. There was no need for each of them to bring out their worst selves to prove the other wrong.

Three hours ago, it had all been very different. They had been arguing, storming out of rooms and storming back in again to finish a point or win a round. The volume of their voices rising and falling as they struggled to suppress shouts and swear words for the sake of the kids.

That was a more accurate reflection of their marriage now than this gentle conversation about how to go forward, for all Dan wanted to think better of the two of them.

Anya had finished her drink and was not reaching to pour another.

'I think I'll go up,' she said, pushing her chair back and away from the table. He noticed that the big, oversized jumper she was wearing over her yoga gear was his, and wondered if she'd keep it when it was all done. 'You don't mind, do you?'

'No. I'll be a while,' he said. 'I'll try not to make too much noise coming up.'

'You can have the bedroom tonight,' she offered. 'If you want. I know the spare room's a bit uncomfortable,' she said, referring to the single bed, the half-decorated room, the boxes they were still yet to sort through and now likely never would.

'It's fine,' Dan said, with a kind smile.

'Night,' Anya said.

'Night.'

She climbed the stairs, corduroy slippers against the dark red patterned threadbare carpet that reminded her of a pub.

When she got to the top, Anya turned left, to the master

bedroom, which hadn't been theirs for five weeks now. Dan would turn right, to the spare room they'd told the kids he was sleeping in because of his back. And as she closed the door of the room, Anya sighed and began to cry. Downstairs, Dan did the same.

NOW

'Okay,' Margot began. 'I've spoken to you both individually. But I like to start these sessions with a little reminder of why we're here.' She handed both of them a stack of A4 pages, stapled together in the top corner.

On the front, it read *The Kinder Separation: a methodology from Margot Larkin*. Anya had read it already when Margot had sent it over email after their call. Mostly, it seemed to be well meaning but vague philosophies about why families disband and how to do it, along with a less vague sales pitch for her book about couples therapy, sex and divorce.

'Mediation is a way of ending the period of your life together that's defined by your marriage,' she said, clasping her hands together. 'And beginning another period as two distinct, but connected, people.' Her hands fell apart. 'Here, we put people at the centre, and kindness... at the core,' she concluded with a sort of satisfied smile, somehow placing more emphasis on her pauses than her words.

'Great,' Dan said under his breath. 'That... that sounds great.'

'Now. You both have decided to have a legally supported mediation,' she said, with what Dan thought was a disapproving look at Charlotte and Matt. 'This means that your representatives will have a full understanding of everything we discuss here. But it does also mean that there are extra people in the room. And, if I may, I would ask that you place your focus on each other as much as is possible.'

They both muttered, 'Sure,' as though they were at a briefing for a parachute jump and were slightly too anxious to listen to the instructions.

'As you know, my method is a blend of counselling and mediation. So in the course of our time together today and tomorrow, we'll cover the emotional side of your relationship and the physical. We'll go through how you want to manage your family and shared property when you separate. And how your relationship – your *partnership* – should look when you're on the other side of this river we must cross together.'

Margot smiled. Dan and Anya returned the gesture. Charlotte and Matt's gazes were fixed to the papers they had on their laps.

'Mediation is not about blame. Or scoring points off of one another for the things you each believe that the other did wrong. We'll explore the past. But our focus is on the future only, and ensuring that we come to an understanding that is mutual, kind and created by you, not enforced on you. As we proceed, you will see me filling out some documents and taking notes. These will become the Minutes of Agreement and relevant forms your solicitors and I must lodge at court to obtain your decree nisi. There will also be a memorandum of understanding that stipulates the background to your separation. You will, of course, be given the opportunity to review all of these. Now, does anybody have any questions?'

Anya shook her head. Dan said 'No' but only because the questions he did have would show everyone that he hadn't read any of the material Margot had sent before the session and was really flying a bit blind.

'Just a few preliminaries first. Now, Dan, you are Daniel Peter Moorcroft. Thirty-nine years old. Living in Suffolk. And you are a...' She paused. 'It says here: repair man.'

'Sort of. I repair instruments. Guitars, mainly.'

'Lovely. And Anya Siobhan Moorcroft, maiden name

O'Hanrahan. Forty. Also living in Suffolk. And you are a writer,' Margot said with a little inflexion that revealed her interest in Anya's job.

'Yes,' she said. 'Kids' telly, mainly. But other bits, too.'

'Oh right,' Margot said, now a little flat. Perhaps she had been hoping for an author or a journalist. Either way, she'd obviously not googled the two of them extensively enough to find the long IMDb page for Anya O'Hanrahan's work. 'Anything I might've heard of?'

'A few things. I wrote—' Anya began, then suddenly stopped. Dan knew that she was about to say his name. But she couldn't bring Kelvin up this early in proceedings. '*Snugglebugs*,' Anya continued hurriedly. 'And a couple of episodes of *Postman Pat*.'

'Hmm.' Margot smiled. 'And you both still live in, what we'll call for the purposes of today, the family home.'

'Well,' Dan said. 'Officially, yes. But I've not been there for a while now.'

'Oh?'

'No. We have another place. In London. The tenants moved out and we were looking for new ones. So I thought I might... you know.'

Margot's look suggested she didn't.

'Give them some space. Anya, I mean.'

Margot didn't reply. Instead, she scribbled something down in her notebook.

'That's okay, isn't it?' Dan said, now a little panicked and wondering what this might mean for the rest of the day. Charlotte knew, didn't she? Dan was sure he'd told her.

'Of course,' Margot said, without looking up. 'It's good to know these things.' She closed the notebook with her pen inside it, keeping her place. Then removed her pink glasses and fixed both of them in her gaze. 'Now, to begin, I'd like you to both talk about how we arrived here. What caused what I'm sure was a strong, loving marriage to come to its end.'

Everyone, it seemed, shifted in their seat. Except for

Margot, of course. This sort of thing was a more mundane part of her day. Anya wondered if the two of them would be able to say or do anything to shock her, when Dan spoke up.

'Well it was the tumble dryer thing, wasn't it?' he said, looking directly at her.

'Sorry?' Anya said, confused. As if Dan had chosen to open a play with a bit of ad-libbing.

'That was it, wasn't it?' he continued. 'The last argument we had before we decided to do… this.' He looked over at Margot. 'It was one of those silly things. I'd put a jumper in the dryer. Turned out to be cashmere. We had a row about it and it just sort of snowballed, really. One minute we're bickering about me not paying enough attention. The next minute we're bringing up every mistake either of us has ever made. Then we're at the kitchen table talking about getting a divorce.'

'Dan, I'm not sure—'

'Thank you, Dan,' Margot said, gently cutting Anya off. 'It's good to know… that. But what I am really looking for is for you to both explain how the marriage came to be here – what went wrong, I mean. Not the last argument you had before you chose to seek an alternative life situation. Although I understand that's important, too.'

'Oh,' Dan said, feeling as he had done several times in school classrooms. 'Sorry, I thought that…'

'You'd be surprised how often it happens,' Margot said, kind but clearly lying.

'Right, I'll go, shall I?' Anya said nervously.

'I can,' Dan said. 'If you want?'

'No. No, it's fine. Well, I suppose it was the… well,' she said, with another regretful look at Margot. 'The infidelity, really. Our… infidelity.'

As soon as she said it, Anya was aware of how infrequently she used the word. Usually, she went with 'cheating'. She had cheated. He had cheated. They had cheated, were cheaters, cheating on each other.

'And I know,' Anya continued, 'that it's a symptom. People do it because they're unhappy in other ways. But I think, and I don't know, Dan, if you agree with this. I think that if it was just the problems that made us unhappy, then maybe we could've worked it out. It was the... cheating,' she said, relaxing back into the more familiar, colloquial term. 'We just couldn't recover from it.'

'Dan?' Margot said, like the host on a panel discussion.

'Yeah,' he said quietly. 'Yeah, that's true.'

'Okay. So let's start there, then. With the physical side of your relationship and how that contributed to the breakdown of your marriage.'

Dan and Anya looked at each other, both unsure if they had really signed up for talking about this stuff in front of three people they'd really rather keep it well apart from.

'Anya,' Margot said. 'Could I ask you to continue?'

SEX

FIFTEEN MONTHS AGO

Queen's Park, London

Dan was midway through a service job when his phone buzzed.

> *George: Hello mate. Long time and all that. Look,
> not my business to pry. But is everything all right
> with you and Anya?*

> *Dan: Yeah fine. Why do you ask?*

And instead of replying, George picked up the phone and called him.

'Hello?' Dan said, putting his tools down on his workbench and wedging his phone between his ear and shoulder as he cleaned his hands on an old T-shirt he used as a rag.

'You all right?'

'Not bad. What's up with the cryptic message?'

'Look. I wasn't sure whether to even send you it. I feel like a fucking private detective or something,' he said. George was, in fact, a partner at an advertising agency, the same one he'd joined as a graduate when he and Dan moved into a drafty, permanently unclean flat in Crouch End almost fifteen years ago. They were close friends. But of the type who saw one another maybe twice or three times a year.

'What is it?'

'Fuck,' he said, audibly pained. 'Right, I might be wrong. But I saw Anya earlier. She didn't see me. And she was with someone.'

'Oh. Yeah… fuck,' Dan said. His stomach had lurched at the word *someone*, but he tried to disguise any discomfort. 'Someone?'

'Yeah. Someone. As I say, I don't know what I saw properly. But they looked close. That's all I'm saying.'

Suddenly, signs were everywhere in retrospect. Making sure her phone was screen down against the couch. Adding a passcode lock to it for the first time ever. She had been staying away from home more, too. Attending shoots all over the place and meetings in Manchester, where it made more sense to stay over than to come home on one of the late trains that just about connected the two cities.

She'd actually seemed a bit happier recently. Dan had mistakenly put that down to things improving a little between the two of them. Fewer arguments, one or two date nights, less irritability on both sides. Their marriage repairing itself.

'Did you recognise him?' Dan said.

'Well, I thought I did. But it couldn't have been.'

'Who?'

'The bloke from the telly. The kids watch him. Irritating fucker. Captain something-or-other.'

Kelvin, Dan thought.

That made sense, too. They worked together a lot. Travelled together. And they got on well enough. Too well, it seemed.

'Jesus,' Dan said, dreading having to say his stage name out loud. Confirming it was happening. 'Captain Funtastic?'

'That's him. But surely not?'

'They work together.'

'Shit, mate,' George said after a moment. 'I'm sorry. I didn't want to be the one to… you know.'

'It's fine, mate.'

'As I said, I didn't see them clearly. But…'

The line went quiet.

'Beer soon?' George said, suddenly quite chipper. Like he had called to chat about football results or arrange their annual camping trip.

'Sure,' Dan said. 'I'll let you know when I'm next down.'

There was a brief, uncomfortable silence before they said their goodbyes. This had never meant to be part of their friendship – not in the deal. Dan sat down on the wooden chair he kept in his workshop shed.

Captain Funtastic.

Anya was having an affair with Captain Funtastic.

He googled the name and was presented with a selection of photos and the Wikipedia page for the overly cheerful, lanky, tousle-haired kids' television presenter whom she had been working with on and off for the past eight or nine years – her biggest career gig so far. She'd started as a writer on his show, proving her worth over the first couple of years before becoming an executive producer.

At the same time, Dan's own work as the owner of a guitar shop in Crouch End was winding down, and gradually they had swapped household roles – her working away and spending nights at her desk, him doing school runs and working from home fixing instruments to sell online. He barely left the house, she spent more and more time with a man who was, he knew, funny and charismatic as well as able to do a pretty decent pratfall.

Captain Funtastic, though.

The man Dan's kids watched endless YouTube highlights reels of, as he went round farms, zoos and parks, making some blend of education and slapstick, and who was a seemingly irremovable part of children's television. Who had been to their house, come to parties and met their friends. Whose real name was Kelvin Fisher, and who lived in an absurdly nice town house in Hampstead except during panto season when he'd be the star turn at some rep theatre in places like Aylesbury, Dudley and King's Lynn for a few weeks. (Which at least explained why Anya had an unavoidable work trip to Lincoln in her diary.)

As he scrolled through photos of Kelvin feeding sea lions, juggling and going down a slide in a play park, Dan thought about Anya's movements over the past few months and if the affair might have been the motivating factor behind them. Were those nights away spent with him in hotel rooms after shoot days? Anya in lingerie. Kelvin having just removed the make-up and polka dot jumpsuit his character sported.

And the truth was that almost every time she was away, Kelvin would've been there.

The thing was that Dan had always considered children's television presenters to be kind of sexless. So, while he knew that Anya was close to Kelvin, the thought that it might become anything more had never crossed his mind. Jesus, he couldn't for the life of him imagine the *Blue Peter* and *Newsround* presenters he had watched growing up having private lives full of sex and booze and whatever else everyone else did. They were celibate, surely? Or, at the very most, strictly missionary position; sex to procreate.

It was a surprise to find a raft of Mumsnet forums dedicated to how attractive Kelvin was. And to read the deeply speculative and woefully under-informed articles in the tabloids about his private life.

Dan left his shed for their small kitchen, half-painted and with the floor unfinished after he had started a job he couldn't find the time or will to finish. He checked the green blinking digital clock above the oven (2:56) and took a beer from the fridge.

He wasn't in the habit of mid-afternoon drinking. But it might steady his nerves before Anya got back from dropping the girls at their respective after-school football and gymnastics clubs.

There was a decision to make.

Either confront her when she got in, knowing that one or the other of them might have to leave a fairly pivotal conversation about the future of their marriage to pick up the girls forty-five minutes later.

Or wait. Until the evening. When Edie and Martha would be asleep and they could go talk it out properly.

But that meant going through all those family things they did and pretending nothing was wrong. Listening to the girls' stories about their days and all the minor achievements, injustices and score settling life involves when you're eight or six. Then dinner together as a family and their prolonged, argumentative bedtime routine.

Confronting her felt too urgent, Dan thought, as he tipped the bottle of Moretti down his throat. But waiting required the kind of patience and ability to compartmentalise that he simply didn't have.

* * *

Around an hour later, Anya bustled into the small hallway. She was carrying two rucksacks, two book bags, a recently completed painting and a violin – in addition to her own handbag and a canvas tote in which a cake tin rattled against her lunch box.

'Give me some help with all this crap, would you?' she called out, not bothering to check if Dan was home because Dan was always home.

She was lowering the violin to the floor, trying to be careful not to knock any of the pasta shapes off Edie's painting, when he appeared in his tatty jeans, flip-flops and a white T-shirt on which the logo of a band she'd never heard of was just about visible.

'You're drinking?' she said, surprised to see him holding a beer bottle by its neck. And not aware that it was his third of the afternoon.

'Just one,' Dan said, taking the painting and one of the book bags, then moving the violin so that she could make it through the hallway to the coat rack.

'Dan.'

'What?'

'We said. If you were going to work from home, you couldn't just do this sort of thing. You still have to have some sort of structure.'

'Tough day,' was all he said, turning away from her, walking past the stairs and towards the kitchen.

Anya was tempted to ask how. It would be mean, she knew. But she often found it difficult to understand what could make a day fixing nice guitars or checking the reader statistics on his blog tough.

She hung up her duffel coat and followed him through to the kitchen, where he was now sat at their little drop-leaf table, slouched with the beer in front of him. Anya opened the cupboard where they kept the kids' snacks, unlocked the box where they kept the weekend-only treats and pulled out a Wagon Wheel.

'Want one?'

'Not for me,' he said sullenly. Then, 'Actually, no, yes. I will.'

She frisbeed one over to the table, where it slid towards him like an air hockey puck. Knowing that he desperately wanted her to, she asked, 'So what happened, then? Work thing?'

'No. Work's fine.'

'Right.'

He looked miserable. But Anya was struggling to figure out what else might have caused him some anguish.

Family? Probably not – and if someone had died, he wouldn't be playing this silly game of *guess why I'm upset*. Money maybe? But then she'd probably know, unless he'd been keeping something from her, like a whopping great credit card bill or that he'd remortgaged the house without her knowing.

Maybe it was something more trivial? Or trivial to her at least. He'd spilled Vimto on one of his precious band T-shirts, or Newcastle United had sold one of his favourite players.

'Are you going to tell me, then? Or do I have to guess?' she said.

'I spoke to George today.'

Shit, Anya thought. *George is ill*. Cancer maybe. They were men of that age now. When things start going a bit wrong here and there. And George had never been the healthiest. Big drinker. Still smoking.

'Oh?'

'Said he saw you the other day.'

'Where's that, then? I don't think I saw him.'

'Soho,' Dan said, sipping from the beer bottle. 'You and Kelvin.'

And right away, it all made sense. His sullen tone and dourness, the mid-afternoon beer.

They'd been spotted.

She had been worried that they were getting a bit lax recently. Too many affectionate touches in public. The occasional kiss or a few metres walked hand in hand. It was especially stupid to do it in London, where they were most likely to be found out.

And so it had been.

'Right,' Anya said. 'I see.'

NOW

'And could you tell me what happened then?' Margot said. Matt was on the edge of his seat; it was almost as if he was enjoying the behind-the-curtain elements of his friends' marriage being played for the court.

'I came clean,' Anya said, unsure if that was the right term for it. Coming clean was what criminals did. Not unfaithful spouses. Particularly when that lack of faith was at least in part understandable. She was already tired of talking about this chapter of her marriage, even if it was strictly very much outside of that marriage. And although she was desperate to avoid having to go over it again, she knew that she'd have to. They'd employed Margot for this sort of blister popping.

'Tell me about the conversation.'

'I said it was true. That it was me and… Kelvin. That we'd been together.'

'How—'

'A year. Well, almost a year. Sorry, but don't you already know this? It's in the stuff I sent you.'

'I do. But the process is—'

'Yes, sorry,' Anya said. It was less than half an hour into the first day, and already she regretted hiring Margot. 'The process. We were colleagues. Then friends. Then it just sort of happened, I suppose. Kelvin and his wife had split up the year before. Things weren't brilliant between me and Dan. We were away on a shoot one night.'

'Where?' Margot interjected.

Everyone around the table looked a little surprised at this. Process aside, it just felt like nosiness rather than legitimate professional interest.

'Belfast. We'd been filming at the Giant's Causeway and were flying home the next morning. The crew went out for dinner. Usually, the young ones stay out a bit, go to a few bars. But I was in a bit of a fuck-it mood, so I went, too,' Anya said. 'So did Kelvin.'

Immediately, Anya was out of the office in Holborn and back in the bars and pubs of Belfast on that Saturday night. She remembered feeling like a different, younger version of herself, abandoning her choosiness about white wines to take whatever was on offer and getting involved with the rounds of tequilas. She had tied a rope around the knowledge that tomorrow would bring a hangover, a flight and childcare, then attached it to a stone and dropped it to the bottom of the ocean.

She and Kelvin had stuck together throughout the early part of the evening, then surprised the assistants and runners by staying on for the next drink, the next bar and the noisy, pounding club at the end, where Anya couldn't believe a room could be so bright and so dark at once.

She recalled the slightly juvenile thrill of people recognising Kelvin. Though she denied it, proximity to fame always excited her. Even if Kelvin was primarily noticed either by hen party mums who couldn't quite believe that they were in the same bar as Captain Funtastic, or by pissed-up blokes who sang his old theme song at him like it was a football chant. Anya had written the lyrics to 'Cheerful, Golly, Jolly, Whoosh!' and was delighted that so many people seemed to have it engrained in their memory.

Anya was drunk when the first proper move was made. But she remembered it so clearly that either her brain had battled through the Sauvignon and shots to store it, or she'd made it up afterwards. She and Kelvin had distanced themselves from the group and were dancing close together when he moved towards her. And from the first kiss, the path seemed clear: taxi back, his hotel room and drunk, clumsy sex.

'What about the next morning?' Margot asked. Anya was trying not to look at anyone, but could see Charlotte taking notes, backup for if things got messy and the legal representatives had to step up from their somewhat administrative role so far.

'I felt anxious,' Anya said. 'I was a bit hung-over and I'm one of those people who worries about what she's done when she's pissed. Even though I sort of knew. So yeah, anxious,' she said.

She could see Dan was waiting for the next bit. He'd heard it before in the talk in their Queen's Park kitchen after George had seen her with Kelvin. Then again when they briefly, ill-advisedly tried marriage therapy. How she had looked over and seen Kelvin there in bed. That they had gone for breakfast together. She suspected that, in Dan's mind, whatever had happened over eggs and coffee was how it went from sex to affair, mistake to plan.

'But I didn't feel guilty that I'd cheated on him,' she said.

'And that's because Dan had himself strayed from the marriage?'

'Yeah,' Anya agreed. 'I know it shouldn't feel like it. But to me, it was one–all.'

TWO YEARS AND NINE MONTHS AGO

Stoke Newington, London

As soon as they had finished, Dan knew that it would be the last time. Really, it should've been the last time the first time.

Eleanor was lying next to him on the bed, the duvet covering up to her belly. She rolled to her right to check her phone, conscious of the time and probably worried about the terrifying sound of her husband or daughter's key in the latch, followed by all the explaining that would entail.

But he stayed flat on his back, looking up at the ceiling and the large, elaborate decorative lampshade around the light he recognised from the IKEA catalogue.

This, Dan thought, was one of the uncanny things about it all. The room. He honestly couldn't remember the last time he'd had sex anywhere besides his own bedroom or occasionally a hotel, if the kids weren't staying with them.

It felt unfamiliar, but also not. Bedrooms were all pretty consistent in their own way. A mix of comfort, storage and little piles of mess that had sort of become furniture – stacks of books, jackets and shirts draped over a chair no one would ever sit in, that sort of thing. The noticeable, uncomfortable difference was in the particulars: the unfamiliar mattress, lumpy in places and slightly too soft for his liking, the patterned wallpaper on the opposite side of the room to the bed, the lack of glasses and mugs sitting around from two or three nights ago.

'That was good,' Eleanor said, rolling over to rest her cheek on his shoulder. Never had such a slight, affectionate gesture felt so incredibly awful and unwelcome.

'Yeah,' Dan said.

He felt her shoulder-length light-brown hair fall across his chest.

'I could stay like this all day.'

'Yeah,' Dan repeated, inwardly questioning what Eleanor thought this thing between them was. Was she thinking it might develop into something more? That they would both leave their respective partners to begin again together? Or that they would simply carry on for a bit longer?

They'd never really set out the terms and conditions at the start of their irregular tryst. So, neither could say for sure whether it was fun but generally meaningless sex, a problematic but essentially doomed affair, or something more serious that would eventually end in mutual acrimony and alimony.

It hadn't been spontaneous, with both of them struck off the course of fidelity by unavoidable, disarming passion. Instead, the beginning had been relatively benign. Eleanor's husband Dev was one of Dan's regular customers. A well-to-do financier born in Solihull to Pakistani parents, who had, over the years, developed a fairly serious and extensive collection of vintage guitars that Dan serviced, repaired and restored. A few months ago, Dev asked Dan to fix up an old acoustic for his wife, and put the two of them in touch.

Dan realised he fancied Eleanor on first meeting. She was short, with bright, clear skin, a small frame and sort of deliberately messy hair. She dressed in striped T-shirts, white trainers and oversized coats.

But his attraction to Eleanor was a low-level thing. In his head, it would never amount to anything and was as much driven by lifestyle as looks. In the way he occasionally found himself fancying a food writer for her Instagram page, or a journalist because she wore cool jumpsuits and had nice garden furniture. Attraction that never even got as far as lust or the vaguest sexual interest. More a 'wouldn't it be nice' than a 'would like to meet'.

But one day, shortly after Dan had dropped off her guitar, he got a WhatsApp message from Eleanor.

What do you think to this? xx

In hindsight, the two kisses were a giveaway. Although at the time, the more obvious tell was the picture of her in front of a mirror, wearing shorts and a bikini top, holding the guitar on her lap.

Hope it plays well? x Dan had replied, agonising over the number of *x*'s to sign off with for a good few minutes.

It's great. But maybe you could show me one day... xxx

From there, the flirting escalated for a bit before Eleanor asked Dan over to *have a look at the guitar.*

That all? xx

Depends... xxx

Are we really going to? xx

Depends xxx

And they did. In her bedroom at eleven in the morning, when Dan would normally be having a cup of tea and two custard creams in a self-bestowed break from work. And while their combined five children were at school, two partners were at work, and a late spring London rain lightly pattered against the window that overlooked Eleanor's garden.

And now, three weeks after that first time, they were here again.

'I'd better be off soon,' Dan said, looking at his watch. 'I've got someone dropping off their amp at two.' It was a lie. But good enough to get him out of the bed and dressed.

'Sure,' Eleanor said, as he hurriedly pulled jeans on and found his creased Guided by Voices T-shirt underneath her bed. 'What are you doing next week? Tuesday, I thought.'

'Oh. God, I don't know. Work probably. Got a busy couple of weeks coming up.'

'Well, let me know. Dav's in Amsterdam for a few days. Thought we could even leave the house or something. Get a drink somewhere.'

'Right,' Dan said. 'Yeah… I mean… well.'

'No pressure,' she said, sitting up in bed, pulling the duvet with her.

'Sure. It's just… no.'

'No?'

'Yeah. No,' Dan said, wondering whether he'd removed his shoes when he came into the house or if they were somewhere in the bedroom. 'Look. I can't do this again. I'm sorry. It was—'

'Don't say it was a mistake.'

'It wasn't. No. Sorry. All I'm saying is that I can't now. I just… can't.'

He had been avoiding eye contact with Eleanor. But when he looked up, she didn't seem cross or even upset. More put out.

'Nice of you to say that *after*.'

'Sorry. I thought… I don't know what I thought.'

'It's fine.'

'Is it?' he said hopefully.

'No. But I'm not going to sit here trying to change your fucking mind, am I?'

'Right. And…'

'I'm not going to tell Dav, either. If that's what you're worried about. Fuck, Dan. You'll be stunned to hear it, but our marriage isn't exactly like a rock. This wouldn't be the first time for either of us.'

'Okay.'

Dan stood there for a minute longer. He felt like he'd been thrown back decades to the awkward break-ups of his teens and early twenties, ending relationships that, of course, had no prospect of longevity but were still a bastard to call time on.

'I'd better…'

'You don't mind if I don't show you out?'

'Sorry,' he said.

'Nothing to apologise for,' Eleanor said, and he turned and left.

* * *

Dan was barely out of Eleanor's house and cycling back to Queen's Park when he made up his mind to tell Anya. He'd read hundreds of articles about infidelity during the weeks that he and Eleanor had been texting often and meeting occasionally. Some justifying it, no doubt by writers who had found themselves in his position. Others decrying it as weakness or selfishness. All, however, landed on the same conclusion: that progression and healing started with full, terrible honesty.

But it would take another week of reading, self-critiquing and prevaricating before he found himself compelled to actually take that step.

* * *

'I slept with someone.'

Anya had known it was coming. Dan had sat her down at the kitchen table five minutes ago, pouring them each a glass of wine. She knew then it would be bad news of some sort. The only question was how bad.

Nonetheless, the words winded her. Before she could react, the thought of it was there, a mental image more fully realised than any dream she'd ever had. Dan and another woman, naked. The fumbling and foreplay. Him experiencing that half-joyous, half-disconcerting feeling of discovering someone's body for the first time.

'Right,' she said, biting her top lip with her bottom front teeth. 'Shit.'

'I'm sorry.'

'Who?'

'You mean—'

'Yes, I mean who did you fuck?'

He paused for a second, before meekly saying, 'Eleanor.'

Anya went through a mental Rolodex looking for the name. But an Eleanor didn't exist in their lives.

'A customer,' he clarified, perhaps noting the confusion on her face.

'You're not serious?'

'Well. I suppose her husband is actually the customer. But—'

'You barely even have a business. But still manage to have an affair with one of the customers,' she said. Dan didn't respond, taking the blow on the chin.

They both took a drink, steadying nerves for round two: the context behind the infidelity.

'I knew there was something,' she said.

'Really?'

She bit her lip again, harder this time. She could sense that she might cry and willed herself to hold it back.

'You can be a bit obvious, Dan.'

'Sorry,' he said again.

'For which bit? That you did it or that I knew?'

'Both, I suppose.'

Dan wouldn't look at her. She could imagine how much this had been eating him up. The hours he'd have spent afterwards going back and forth over whether to tell her. Deciding then he'd have to, before more agony about where, when and what they'd do with the kids for a couple of hours while he threw it all out into the open under the kitchen lights.

It was why he'd picked a Wednesday, when her mum and

dad came into London to pick up Martha and Edie from school and take them for dinner.

'When?' she asked.

'The first time was weeks ago. Then—'

'More than once, then?'

He nodded.

'The last?'

He said nothing.

'*The last, Dan.*'

'A week ago. Six days.'

They both sipped at their wine. Anya looked at the small faux-vintage clock on the wall. It was half four. Her parents would drop the girls back at six, after they'd eaten dinner. She felt remarkably sanguine about it, surprising herself. Wasn't she meant to be screaming and throwing his most breakable stuff at the wall?

'Dan, are you trying to tell me that you're having an affair or that you fucked someone? Because I'd really like to know.'

'It was three times,' he said.

'Where?' she asked the second he'd finished answering.

'Her house. Never here. She's never been here.'

He said it with confidence, but Anya didn't know if she could believe him. Maybe she would burn the bedsheets anyway, to be on the safe side.

The whole thing just felt so awful. For weeks Dan had been behaving strangely, but not distant- or cold- or angry-strangely. Instead, he had been over-attentive, faultlessly kind and always willing to be the first to back down in any argument, no matter how big or small.

It only added to the heartbreak that it had to be infidelity to bring that side of him out.

It was odd, though. Whenever he vaguely fancied someone he'd met through work or friends, he would drop her name and anecdotes about her into conversation, no matter how banal they were. As if he was confirming that Anya could still be annoyed or jealous, despite their years together. With Eleanor, there had been nothing. Though… a few weeks ago, there had been some vaguely disparaging comments about a house after he'd delivered the guitar back ('ostentatious', 'showy', 'too big if anything'). Maybe that was hers?

She should've known then, really.

But Dan wasn't a philanderer or an adulterer. Like her, his mind probably wandered, subject to those not wholly unpleasant daydreams of who might come along next should their marriage go belly-up.

So what, Anya wondered, had made this one the exception? The time he didn't stop at a brief flirtation, but carried on to exchanging numbers, text messages and actually meeting up. All those things that preceded sex (she knew enough about Dan to be sure that the process hadn't been instant attraction to undressing). He had all those milestones to stop and realise that he was getting into trouble. But he had carried on, a driver passing the last petrol station.

'Was it good?' Anya said, thinking maybe he'd fallen for some overwhelming, base attraction. The kind the two of them had when they met and that he might be justifiably missing after almost thirteen years.

'Fucking hell, Anya.'

'Dan.'

'Really?'

'Was it good?' she asked again, asserting the question a little more.

'Do you really want to?'

'Yes. I want to hear it from you.'

'Fine,' he said, relenting. 'It was, well… it…'

'Dan, you can say it was good. It was sex. Sex is good. Fuck, if it wasn't good, why'd you go back again?'

'Okay! Fine,' he said, looking away from her. 'It was good.'

'Fucking hell,' she said, pained.

'What? You told me to say it.'

'But hearing you say it.'

'I'm sorry,' Dan said.

* * *

Dan could handle making Anya angry. Knowing that she was so badly hurt and that he was the cause of it made him feel sick.

It was strange that he had felt almost justified in sleeping with Eleanor when it happened. At no point had he felt compelled to do it by some fierce, burning passion. Instead it was that Eleanor fancied him, and his sex life with Anya had been put into a coma by too many nights apart, running around after two kids, and a general jogging-bottoms-in-front-of-the-TV lethargy. Besides, it happened all the time. Couples cheated. It didn't always cause irreparable harm. Or so said the search results about the ethics and morality of infidelity.

'It was different, too,' he said after a moment.

'Well, I should fucking hope so.'

'Sorry. I—'

'Different how?'

'I don't know. I can't put these things into words. Just… different.'

'Well, it's good to know you can readily exchange me for any old bit of stuff that turns up on the doorstep.'

'No. Look, you know it's not like that. You're you.'

'Right,' Anya said. She seemed determined to string this out, to coerce the words out of him, no matter how much he mismatched and mangled them. It felt a little cruel but was probably fair.

'All I mean is, like, sex is sex, isn't it?' Dan said, aware on looking up at Anya that he was on the wrong path, but nonetheless had to get to the end of it. 'It's hard to look back and say what exactly was different. Like, specifically.'

'You're making it sound like you were buying a new pair of slippers.'

'Anya.'

'"Broadly the same, but these were just a bit more firm underfoot."'

She always put on a slightly nasal voice when she mimicked him.

'That's not what I mean. You know that's not what I mean.'

'How did it happen?' she shot back, with a look up at the clock to see how long they had before the girls got back and they had to put on a show of being normal, contented and in love. Rather than fractured, unhappy and hopefully still in love. Whatever it was, they'd need fifteen minutes to make the transition back to the people Martha and Edie believed them to be. 'Well, then?' she prompted when Dan didn't reply.

'I went over to drop off the guitar. We got talking and… I don't know, it sort of happened.'

'Right. And that was it? She went from customer to the other woman in the time it took for you to drop off a guitar?'

'No. Look… I mean. We texted a bit. Just the odd message back and forth since she first came round.'

'Flirting,' Anya said.

'No.'

'Dan. You shagged her three times. If there wasn't any flirting beforehand, you're a fucking miracle worker.'

'Fine. Yes, then. Probably a bit flirty. Then, I don't know, we had a coffee. We kissed. And it happened,' he said, remembering the drinks they'd had in her garden, the way they'd moved gradually closer together over the course of an hour, her hand on his thigh, and how she had leaned over to kiss him, and he'd sat up a little to meet her lips. He remembered the stale coffee on her breath. The way her mouth and tongue felt so different. The force with which she kissed – just that little bit harder than Anya.

Dan remembered the last words either of them spoke before it happened.

'Is this all right?' Eleanor said to him. Clarifying that he was broadly okay with corrupting his marriage, betraying his wife, and laying a gut punch on everything the two of them had built over the years.

'Mmhmm,' was all he replied, not even a word.

'And her husband? Kids?' Anya asked.

'Married. But on the rocks,' Dan said. 'Three kids.'

'Fuck,' Anya said, laughing. 'So what, you had to keep the noise down because of them, did you?'

'They were out—'

'Ah! So you had to wait until the coast was clear. Like a fucking teenager or something.'

Dan almost tried to defend himself. To tell her it wasn't like that adolescent lust, when sex was as much logistics as desire. But that's exactly what it was like. Empty houses, furtive texts, more time spent removing footprints than creating them, knowing that a forgotten sock could blow the whole thing apart.

'And you went back. Twice,' she said, switching from cruel humour to disappointment, changing direction with the deftness of a swift in flight.

Dan was about to answer her. To tell her about the second time, how he had given into base impulse, and the third when he knew he couldn't do it again. But the doorbell went, and he could hear the girls' voices outside.

Without a word, Anya wiped her lower eyelids with the outsides of her forefingers, and got up from the table.

NOW

'So is that how you see it, too, Dan?' Margot said, clearly a little uncomfortable after he'd finished explaining his infidelity. The not-quite affair, not-quite one-off mistake with Eleanor. 'One–all? As Anya said.'

'Well,' he began. 'Given the circumstances, it's probably more like two–one. To Anya, I mean.'

'Now, come on,' Matt said, straightening his papers like a newsreader at the end of a broadcast and trying to look all important.

But Anya was laughing now. 'It's fine,' she said. 'I mean, he's right really. I mean, he fucked up. And, I might add, he fucked up first. But I fucked up for longer.'

'That's as may be. But I'm not putting "two–one" down on anything official. I'm sure Charlotte agrees.'

'Matt. It was just a joke,' Anya interrupted before Charlotte could reply.

'If I could,' Margot interjected. Everyone turned to look at her. Like they were unruly students. 'I'd like to move on from your infidelities,' she said to both Dan and Anya's relief. 'And quickly discuss how what happened outside the marriage affected your physical life together.'

'Oh.'

'Dan?' Margot said.

'I mean,' he said, looking at Matt, desperate to avoid having to go into any of the details of his and Anya's sex life with him sat there. Part of Dan always suspected that Matt half fancied her. Some lingering crush from their student days in Durham.

He could picture a floppy-haired Matt in a French Connection slogan T-shirt and boot-cut jeans lurching towards Anya on a nightclub dance floor for a kiss. Her moving out the way like a boxer swerving a punch. Him pretending that nothing had happened and keeping up the pretence for the next twenty years.

'Yes?' Margot said.

He looked over at Anya. Surely she thought the same? Anything but this.

'I…'

'The petition mentions separate bedrooms. A lack of intimacy?' Margot said in that questioning tone of hers.

'Yeah,' Dan said.

'That's right,' Anya said.

* * *

The sunbeam that hit her through the window might as well have been a spotlight for all she felt pushed out onto a stage. Charlotte was staring at her, mouth almost gaping. At what point in life did adults stop being so childishly fascinated by gossip about other people's bedroom problems? Did they ever? Even in an apparently professional setting like this.

'In your own time,' Margot said kindly, hurrying Anya along. 'I understand this can be hard.'

'No,' she said, taking a deep breath. 'No, it's fine. I suppose we just… well, we just stopped really,' she added, with a look over at Dan.

Was this a fair representation of the gradual halt of the intimate side of their marriage? There had been no actual agreement that they were done with it. Just that, over time,

50

they had come to accept that their evenings didn't include that sort of thing. There was time for dinner, then either a couple of episodes of something on the telly or sex, but not both. And they had seemed to tacitly decide between the two of them that *The Sopranos* was a better use of their time.

'Yeah. I suppose that's right,' he said.

'And could you elaborate?' Margot said.

Fucking hell, Anya thought.

FIVE MONTHS AGO

'You've been on that page for ages,' Anya said, not looking up from her Kindle, swiping the screen every few seconds or so to turn her virtual page. As ever, it was resting on her thighs, raised up beneath the light grey duvet cover.

'I'm not really reading it,' Dan said. 'Just looking at it.'

'Are you not enjoying it?'

'No. I am. I mean, it's not, like, a page-turner,' he said, closing it briefly to look at the cover and privately wondering if he ever really believed he would read a six-hundred-page investigation of modern economic inequality, and if the book would ever be over (he was still less than halfway through after three months). 'But it's interesting. Dense, though.'

'Not bedtime reading?'

'Maybe not. But then if I don't have bedtime reading, then I probably don't have reading.'

'Holiday?' she said, not looking up from her digital page. Dan was constantly amazed by her ability to hold conversations while reading or watching TV and barely break stride with either activity.

'Not really a beach read, is it? I prefer a Lee Child for that sort of thing.'

'Hmm.'

Dan shifted in the bed and pulled down the bottom of

his ratty old Pavement T-shirt (not an official one, bought from a vendor selling them on the floor outside the Brixton Academy), which had rucked up around his belly. In doing so, he shifted closer to Anya, brushing her thigh with his knee and leaving it to rest there, bare leg on pyjama trouser.

That, it turned out, was the spark. She sort of pushed her thigh against his, moving it up and down very slightly, all while keeping her eyes fixed to her book. With nigh-on fifteen years of experience of Anya on his side, Dan recognised this as a clear sign and took one of his hands off the large hardback edition of Thomas Piketty's *Capital in the Twenty-First Century* and placed it just below her knee. She responded by moving slightly closer, just an inch or so, climbing out of her indented shape in the memory foam mattress.

They stayed like this for a moment – three pages for Anya, one for Dan, who was struggling to hold his book steady with one hand – before he gradually made his way up her thigh, stopping at the top of her flannel pyjamas that were decorated with penguins on ice skates. To him, it was still slightly too warm for winter bedwear and the thicker quilt. But she was always much colder.

Anyway, he tried to dispel his opinions about dressing for the weather as he placed the very tip of his middle finger underneath her elasticated waistband, against Anya's warm, soft skin. If she didn't move him on within the next minute or so, that would be another, more certain, sign.

* * *

'Shall we?' Anya said, looking up from her e-reader.

'Do you want to, then?'

'Maybe. It's been a little while, hasn't it?'

'It has.'

'Well, we could…'

'If you… I mean, only if—'

'I think I do,' Anya said, struck by how much negotiating

the terms of sex with her husband of ten-plus years reminded her of the first time ever: all doubt, second-guessing and earnest, well-meant questions cut through with clear and obvious desire.

'Okay,' Dan said, and leant over to kiss her in a way that he hadn't for so long that his lips and stubbly chin felt almost unfamiliar to Anya. As he did, he pushed his hand further down into her pyjama trousers, his wrist raising a couple of the ice-skating penguins up so it looked like they were going downhill.

'Is that—'

'Yes.'

'Okay,' he said, kissing her again. But in a way that suggested obligation rather than want. As if he shouldn't be down there unless he was also prepared to show some affection up here. 'Just tell me if you want me to.'

'What?' she said.

'Stop. I mean, if you don't… you know.'

'Right,' Anya said, wondering why neither of them could stop fucking talking. In the spirit of the whole thing, she, too, reached down and rested her hand on his crotch.

Of course, there it was.

Fuck, she thought, questioning if they were actually going to do this. Hadn't they sort of accepted that this was now a non-physical relationship? Not of convenience, as such. But of practicality maybe.

'Maybe we should just,' she said, lifting her bum into the air and pulling the penguin trousers down and off, reluctantly also removing the socks she would usually discard seconds before sleep. Next went her bed T-shirt, an end-of-shoot commemorative Fruit of the Loom thing from a children's television programme she had worked on. On the front a well-loved geriatric actor was dressed as a pirate. Dan did the same with his T-shirt and boxers.

This, Anya thought, was a reminder of where they were as a couple. Bedclothes scraped off under quilts instead of lingerie peeled seductively. Limbs scared of the cold air outside the bed. Half a mind on where everything landed, so the clear-up-and-back-to-bed operation would be fast and easy. Both of them were now naked, lying on their respective pillows.

'Do you want to get rid of that?' Dan said, moving towards her.

'What?'

'The cream,' he said, gesturing to the line of white emollient across her forehead, just above the eyebrows, and the Alice band keeping her hair from falling down and sticking to it overnight.

'No, it's fine. Isn't it?'

'Sure.'

'What?'

'Nothing.'

'No. What?'

'It just… remember what I sang the other night? When you came in wearing it?'

'"Prince Charming",' Anya said. 'Fuck, Dan. Are you saying that I look like Adam Ant?'

'No!'

'Because—'

'No. Honestly, it's fine.'

'I don't want to have to put it on again,' she said. 'You know it costs a bloody fortune. Can't you just live with it?'

'Yes. Sorry. Look, forget I even mentioned it.'

They waited there a moment. Anya wondered if she should, in fact, take the face cream off. It was only face cream, after all.

'Do you want to go, then?' he asked. 'Or shall I?'

'You maybe. To start. Then we'll see,' Anya said, as Dan hoisted himself up and across her body, parting her legs with his thighs.

'What about anything else?'

'No. Just crack on.'

He relaxed his arms and lowered himself down onto her,

kissing her neck and cheeks, then occasionally her lips. Anya felt impossibly nervous, so out of the habit of regular sex with her husband that she could barely remember the little touches and strokes that they'd honed over the years to the extent that they worked together like a reliable old engine.

Then, suddenly, she felt it. Dan pushing inside her, missing the mark, then trying again with more success.

'Is that okay?'

'Go slowly,' she said

'Okay,' he said, pushing again. 'I don't think I'm quite—'

'Hang on.'

Anya shifted around a bit, hoping that her discomfort was physical rather than emotional.

'Now?'

'Okay,' she said, and he went again. 'No. Jesus, sorry. Stop,' she said. 'Stop.'

Dan pushed himself up so that he was above her, looking down.

Everything about his face and his body was so familiar and natural to her. Of course, both had changed over time. But she had barely noticed his hair begin to fleck with grey or his stomach distend slightly with comfort and craft ale.

And yet for all that – for all she had become accustomed to Dan – it felt uncomfortable and alien *being* with him. Her body wouldn't accept him as it once had.

Sure, they'd had sex before when one or the other of them was phoning it in a bit. Like when they were trying for a second kid and were so exhausted by the first they barely bothered getting undressed. Or on date nights when it felt almost obligatory to end it in bed. But Anya had never felt like she absolutely didn't want Dan, no matter how much her head tried to convince her that she did.

'Is something wrong?'

'Sorry,' she said, forcing a smile as he sat upright, backside resting on his thighs. 'It just doesn't feel right tonight.'

'Oh. Sorry, I—'

'No. It's not your fault. I should've said earlier. I thought I could be. But it didn't…' She trailed off.

'It's fine,' he said, laying down beside her, deliberately keeping a little space between their arms, and pulling his red and black checked boxer shorts and his T-shirt back on again.

'I am, though. I wanted to. But… I don't know. Something just didn't feel right.'

'Honest, it's fine.'

Dan picked up his book from his bedside table, where it had been sat next to a pack of blister plasters, a pint glass of water and precisely three pounds and sixty-four pence stacked in a neat little pile. He propped his head and neck up against a pillow and began to read again.

Anya grabbed her pyjama trousers from where they had been thrown on the floor, unwillingly getting out from beneath the duvet to put them back on again.

'I'm just going to nip to—'

'You know we haven't since…' Dan interrupted.

'I know,' Anya said, stopping short of the doorway.

'What's that, a year?'

'Not quite. Nine months.'

'Yeah,' he said, eyes on a page, hardly reading again. 'Do you think we ever will again?'

'Dan.'

'It's a legitimate question.'

'It's late. I've got to be on a train at half six,' she said, looking over at the sunrise alarm clock on her bedside table (much more sparse than Dan's – only that and her Kindle). It showed 11:43.

'Just answer me one question.'

'Please, Dan. Not that.'

'What?'

'Don't do that "was he better than me?" thing,' she said, mimicking a thuggish bloke's voice.

'Jesus. I'm not asking that. Who the fuck asks that in real life?'

Anya looked at the clock again. She didn't actually need the loo. Just wanted to get out of the room to have a bit of a think about all this. 'Go on, then.'

'Is it done for us? Sex, I mean. And be honest. Because I'm starting to think it might be.'

She thought for a moment, despite being fairly sure of her answer. Because what is a marriage without sex? Especially when you're still young enough to actually have it.

'I don't know,' she lied. 'Maybe. It just doesn't feel—'

'I know.'

'And we both—'

'I know.'

Neither of them spoke for a minute. Without a word, she slipped out of the room and into the toilet. When she came back, Dan's light was off and he was on his side, eyes closed, pretending to sleep.

NOW

Margot turned to a fresh page of her notebook. By Dan's count, this was number twelve, and it wasn't even lunch yet. Whatever came from the next two days, there would certainly be a conclusive record of his marriage and why it went wrong.

'How long after that did you move into a separate room?' she asked.

'Couple of months.'

'And you feel that this contributed to the breakdown of your marriage? The, what's the word, demise of the physical side of your relationship. The fact that you no longer had an active sexual partnership.'

'Well… yeah,' Dan said. He had never really thought of it in that way. To his mind, they were getting divorced because they couldn't stand to live together any more. Let alone share a bed. 'I suppose.'

Another note. Another nod of the head from Margot.

'Okay. Well, I think we've established the underlying reasons for the separation. What we need to do now is look at the application,' she said, shuffling through some papers before she found what she was looking for. 'Now, I see from this that Dan—'

'We're not going to be blaming each other,' Anya interrupted, almost gabbling.

'Yes, I understand that. But—'

'I know the rules. One of us has to petition. I'm just saying that, like, for the purposes of today, we're equal.'

'Of course. All I want to do is read the application.'

'Fine. But—'

'Anya,' Matt said, curtailing her next interruption. 'We understand. No blame. But I explained the legal position on this is that one of you has to petition.'

'It's a fucking bullshit law.'

'And it's being changed. But we're not quite there yet.'

Anya folded her arms and looked away from Matt. Despite the equitable way they wanted to apportion blame, the fact remained that one of them still had to carry the weight of it for the sake of the divorce. Yet instead of filing a petition for adultery after Anya had been seen with Kelvin, they had bought a new house in a new town, under the misapprehension that a fresh start and a relocation might save them. There was no desertion on either side. It left them with one option.

'I've agreed to petition her,' Dan said sheepishly, as Charlotte took printed-out copies of the divorce petition and handed one out to everyone in the room. 'Anya, I mean.'

Dan remembered how they had come to the agreement that he would file rather than her. He had been chivalrous and offered for it to be the other way around. But there were more possible boxes to tick for unreasonable behaviour on her side than his. Partly because he rarely left the house for any length of time and barely socialised unless forced to than any actual unreasonable behaviour.

Anya had been cross that it had landed this way. Future generations looking at family trees and the nuanced lives of their long-dead relatives would see Daniel Moorcroft as the petitioner and Anya Moorcroft (née O'Hanrahan) as the respondent. Him the wronged party, her the blamed. When really what they were looking at was a quirk of admin, a necessary workaround for a process that hadn't moved with the times. Or at least a couple who weren't prepared to wait for no-fault divorces to work their way into law before ending their marriage.

Dan looked down at the paperwork he'd been given.

Most of it was boxes ticked and perfunctory information that could be found on any job application, passport form or permission for GiftAid on a donation. Overleaf were the details – the specific examples of that unreasonable behaviour.

He and Anya had chosen them together from a list of 'popular reasons for divorce' on a family solicitor's blog, spending an evening in front of an open fire with a bottle of wine, picking the excuses they'd give the court for ending their marriage. It was surreally calm and peaceful, Dan remembered.

1. The Respondent and the Petitioner stopped socialising together, which led to the Petitioner feeling lonely and alienated from the marriage.
2. For six months, the Respondent has been pursuing an active social life with her friends, leaving the Petitioner to feel abandoned.
3. The Petitioner and Respondent do not share any common interests and only spoke to each other in the latter part of the marriage regarding the children.
4. For three months, the Respondent has slept in a different bedroom to the Petitioner, which has made the Petitioner feel isolated from the marriage and alone. There is also a lack of intimacy in the marriage, a state of affairs that has lasted for upwards of six months.

The veracity of the words didn't matter. They were a means to an end. Something to get a judge to grant them a decree nisi, to rubber-stamp the end of the marriage.

Had they been honest, they knew the divorce might not be granted. A couple that had so recently relocated, been on holiday and undergone couples therapy didn't cut things off with such finality. To someone looking in, they were still trying – mechanics who had found the fault but didn't know quite how to repair it. Whereas the view from within was that it was hopeless, and that carrying on after Kelvin and Eleanor and everything since had been little except an attempt to convince themselves that they weren't giver-uppers.

All that was needed now to proceed was for the two of them to stick to the terms they'd agreed on going into this. The last time they had spoken, on the phone a week ago, they had promised not to spring any surprises, no requests the other wouldn't be expecting or claims that were outside the scope of what they'd already discussed. If they followed their own rules, they'd be fine.

Dan didn't trust Matt, though, and was sure he'd be the type to throw something in at the last minute.

Would it start here, he wondered? He would contest the fault attributed to Anya and go ahead and make the whole thing worse.

'Well,' Margot said, looking up from the application paperwork. 'If all parties are happy with this…' She looked at the four of them. Dan held his breath and felt a sort of nervous righteousness, as he might have when knowing an argument was brewing. But Matt and Anya nodded and Margot smiled. '…Then I suggest that we continue.'

* * *

Dan and Anya looked at each other. They knew that all the talk about how they had got to this point was, in essence, preamble. Nothing more than a bit of background to set the scene and remind everyone of the context that had landed the two of them in a lawyer's office in Holborn while her parents took their kids to the London Aquarium and then tomorrow to Woburn Safari Park, in the hope that the animals and fish would distract them from the demise of their family unit.

This next bit was when it got serious. When specifics were picked through, their lives truly disconnected and their marriage moved from present to past tense.

On Margot's instruction, they all opened the nicely bound booklet that Matt had someone make for him. Inside was everything they would go through today and tomorrow, organised by chapter and kept inside a plastic wallet. It even had a front cover reading *Moorcroft Lawyer Supported Mediation*, below which was the logo of his firm and the month and year.

The first chapter was headed *Assets* and followed by an introductory paragraph with mostly unnecessary context about the mostly equal way ownership and payment for houses, cars and property would be taken care of. Below which was a list of owned items, suggested ways of separating everything, and a load of legal language that neither of them could pretend to understand.

Charlotte and Dan had their own version of this, covered in notes and minor amendments in red pen. It worried Anya. Were the things they had agreed on or thought they were in broad alignment on about to be questioned and pulled apart? What if Dan had changed after he moved out?

The past six weeks were the longest amount of time they had ever spent apart, only meeting to exchange the girls at a service station car park in Colchester, more or less an equal distance between their home in Suffolk, and his temporary set-up back in London.

'Now, you will both have some ideas and suggestions for how you wish to separate your assets, including property.'

'Sure,' Dan said.

'And I understand that you still own the first property you shared together. Which is where you, Dan, are living.'

'Yeah.'

'Well,' Margot said, clicking her pen. More notes. 'If you'd like to talk about how it came into your lives first, then maybe we could discuss what happens to it in the future.'

HOME

FIFTEEN YEARS AND ONE MONTH AGO

Crouch End, London

Anya took stock of the building in front of her. A shopfront, covered by shutters, behind which she could see three or four guitars, a couple of amplifiers and a drum kit. The type of window display to attract a type of person. Above it was a large sign, the shop's name spelled out in pink neon lights against a black background.

String Theory.

It certainly stood out against the neighbouring pizza takeaway, Sicily Joe's, and William Hill betting shop.

'Do you leave it on every night?' Anya asked.

'No. Only tonight.'

'For me?' she asked, with a knowing smile.

'I wanted you to see it.'

'Well, I feel very privileged,' she said. 'Did you not worry about burglars? Advertising a guitar shop with a bloody great sign like that.'

'Nah,' Dan said. 'Mehmet next door is here all night. He'll know if anyone's trying to break in.'

'Is he not called Joe?'

Dan looked confused.

'The sign says Sicily Joe's.'

'Oh yeah. No. There might be a Joe somewhere. But it's owned by Mehmet. And he's from Istanbul, not Sicily.'

Dan, she could tell, was really trying. He had been since their first furtive messages when they had both claimed to be new to online dating. Part of her wished he would relax. Although she loved that he'd left the light on for her.

Tonight, he was wearing a nice white shirt beneath his overcoat and smart shoes. Although the real Dan was still evident, in the fact that his shirt was unironed and shoes scuffed and worn.

She, meanwhile, was in a dark grey knitted dress with a roll-neck, burgundy tights and high-heeled shoes that were not suited to the icy pavements of mid-January.

'Dan,' she said while they were both still looking up at the pink lights. 'Nice as it is looking at the sign. I am fucking freezing.'

'Oh shit. Of course,' he said, fumbling in his coat for his set of keys. 'Do you want to... like, come up?'

'I thought that was the whole point of coming here.'

'Sure, yeah. Just thought you might've changed your mind or something.'

'Dan.'

'Right,' he said, unlocking the door next to the shopfront, and turning on the single light bulb hanging from the ceiling to reveal a tiny hallway – the floor of which was covered with takeaway menus – and the steep stairs to his flat.

She could see that he was worried about the first impression the flat might make on her. The pretty knackered green carpet, damp walls and an odd, slightly sweaty smell. He was probably used to it, but still recognised that it wasn't the best introduction for new people. He hesitated, then seemed to lead her upstairs in a rush, as though he was trying to beat the timer on the hallway light.

'This is me, then,' he said, opening the door and ushering Anya inside.

The place was somewhere between a bachelor pad and a teenage boy's room. Dan had books on the shelves, and the odd photograph or keepsake. But the posters were Blu-Tacked to the walls rather than framed and hung. The little living room was home to a TV on a dusty and scratched wooden table, and there was nothing between it and the grey, well-sat-on sofa to put a mug of tea down on. There was also no dining table Anya could see anywhere, suggesting that Dan and his flatmate George rarely ate a meal when they weren't either standing and scoffing, or sat with plates on their laps.

'So what's the deal with this place, then? You said it comes with the shop,' Anya said, as she followed him through the flat, slightly worried about how bone-achingly cold it was.

'Sort of. It belongs to Eddie.'

'Your boss?'

'Yeah. When he gave me the manager's job, he said I could either have a pay rise or live here. He was going on tour for a year. Then he just sort of stayed in America.'

'But he still owns the shop?'

'Yep.'

'And the flat?'

'Yep.'

Anya put her handbag down by the front door and waited as Dan went into the small kitchen.

'Who was it you said he plays with again?'

'All sorts. Eddie's a session musician. But he used to be the sort of stand-in bassist for Jamiroquai. When the normal bloke couldn't do it. You'd recognise him, I think. He's been on Jools Holland.'

I bet I wouldn't, Anya thought.

'Big fella. Dreads,' Dan continued.

'I think I know the one you're talking about,' Anya lied. 'And what, George works there, too?'

'Nah. George is here for the low rent. He works in advertising. Anyway, drink?' he said. 'Tea? Coffee? I've also got wine, whisky and, err,' he examined the bottle rack, 'Blue Curacao.'

'As tempted as I am by the Blue Curacao, I think wine's good,' she said. 'But only if you're opening it.'

'You coming over was the only reason I bought it. So, yeah,' he said, as she heard the pop of a cork and the glug-glug-glug of wine pouring into a glass. When he reappeared, Dan was holding two little round bowl glasses, almost full to the brim with red. She wondered if he'd bought them when he bought the wine.

Dan showed her to the sofa, still visibly indented by whoever had been sitting on it last. Anya looked around for a blanket, slightly regretting removing her coat and wondering if this would be one of those London flats where whatever heat the rickety old boiler managed to generate disappeared straight out of the thin, single-glazed windows.

But before she could ask if he had anything to keep her warm, Dan leant over and kissed her, placing a hand on her thigh. She kissed back, but pushed him away with her lips until he was back on his side of the couch again.

'Hold it there, mister. Not so fast.'

'Come on,' Dan said, pretending to be frustrated. 'We've been out together for what, four hours?' he added, looking at his digital Casio wristwatch, the annoying type that beeped on the hour.

'It's called a date, Dan.'

'And you made me sit through that bloody film.'

'You said you liked it! What was it? "A compelling portrait of jealousy."'

'Yes. I was trying to sound as though I knew what I was talking about. But if I'm being honest, I can't stand Woody Allen.'

Anya feigned shock.

'What?'

'I swear you said you liked Woody Allen. On our first date. At the bar.'

'No. You said you liked Woody Allen. And asked me if I liked him.'

'And you said yes.'

'I said he's all right. *Manhattan*'s all right. *Annie Hall*'s all right.'

'*Annie Hall* is a masterpiece.'

'Wrong.'

'What do you call a cinematic masterpiece then? And so help me if you say *The Godfather*.'

There was a pause as Dan thought of his bedroom, and the large poster of Marlon Brando as Don Vito Corleone, black-and-white except for the red rose in his pocket. It was stuck above his bookshelves and CD racks, which themselves contained hardback editions of *The Godfather* and *The Sicilian* novels.

'I don't know. *Apocalypse Now* or something. That's a masterpiece. Anyway,' he said. 'It's not just the films, is it? Woody Allen himself...'

'What?' Anya said.

'Well, he's a bit of a twat, isn't he?'

'Dan! You can't judge the art by the artist.'

'Not true.'

'Of course it is. Take, I don't know, Caravaggio. An actual, literal murderer. Killed someone. But that doesn't make his paintings bad.'

'Like Phil Spector.'

'You can't compare Caravaggio and Phil Spector.'

'Both artists. Both killed someone. If we save Caravaggio, we have to save "Then He Kissed Me".'

'Fine. Well, maybe there should be some rule about the quality of the art versus the crime. See what gets saved. And I think *Annie Hall* should make it through. No matter what the artist has done.'

'Hmm. I'll give you *Annie Hall*, then,' Dan said, shifting towards her. 'But only because I can't be bothered to argue about it any more. Tonight's film can go with his reputation, though.'

'Deal. I am prepared to sacrifice *Melinda and Melinda*. Even though it'll go down as the first film we watched together.'

'I'll buy you the DVD,' Dan said, leaning over to Anya again. This time she put her wine glass down and moved towards him.

They sat kissing on the sofa for a few minutes, until Dan's hand began to move up her thick burgundy tights. The tense, shivering thrill of it was like nothing she had ever known before. And her breath left her for just a second. Anya wondered if this was what it was meant to be like when it was right. When the feeling of something so simple as a kiss was so noticeably different from anything she'd known before.

'Wait,' she said, and Dan's face reappeared from where it had been burrowed in between her neck and chin. 'What about George?'

'He's out for the night. Staying out.'

'You sure?'

'He fucking better be,' Dan said firmly, which sounded like he wanted privacy for Anya's and his first night together. But was really because he'd given George ninety pounds to stay in a hotel for the night and treat himself to a full English the next morning on the understanding that he didn't reappear before ten.

'Shall we go to your room, then?'

'Sure,' Dan said. 'Just give me twenty seconds.'

And he got up from the couch and ran into his bedroom to remove the poster, before motioning to Anya to come through.

* * *

Anya woke up the next morning to no Dan but a note on his pillow to say that he'd gone to get them breakfast.

Alone, she got out of bed and had a look around the room, having only seen it the previous evening by candlelight, after he'd lit some tea lights and placed them in ashtrays stolen from pubs to give the place a bit of a mood.

She was right about Dan's flat. It was incredibly cold. The kind that seemed to seep through skin and muscle, freezing the body from bone marrow out. She wasn't helped by the fact that she was wearing only her tights and one of his T-shirts, not being so presumptive as to pack a pair of pyjamas and a hot water bottle.

Dan's bedroom had the feel of a place holding its breath. The moment she left, a mess of clothes, unopened post, tea-stained mugs and cigarette packets would burst out, littering his desk, bookshelves and chest of drawers. She pictured him frantically tidying yesterday, bunging whatever it was wherever it would go, knowing that he didn't want to present a bad first impression of his living space.

Preternaturally nosey, she started browsing his music collection, which was far too extensive to offer any information about Dan that she didn't already know. Marilyn Manson shelved alongside The Supremes and Willie Nelson spoke to a man who was almost completely undiscerning in his tastes, and who was perhaps too easily pleased by anything with a tune (or not).

Next was books. Mostly biographies of musicians, comedians and actors. Plus a bit of crime and the entire Adrian Mole and Harry Potter series, arranged in their chronological orders. She also noticed a poster, rolled up and stuffed behind the shelf, which, when she unfurled it, turned out to be of *The Godfather.*

'Got you,' she said to herself, then checked her watch.

It was almost half nine. She didn't know when he had left, but hoped he would be back soon. She was starving and wanted to get home to Clapham to shower and change before she met her friends for Sunday lunch later.

For a second, she wondered if it would be a step too far to pry any further, but justified it to herself because they had met online rather than through friends or at work or something. He said it was the first time he'd done internet dating, but who knew? Maybe snooping was actually due diligence?

Gently, she pulled open a drawer to reveal a mess of underwear and socks. Nothing incriminating except for a few holes where big toes should go and a pair of *Star Wars* boxers, which, had he worn them last night, would've certainly changed the course of events. There was nothing to spoil the mood like Chewbacca decorating a man's crotch.

The next drawer down was jumpers and jeans, most of them bundled rather than folded. Dan clearly wasn't the kind of man to worry for lack of an iron.

She was about to give up and slip back under the thin duvet when she decided to give the last drawer a go, pulling it out to reveal hundreds of immaculately folded and presented T-shirts, all organised by colour and bearing countless logos she didn't recognise.

'Nosey,' a voice behind her said.

'Fuck! Dan. You gave me a bloody heart attack.'

He was standing there with a paper bag in one hand and two Starbucks coffees in a cardboard holder in the other.

'Which I probably wouldn't have done if you hadn't been going through my things.'

'I wasn't "going through",' she said. 'I was just looking. To see.'

'To see what? My bloody underwear,' he laughed, closing his top drawer, which Anya was embarrassed to see that she had left open.

'To see...' she began, wondering if it was worth explaining that she had assuaged any concerns about intrusion of his privacy on the grounds that there was no evidence, as yet, to say that he wasn't a maniac.

'It's fine,' Dan said. His laugh put her out of her misery. 'You found the collection, then.'

'Yeah.'

'I know it's a weird hobby,' Dan said, taking a sip of coffee and pulling an almond croissant out of the paper bag to take a bite. 'I ... I didn't know whether to mention it on the site, y'know. Some people might see it as a bit of a turn-off.'

Anya looked at the drawer again, still open. Some of the logos and names were familiar. Mostly from HMV CD racks, or posters for music festivals.

'What's wrong?' he said.

'Nothing. It's… well, it's more serious than I thought,' Anya said. She had imagined it might be a few memorable take-homes from favourite bands and gigs rather than this somewhat more industrial-level operation.

'Anyway. I know it's a strange one. I sort of got into it a few years ago through a mate. Then he gave up and I carried on. Now I run a blog about them.'

'A blog?'

'Yeah. It's like a sort of diary essay thing but on the int—'

'I know what a blog is, Dan. I meant you run a blog about… this?'

'Yeah. I pick a T-shirt every week. Then write a little post all about it. Where I got it. If it was from a gig. The tour it was part of. The set list. Loads. A T-shirt is like a moment in a band's history.'

'And people read it?'

'Oi,' he said, feigning offence. 'And yes. A few anyway,' he said. Anya wondered how many. Surely no more than fifteen or twenty? 'My most popular post had almost five hundred readers. But only a hundred and fifty or so are regular,' he said.

She was surprised, and immediately found herself bemused at the idea of this subcommunity of anoraks, of which Dan was seemingly a key part. 'I sort of dread asking. But how many do you have? T-shirts, I mean.'

'Well, there's these. They're sort of my favourites. Then there's a box in the wardrobe. And a few that I actually wear hanging up.'

'So what, you don't even wear these?'

'Not really, no. Unless in emergencies.'

'And in total?'

'Maybe a hundred. It's hard to keep track of,' he said.

* * *

This was a lie. Because he actually had an Excel spreadsheet containing the fine details of every band T-shirt he owned, saved on both his computer and on an external hard drive. 'Is this going to be the thing that means I never hear from you again? Because if it is, I'd rather you said so now and gave me the other half of that croissant.'

'No, on both counts,' Anya said, after a sip of coffee. 'Despite the obvious sad-bastardness of it, it's kind of sweet.'

Dan smiled and kissed her, and the both of them slowly edged backwards towards his bed.

'And I hope this isn't jumping the gun. But if we ever live together, they're not all coming with you.'

'We'll see about that,' he said.

Their coffees and pastries on the floor, they fell onto Dan's mattress. As they did, they heard the door open, a voice call out and a set of keys land on the kitchen counter.

'Ahoy there! She still here then or what?'

'And I think that's probably my cue to go,' Anya said.

With that, she got up off the bed and dressed in her clothes from the night before.

She kissed Dan again, and he walked her past their wine glasses and shoes, still by the sofa, to the door, briefly stopping at the kitchen to say, 'That's George,' and pointing at the skinny, long-haired man who was making a large pot of coffee.

Outside, a fine layer of snow was settling here and there – just for a few brief seconds before hurrying feet trampled it away again.

* * *

Anya looked back up at the shop and the sign above it, no longer glowing pink. It was, in many respects, a terrible London flat. But she'd rarely felt so immediately comfortable anywhere.

NOW

That drafty little two-bedroom flat above the old shop in Crouch End had had so many different roles in their story. Their first shared place. Home for a good many years. And the root cause of a change in their circumstances that transformed what was possible for their life together.

Anya had moved in when they had been together for nine months. Of her three housemates, only Sarah was a friend, having offered Anya the room when one of the original group of renters had relocated to Berlin. Not a day went past that she didn't feel that keenly through a mention of 'what Bethany used to do'. And while she liked Sarah, she was desperate to get away from the others. And just as desperate to move in with Dan.

Then, after just over three years of living with him there, everything changed.

'Now, Dan,' Margot said, her glasses falling down to rest on her nose as she fixed him in her gaze. 'I gather that you came into the ownership of the property in July, two thousand and eight.'

'Yeah,' Dan said, hesitant about what was to come. 'That's right.'

'When a Mr Edward Webb left it to you when he passed.'

Mentally, Dan had prepared himself to go over the finer

details of his marriage, his and Anya's respective faults and mistakes, their parenting. He hadn't prepared himself to rehash this.

'Mmhmm,' he said. He could tell from Margot's look that she wanted more from him. A simple affirmation wasn't going to be enough. 'Eddie died pretty suddenly in Australia, when he was on tour. And we found out that he'd left the flat and the shop to me.'

'Which came as something of a surprise, I gather?'

'Yeah. I mean, like, Eddie was my boss, really. He was a friend as well,' Dan added, correcting himself, always slightly defensive about the circumstances in which he had become the owner of a flat and a retail premises in North London. 'But he'd never mentioned anything about leaving me anything. I've always thought it was because he didn't have any kids or anything. And probably felt a bit sorry for me.'

'How so?'

'Eighteen-year-old kid shows up asking for a job. No parents. Nowhere proper to live,' he said, realising how much his story of arriving in London made him sound like a Dickens character who then wound up fixing guitars.

'Because of your own family situation, then?' Margot said.

'Yeah. I suppose. I'd been working in a pub in Newcastle and living with my nan. Then one day I thought *fuck it* and got a train to London,' Dan said, wanting to provide as much context to Margot as possible. Just in case Matt had convinced Anya to coerce him into selling it quickly. The flat was the only thing he was stridently protective of. The manifestation of the only time in his life that someone had thought to provide some sort of safety net for him – until he met Anya, of course.

'And you and Anya stayed there for another seven years together?'

'Yeah,' Dan said, noticing Matt scribbling down a few notes of his own, though he couldn't imagine what about. Matt knew Dan's story as well as anyone. Although what Dan saw as the heartbreaking early death of his mentor and friend,

Matt had always seemed to see as a stroke of luck that ended up with Anya being the beneficiary of a mortgage-free flat in a decent part of London.

They'd had Matt and his wife Emma over for dinner occasionally back in the day. Every time, Matt would comment on how it 'looks like student digs, no matter how much you tart it up' or that 'there's value here, but you'll have to do a lot of work first'. All the while trying to convince them to sell up and move down south, to Battersea, where he promised they'd get more for their money and an area that offered a better return on investment than North London.

Every time, Dan said no. Not while the shop was downstairs.

'Ah, the ten-second commute,' Matt would say.

And then eventually that excuse wore out for Dan when String Theory succumbed to what had felt inevitable for as long as Dan had been the proprietor of the business and closed its big metal shutters for the last time. The letter he pinned to the door told most of the story – they had been beaten by cheaper online shops, escalating business rates in London, and the aftershock of the financial crisis.

The bit it didn't reveal was that Dan had no head for business and was never able to really get his head round the endless lists of tasks that seemed to be etched inside his eyelids. Whether it was ensuring they had enough change in the till, the baffling marketing stuff, or remembering to pay his three employees and noting down when they were going on holiday.

He had got a job fixing guitars and ended up an entrepreneur. Apparently, all by accident.

'Anyway,' he said, remembering where they were in the conversation. 'We moved out just before Christmas 2012. When—'

'I was five months pregnant,' Anya chimed in. She was smiling, Dan noticed. Was that a good sign?

'Yeah.'

'And that was to your house in Kilburn,' Margot said.

'Well, Kilburn–Queen's Park area,' Anya said, echoing what the estate had told them on their first and only viewing all those years ago.

'The Crouch End flat was too small for all of us. And Martha needed a garden,' Dan said. 'When Anya got pregnant again, we moved,' he said, looking at Matt, willing him to break his professional poker face and make a joke about the commute – how it went from ten seconds to twenty-five minutes.

'And you retained ownership of the flat above the shop?'

'Yeah. We took a mortgage out on that one, rented it out and used the money to put the deposit down on the new place,' Dan said, remembering how strange he had found the whole process of becoming an owner of two properties in London, having arrived in the city with nothing except for his clothes, a Discman and some CDs, and an almost knackered mountain bike he used to get around because he couldn't afford the Tube.

He hated to think of Eddie's death as good fortune. But there were times, like now, when it did look rather a lot like it.

'Good,' Margot said, bringing Dan's story of their first home to a close on his behalf. 'So, now I'd like to talk about how you feel the property should be divided between you and your wife when you're no longer married.'

* * *

'Well… look,' Dan began. Anya could recognise how uncomfortable this part was making him. He was happy enough talking around these things, explaining why this and how that. But now it was time to make his case and he could barely even begin.

'I've got two things I'd like to talk about. If it helps?' Anya said. Was she rescuing him or taking advantage, she wondered as she intervened. Offering a lifeboat but demanding a grand to use it.

'Sure,' Dan said, with a look at Margot.

'If you're happy to let Anya proceed.'

'Yeah.'

'Right, well. Look, I'm okay with most of what's been set out. I'll have the car. You can have some of the furniture and the instruments and all that.'

'They're my instruments,' Dan said.

'Exactly. So, you can keep them,' Anya said. She took a deep breath, still unsure if she was really going to say it. But then Matt had told her she had a right *to* it and had a case *for* it. 'But… look, I don't think twenty-five per cent is fair, really. For Crouch End, I mean.'

'What do you mean?'

'Dan, we both lived there, didn't we? We had Martha there. And it was me who made the place look half-decent.'

'Half-decent?'

'Please,' Margot said, managing to get above both their voices without raising hers. 'If I could remind you both to keep this conversational. Anya, if it helps, you can address me rather than Dan. That's what I'm here for.'

Anya took a sip of water and brushed a hair off her face.

'My point is that there wasn't even any proper furniture when I moved in.'

'Not true. We had a couch. A bed.'

'Yes. But you didn't have a table. Or actual chairs people could sit on. There were no cushions. You didn't have a rug.'

'Right, so you buy a rug and suddenly that entitles you to half the flat?'

'I lived there!'

'Well, in that case maybe fucking George gets a share, then? Maybe Eddie still gets a share. I'll take ten grand out and stuff it down his grave.'

'No, Dan,' Anya snapped. 'It was my home. I built it up with you. Christ, I'm not forcing you to sell the place. I'm just asking for a fairer split when you do.'

Both of them stopped for a second. A brief slideshow whirred in her head, full of memories and poignant moments she felt all the more keenly, now knowing that they were contributions to a lost cause. The day they moved in. The night of their wedding, when they ended the evening eating cake in the living room rather than having sex. The moment she discovered she was pregnant in their cold and damp bathroom early one morning while he was still asleep, not sitting together staring at the pee stick like couples on pregnancy test adverts.

The old flat held a funny sort of allure for her now. In the months before they decided to leave, Anya couldn't wait to trade it for more space and a property more suited to a family. But when they did, it was like losing a relative.

'Besides,' Anya continued. 'I'm not asking for half. I wouldn't.'

'How much, then?' Dan asked, refusing to meet her eye.

'Forty.'

He seemed to take forty worse than when he thought it was fifty. Scoffing and looking around the room – anywhere except at her.

'I'm guessing this is you, then?' Dan said finally, looking at Matt.

'Dan.'

'I knew it. As soon as you got involved, I fucking knew it.'

'Mr Moorcroft,' Margot tried to intervene.

'You get in her ear. You tell her to—'

'Dan,' Charlotte said firmly. It was the first time anyone had heard her speak for what felt like hours. 'Margot, Matt, Anya. I wonder if you'd mind if Dan and I stepped outside for a moment? Or had the room, perhaps?'

Matt paused for a moment before saying, 'Sure. Bathroom break, maybe? Five minutes.'

And he, Anya and Margot left them alone.

* * *

Anya closed the door on Serenity, noting the irony. She thought of the last time she had been in the Crouch End flat.

It was the day they moved out and dropped the keys with the letting agent. She remembered how heartbroken Dan had been. The shop had become a boutique interiors store; the flat was up for rent. It felt like everything Eddie had left him was gone.

'I'm not sure this is right,' she whispered to Matt as he ushered her towards a small kitchen where two young women in suits were drinking herbal teas out of branded Melrose and White mugs. 'I told him twenty-five.'

'It's not about that, Anya. It's about fairness. Now do you genuinely feel like you have a rightful claim to more of that property? Would you be happy if Dan were to sell it tomorrow for four hundred grand and took three hundred of it?'

'I don't know,' she said. 'Probably not.'

'Well, then.'

'Anyway, there'd be stamp duty and—'

'That's not the point, Anya. The point is what you feel you have a right to.'

'Fucking hell,' she said. 'It's just so awful.'

'Divorces tend to be,' Matt said, putting a decaf Nespresso pod into the machine. 'Look, this whole thing is not going to be a heart-warming chat and the two of you coming out as best mates. Those divorced couples that meet for lunch and all that bullshit? It takes years.'

'Thanks for the honesty.'

'I'm just trying to be clear with you, Anya. Yes, mediation is probably the kindest way to do all this. Yes, you've chosen the bloody hippy-dippiest mediator there is. She'll make sure she goes through all the good times and the happiness as well as the fucking… shit. And there'll be moments when she makes you feel all right about all this. But – and I'm going to be blunt here, because I'm your friend as well as your… you know – the next couple of days are going to be tough. You will disagree. You will have different ideas about how your life carries on after all this.'

'Fine fine fine,' she said, with half a mind on tomorrow, when they were due to talk kids.

'I'm just being honest.'

'But you don't have to enjoy it so fucking much.'

'Anya. Come on,' Matt said, doing a decent job of sounding genuinely hurt. 'Enjoy it?'

He took a sip of his coffee, the foamy crema top sticking to his top lip for a few seconds.

Anya couldn't understand people who drank decaf espresso. Surely it was just for show? Espresso was a drink built on purpose rather than desire. People had it because they needed a kick up the arse to start their day or a way to stay awake at the end of a meal out. Remove the caffeine and what was the point?

'You did sound like you were.'

'Anya. This is very difficult for me. I've done a few of these. But I never thought I'd be helping out you two. "Danya".'

'You know he hates that nickname, right?' she said, remembering how friends would send emails or texts about nights out, dinners and holidays, addressing them as a singular entity by that portmanteau. It was funny for a couple of weeks, then irritating for the next fifteen years. 'He always says it's just my name with a D at the beginning. Like he's relegated to a single letter.'

'Or that it's his name with a YA at the end?'

'He never saw it that way.'

Matt dropped the little mug in the sink for someone else to worry about.

'What is it, then? Are we going to hold firm on forty or back down?'

She paused for a moment. The kinder, truer side of her wanted to leave it. The evocation of Eddie, and Dan's terrible upbringing, always made her feel guilty. When they had kids, her parents uprooted themselves from Ireland to buy a house in St Albans, a town they had never visited, because it was close to the North London home she and Dan had settled in. Dan didn't even know who one of his parents was; the other was scarcely involved in his life. Eddie was as close to a guardian as anything he had ever known.

Was she really going to take away part of the one thing he had been left?

But then the little devil perched on the opposite shoulder told her she had a justifiable claim to it. They were still married. The flat was their home. She had done it up. They had decided to put a mortgage on it to afford another place together. Forty per cent was a fair reflection of that. Or was it?

'What if we changed? I could ask for thirty. I'd be happy with thirty.'

'Your call,' Matt said, slightly disapprovingly, like he had been about to witness a punch-up outside a nightclub and a spoilsport bouncer broke it up before it even began.

'Thirty, then.'

* * *

Charlotte stood up as the door reopened and Matt and Anya reappeared. Dan was a little annoyed at this. Undue deference during a heated point of discussion.

'If we're ready to continue?' Margot said.

'Sure,' Anya said, sitting down opposite Dan, with Matt beside her.

'Now. I'm sure we've all had time to reflect a little and take a moment. Anya, if I could—'

'Could I?' Dan said.

'Dan,' Anya said. 'Margot was—'

'I know. But I want to say something.'

'I was only going to—'

'I get what you were saying,' Dan said. They were beginning to fill the spaces between each other's sentences, performing the duet they'd honed over the years as a couple.

'I know how much the flat means. And I was going to offer...'

'So I wanted to suggest...'

'...thirty,' Anya said.

'...forty,' Dan said, a few milliseconds later.

And then they both stopped. And looked at each other. And smiled.

'I mean, if you want,' Dan said. 'You were right, you know. About all you did to the place. And how it was our home.'

'No. I mean, so were you. About Eddie and that.'

'To be honest, Eddie would think I was a bit of a prick arguing over it with you.'

'He'd think we were both pricks,' she said. Dan smiled, thinking of the fondness Eddie had for Anya – for the two of them as a couple. He would hate what they were doing now.

'Well, what about halfway, then?' Dan said. 'Thirty-five.'

'Sure,' Anya said with a half-smile. 'Sounds good.'

At this, Margot took her pen from where she had been keeping it behind her ear and began jotting again.

'And you're both happy with that?' she said. 'Upon the sale of the property of Park Road, N8, Mrs Moorcroft will be entitled to thirty-five per cent of the proceeds?'

They both nodded, and Margot once again looked up from her pad.

'Good. Now, as I understand it, you moved from this property to the house on Hartland Road in... Queen's Park. And sold that property approximately a year ago?'

'Yeah,' Anya said sheepishly. 'We decided that, well, after everything ... Maybe a fresh start. Somewhere new and all that.'

'Of course. And that's when you moved to the village of Westleton in Suffolk. Where you, Mrs Moorcroft, currently reside?'

'I do.'

'Well, as we've already had a little break, I suggest we move straight on to that.'

FOURTEEN MONTHS AGO

Westleton, Suffolk

It had only just stopped raining when they stepped out of the cottage and onto the narrow lane that bordered a small common in the middle of the village. The tarmac was dark grey. A rivulet of water ran down the gutter of the slightly sloping road. And the trees on the common were lush, green and heavy with collected raindrops.

The estate agent shook their hands and hurried back to her car, leaving them alone except for a dog walker dressed in shorts and a Barbour jacket.

It was a pretty little place, Westleton. A small village, set halfway between the A12 and the North Sea, bordered by farmers' fields and three separate nature reserves. There were two pubs, a village shop and a second-hand book and record shop that was full of eccentricities. Close enough to the nearest station in Darsham for Anya to get to London when she needed to. And with plenty of space in the garage for Dan to set up a workshop for the repairs and restoration work he currently did in their slowly decaying shed.

'What'd you think, then?' Dan said when the estate agent was a safe distance away.

'Nice. Lovely, I mean. A lovely house.'

'Yeah.'

'It was a bit weird though, wasn't it? Looking around it like that.'

'I was thinking the same,' Dan said.

The owner of the cottage they were viewing had died two months ago, aged ninety-one. Six weeks before that, his wife had gone at ninety. They'd been married for sixty-seven years and living in the house for fifty of them.

Their life together was etched all over it. The lines drawn up the larder wall charted the growth of their kids: Andrew, Mary and Jennifer. The small extension on the kitchen had been built by the owner, Tom. And the stairlift rail leading to the four bedrooms upstairs told of a couple who had no intention to spend their final years anywhere except home.

Dan couldn't quite see how he and Anya would scrub over the history and replace it with their future. It was undoubtedly someone else's. And simply tearing away the dated wallpaper and worn carpet wouldn't change that.

'It's got promise, I suppose. Plenty of room,' Anya said, as they walked away from the house towards their car, parked at the bottom of the hill by a duck pond.

'Yeah. Better than the one down the road,' Dan said, thinking back to the place they had been round in nearby Leiston, which was bigger, but a near-total wreck, complete with an all too visible mouse problem.

'Shall we do pros and cons?'

'Sure. Pub?' he said, nodding towards The White Horse on the corner, empty except for two drinkers outside on a bench.

'I was thinking we could just sit by the pond. I know it's cold but it looks nice.'

'Sure.'

'Fine. Pub, then,' Anya said, clearly guessing from his tone that if he relented to sitting by the water he would be looking longingly over at the pub every thirty seconds anyway.

The White Horse was as deserted inside as out. One bloke

on a bar stool in front of a half-drunk pint and a copy of the *Racing Post*, which he was ignoring in favour of his phone. Anya took a seat in what used to be a church pew as Dan went to the bar, returning with a cider for her, a beer for himself, a bag of crisps and a wooden spoon with the number 7 daubed on it in sky-blue paint.

'What's that for?'

'Chips.'

'Dan.'

'What? We haven't had lunch.'

'You had that sandwich on the way up.'

'That was bang on twelve. It's two now. Anyway, don't pretend that you don't want chips.'

She took a sip of the cold, sharp cider.

'What first, then?'

'Cons.'

'Fine,' Anya said, taking a notepad and a pen from her handbag and leafing to the back, where she wrote *Westleton house* and underlined it, on an adjacent page to a half-written shopping list, an 0800 phone number and *Martha football subs* in Dan's writing. 'Are you going to start or shall I?'

'You.'

'Fine. Well, for one, we'd have to move house. Which would be a fucking ball-ache, as we know.'

'So we might as well give up now, then, if that's the problem.'

'It's not the problem. It's just a con. You've seen our house. There's stuff everywhere. You have no idea what's in the loft.'

'Well, put it down but put an asterisk next to it,' Dan said, between sips. 'And add "new town" to it.'

'Hardly a town, though, is it?'

'No,' Dan said. 'I always worry that people won't like us. Or we won't like them. What do you do if you move somewhere like this and can't stand your neighbours? Maybe we should be thinking of renting instead to see if we like it. We could easily get a tenant for our place.'

'Rent out the house so we could rent one up here?'

'Yeah,' he said.

'No chance.'

'Why not?'

'Do you remember what it was like when we put the flat up for rent? We'd have to decorate from top to bottom. Install fire alarms bloody everywhere. Make sure there's no health-and-safety risks. No chance.'

The barman ambled over to place a large white china bowl full of chips down between them, along with a bottle of vinegar and a dish full of salt sachets, sauces and two sets of knives and forks wrapped in paper napkins, which felt like overkill for the size of the meal.

Dan immediately began liberally sprinkling vinegar all over the chips, along with two packets of salt. He did it all without checking first. It briefly took Anya back to the time she and Kelvin got chips in a pub on a weekend away in Bath. He had poured ketchup over them, and Anya had spent the next half-hour picking out the ones that seemed to have the least sauce on them, realising there were some things that people just knew about their partners. Knowledge built up over time, as vital and comforting as it was mundane.

'You there?' Dan said, bringing her from her reverie back into the pub.

'Sorry,' Anya said. 'Miles away. Anyway, it's what we said, isn't it?' she continued, keeping her mouth wide open to cool a blisteringly hot, oily chip as she was eating it. 'If we rent, then it's not a new start. Because it'd be too easy to go back to the old one. We have to be all in.'

'Fine, fine,' Dan said, holding a chip between his index finger and thumb and gently waving it around. Why could neither of them wait two minutes to start eating?

'I have a pro, actually. If that's okay?' she said, starting a new column to the right of the short list of cons. 'I feel less stressed here. Already. I mean, I know we've only been here for an hour or so to look at a house. But I can tell I'd feel calmer. It feels slower, you know? I could disconnect more.'

'Anywhere outside of London is slower. London is a permanent fucking rush. Even people with no time limit are in a hurry. It does that to you.'

'Exactly. So pro. Calming.'

'Add "big" to that. As in the house and the garden. We'd have a lot of space and the countryside would be good for the kids.'

'Is that a separate pro then? Good for the kids.'

'Sure. And it's not a million miles from your parents or London or anything. Like, it's not as if we're moving to…' Dan stopped, suddenly unable to think of anywhere far away. 'Aberdeen or somewhere. And we said, it's got potential. We could do a lot with it.'

'Right,' Anya said, scribbling down everything Dan said in an edited form and adding *community*, *cheaper* and *near Ipswich* until the pros list stretched halfway down the page. While the cons list was still just a couple of lines, and the chip bowl near empty.

It had started to rain again outside, pat-patting against the single-glazed pub window and reminding her of their first place in Crouch End, where the glass was so thin it sounded like every raindrop was a pebble pinged from under a bus wheel.

The door opened, and three walkers stepped inside, shaking their cagoules off over the coir matting so as not to drip all over the dark blue carpet.

'I knew the duck pond was a bad idea,' Dan said with a smile. 'Anyway. Another one?'

'Half. I'm driving us back, remember?'

Dan picked up their glasses and returned to the bar. She could see him already trying to fit in. To not look like some idiot from the city kicking the tyres on a house once owned by a denizen of the village. Then she looked down at the notepad.

She realised that the pros were superficial, grasped at because neither of them really wanted to address the cons.

The house was lovely, yes. It said family in every stair rod and bathroom tile. Decades of mostly happy years had been trodden into the carpet. She could already tell who would have each room and how Martha and Edie might embellish their decoration with posters and stickers and toys. It was the kind of house she and Dan could've moved into without a second thought, had the last few years not happened.

She couldn't escape the notion that the betrayals had not only sullied their vows, but ruled them out from certain future happinesses. The estate agent should say, 'I'm sorry, Mrs Moorcroft, but the underbidder is a nice young couple who've been entirely kind and faithful to one another, which we feel is more in keeping with the values and aesthetic of the property.' And she and Dan would be relegated to houses where a murder once happened or new builds.

She checked her phone. The last message there was still open, from her mother who was looking after the girls.

All fine here. How are you getting on? All right I hope x

Normal enough. But there was a heavy subtext there. 'All right' meant 'no arguments'.

In a way, one of the worst things about everything that had happened was other people knowing. The journey from new partner wanting to make a decent impression to the woman who cheated was not one either of them had envisaged making. So few relationships featured an almost complete reversal of power, influence and affection.

She would never forget that first meeting with Dan's friends after it became widely known that she had been having an affair with a children's television presenter most of their kids watched every morning. The official line they'd given was that they were 'working through it together' and they'd asked everyone around them to 'keep things normal'. Because God forbid anyone actually tell the truth or confront the problem.

It was tough on Dan, too, of course. She remembered telling her parents about his infidelity; her mother's hurt, her dad's anger at this wrong Dan had done to their daughter. But, at the same time, they had both wanted her to stay – to work it out.

'People make mistakes, don't they?' Angela O'Hanrahan had said in the end, while Anya was staying with them for a couple of nights in the aftermath of Dan's slow, torturous admission in the kitchen of their Queen's Park house.

'Is it a mistake if it happens more than once, though?'

'I don't know, love. What I do know is that this kind of thing seems to happen all the time. And that's just what people say, isn't it? That it's a mistake.'

'You're a long time married,' her dad, Colm, had added. 'Jesus knows you'll do enough to each other in fifty years or whatever you've got.'

'You didn't, though, did you?'

Colm had chosen this moment to drink his tea. As he had sucked the dregs out of his moustache, she worried that she might've been about to discover her father's mistakes (or repeated mistakes). But instead, he thought for a moment and said, 'You're right. I suppose things were different for us, though. People didn't have affairs. Or if they did, no one ever knew about it.'

Life carried on. Her parents had worked through what they needed to work through, without ever really working through it at all.

And now here they were, in a pub in Suffolk, contemplating buying a house in the sticks because they knew they couldn't stay in their own and had apparently spoiled the entirety of London with their savage behaviour towards each other.

* * *

Later that evening, they drove back to London. But not before a short detour to see the coast, and another to find a Chinese takeaway, where they bought Singapore noodles and ate them in the car with plastic forks, the heat from their food steaming up the windows.

Dan was in the passenger seat of their Nissan Qashqai, playing with his phone. Anya could see him scrolling through Instagram, looking at photos of done-up vintage guitars from other builders and restorers around the country. They were a weird little competitive community, each admiring the other's work but at the same time wondering why they weren't asked to do a certain job. But then Dan liked weird little competitive communities, what with the band T-shirt collectors he spoke to through his blog and once insisted on meeting in person during a minibreak to Paris, leading to what may have been the most awkward and cringe-worthy half-hour beer in Anya's life.

They had just passed Colchester. It was a clear evening, the sky big and bright, blue and burnt orange, as the gradually setting sun replaced the clouds and changeable weather of the day. Anya flicked the paddle on the steering wheel to turn the radio down, pushing Laura Marling's mournful folk music to the background.

'We never did the cons properly, you know,' she said.

'Huh?'

'Put your phone down. I want to talk for a minute,' she said. Dan placed his battered iPhone beneath his right thigh. She wondered if he'd always done that, or if it was a behaviour he had developed when he was texting and fucking Eleanor. Just as she'd got into the habit of tucking her phone down the side of the sofa, or ensuring it was always face down on a table until it buzzed. 'I said we never did the cons properly.'

'We did.'

'Dan. We put down that it'd be a bastard to move and that

we had loads of shite. If they were the only cons, we'd have already bought the place.'

He took a sip of Costa coffee, bought from one of the vending machines in a roadside petrol station.

'Well, what do you want me to say?'

'Just be honest. Tell me what makes you not want to move there. Like, I wonder if we're ready for it, you know? Or if we're fucking idiots to think that a nice new house in the countryside is really the thing we actually need.'

'We said, though, didn't we? A fresh start. Even the counsellor thought it was a good idea. We want to get out of London.'

'Fine, yeah. But,' Anya said, trying to find the best way of saying it. 'London is not responsible for why things are... the way they are. I mean the way we are, Dan. We fucked up. We didn't need London to do it for us.'

'Well, yeah,' Dan said. 'So what are you saying, it's a no?'

'No. It's not a no. But it's not a yes.'

The fields, churches and quaint, soporific villages that had seen them out of rural Suffolk had by now been replaced by the trappings of suburbia. Golf courses and service stations augmented with branches of Starbucks. A closed-down American diner that someone had decided to open on an A-road in Essex. It all signalled their drift back towards the city and the home they had jointly sullied.

* * *

You can't go home, but you can't stay here, Dan thought to himself, as he considered Anya's objections.

'Look,' she began again, as she overtook a BMW. Dan was always a little surprised at how fast she drove. As if there was always something she was running ten minutes late for. 'I know you've probably got some idea of us growing old in that place. Sitting in the living room when we're in our eighties, yelling crossword clues at each other. But you have to think about it… not working, too.

'Of course I think about that.'

'Right, well it hasn't sounded like it. If I'm being honest.'

'You want to know what I worry about? If we're wrong for that house. Like we'll go into this home that was owned by this nice fucking picture-perfect family. And we'll make a mess of it with all our baggage.'

'What, you're worried about the ghost of the old fella who lived there haunting you because we both had affairs?'

'You know what I mean. I would love us to be the kind of family that lives in that home. I'm just not sure we are. It's too, I don't know… fucking aspirational or something.'

Anya waited a moment before saying, 'I know what you mean. You're reading far too much into it. But I do know what you mean.'

'Well, that's the cons, then,' Dan said, and Anya turned the radio back up again as they continued towards London.

* * *

Three months later

When they eventually decided to go, the move happened quickly. Their offer for the cottage in Westleton was accepted almost immediately by children keen to get the house gone and their money in. And a viewing day at the house in Queen's Park ushered fifty pairs of strange feet through their family home to pick through their rooms, openly critique their furniture and decoration choices, and wonder aloud at how they might tear everything Dan and Anya had built down, reconstructing it in their own image.

The winning bidders, paying well over the odds for the house, were a young couple expecting a baby. He worked in finance and she in magazine publishing. They met Dan and Anya once on a visit to measure for curtains.

'Buyer's remorse,' Dan said, seconds after they had left. 'They're wondering if they've made a terrible decision.'

'Don't say that,' Anya said, knowing that even the smallest pebble in the road could throw them off the direction they had set for a new house, and a new start.

And then, in a mess of paperwork, frantic phone calls to lawyers and gradual, at times seemingly reluctant, packing, they were gone.

NOW

'They say that moving house is one of the most stressful things you can do, don't they?' Margot said. She had just listened patiently to their story of moving to Westleton. Dan and Anya took turns to explain what happened, why they made their decision, justifying the move to themselves as much as to the others in the room. 'What made you both believe it was the right thing for you?'

Dan knew this would be on him. But he really didn't want to have to explain.

'We had a fight about something. What was it, a week after we had a look at the place?'

'What was the fight about?' Margot said. 'If you don't mind my asking.'

'Right. Well, I came home from dropping a guitar off and Edie was watching telly. Kelvin was on.'

'As Captain—'

'Yeah,' Dan said, feeling ridiculous. Was he really about to heap yet more blame for the failure of his marriage on a children's television character who seemed to spend at least half his time on screen covered in gunge and shaving cream foam? 'As Captain Funtastic. I asked Anya why. Because after... it all... we'd sort of agreed that we wouldn't have him on the TV any more.'

'The girls like him,' Anya intervened.

'And they didn't know?' Margot said.

'No.'

'We decided it'd be best not to tell them that their mum had been shagging their favourite TV presenter. Bit confusing at that age.'

'Dan,' Matt said. 'Come on, now.'

Dan almost bit back. He could quite happily have chucked a glass of water over Matt and walked out of the whole thing. But he caught himself.

'Anyway. We'd agreed that we wouldn't let them watch him any more. But Edie was and I got cross about it… and… Look, aren't we meant to be talking about the house?'

'I'm trying to get a better understanding of why you decided to move,' Margot explained. 'Now, if you feel this incident is important to that, then I'd like you to share. If not, then we can happily move on.'

He looked over at Anya. She didn't have to say anything to let him know that, yes, the argument was important. Not because of what they had said during it, but because of how they got out of it – those terms that ended the hostilities.

'Fine. We argued about it. And for a while it looked like, y'know, we were back where we'd started.'

'Which was?'

'Separate beds and all that. Like, every little disagreement couldn't end with one of us just walking away or deciding the fight wasn't worth it. Everything had to be more than it actually was.'

Dan remembered those nights on the sofa in their Queen's Park house. How going back downstairs after brushing his teeth and getting ready for bed felt like an ignominious rite of passage, so much more than popping back to get a glass of water or checking that he'd shut the back door. Then setting his alarm for five in the morning, so that if Martha or Edie woke early, they'd not see him there, hunched on a sofa that wasn't quite long enough to accommodate his five-foot, eleven-inch frame, beneath the uncovered and slightly stained spare duvet.

'So I said we should do it. I knew that if we left things like they were, we'd never have made it. And,' he said, looking around the little meeting room, at the lawyers, the mediator, the paperwork, 'I know we didn't. But we had to try. We had to do *something*. So we put a bid in.'

'And Anya?'

'I agreed. I mean, it was pretty obvious that we were still in trouble. Despite all the therapy and the making an effort.'

'Making an effort?' Margot said.

'You know,' she said. 'Trying a bit harder for each other. Being more patient, the odd date night. That kind of thing.'

'Of course. Sorry.'

'I can't remember what I was saying,' Anya said, a little testily. It was clear she was beginning to get a bit tired of the amount of detail Margot wanted from them. Maybe a straight-up divorce would've been easier and cleaner, if slightly less humane? 'Anyway. I basically agreed that we should do it. I mean, I think we both knew it was a bit of a last roll of the dice. But, I don't know, I suppose we weren't ready to end things.'

'No,' Dan said quietly.

* * *

Anya tried to catch his eye. She wondered if, like her, he felt a little under the microscope with this bit. Aware that everyone in the room was wondering what on earth possessed a couple wracked with infidelity and aware that their marriage was in its death throes to move house and relocate to an area where they knew literally nobody but each other and their kids. Her only excuse – the one she'd trotted out to parents, friends, colleagues – was that they just weren't ready to admit their collective failure back then.

Whether it was the upheaval, the heartbreakingly difficult

conversations, the sheer amount of effort that it would take to untangle the wires of their long relationship, the move felt easier, almost. In theory, at least.

'Look, it was the right thing to do at the time,' Anya said. 'We both think that.'

'Of course,' Margot said. 'In that case, shall we talk about what will happen to the house going forward? What you plan to do with it.'

'I'm staying for the time being. But I want to sell,' Anya said quickly. 'Eventually. We said we'll split the proceeds down the line. But I want to move out.'

* * *

There was a brief silence while Dan came to understand what she was saying.

'Back to London?' he asked, still unaware of her thoughts about permanent plans.

'Maybe,' she said.

'And Dan?' Margot said.

'Sure,' he said, thinking again about the old man who'd been in the cottage before them. The evidence of decades of family life and everything it entailed, followed by a couple who barely managed a year.

He thought of the day he had left for London. His abiding memory, the parting glance, was of the kitchen. So recently renovated and beautified. It wasn't in their image so much as the image of a collection of magazine pages and lifestyle sections. There was the big dining table. The pans hung artfully from the ceiling. The mugs they kept out on display on a little tree – the nice ones given as gifts that, over the years, had come to hold more sentiment than tea. Martha and Edie were at the table, drawing with multicoloured felt tips. Neither of them knew quite what was happening, except for change and further disruption to the life that'd been carefully established around them since birth. Anya was standing by the cooker, wearing a thick blue jumper, yoga leggings and big, bulky slippers. She was trying not to cry, knowing that an obvious emotional tell would alert the girls to the fact that maybe this wasn't Daddy going away for a little while, or a moment they'd probably need therapy to reckon with in a decade's time.

She didn't follow Dan to the door, didn't watch him climb into his car and reverse out of the small gravel driveway by the side of the house, didn't see him pull on to the road by the green and drive up the hill and away.

They'd lasted just over a year in Westleton. He didn't know if, given the chance, he'd do things differently. Dan just hoped that houses didn't retain a little something from everyone who ever lived there. Otherwise, the next people along the line would be doomed.

'Sure,' he said again, looking down at Matt's paperwork that outlined the terms of the house settlement. 'Works for me.'

Margot scribbled some notes down, underlined something then closed her notebook.

'Excellent,' she said, checking her watch. 'In that case, it's almost quarter to one. So I might suggest we break here for lunch?'

NOW

Anya left the little meeting room with Matt, noticing that Dan and Charlotte were waiting before following on. Maybe Margot would come after that, she thought. Like they were the bridesmaids and pageboys in a bridal party awaiting their turn to traipse down the aisle.

'There's plenty of places around here,' Matt said, as he ushered her through the corridors and back towards the lift. 'Pret, Leon, sushi. Or we could find a restaurant. Have a proper sit-down lunch. I've not told you about Emma's plan for the garden yet, have I?'

'It's fine,' Anya said, struggling to imagine anything much worse than an hour sat across from Matt while he talked at length about bifold doors, new decking and the contractors they were considering to do the job. Matt had a way of subtly mentioning the cost of things – 'a couple of grand', 'a few zeroes on the end', 'pushing 10K, but a bargain when you think about it'.

No. She'd rather go hungry than endure that.

'I might just have a walk by myself, if that's okay? This morning has been… heavy. I'll grab a sandwich and take it to the park or something.'

'Oh,' Matt said. 'Sure. Fine… Yeah. Well, as I say. Plenty of places. And actually I could do with the hour at my desk. Tackle email city and all that.'

'Sure,' she said. 'I think I can remember the way out.'

Anya took the lift down and hurried through the pristine marble and glass of Melrose and White's office, past the two automaton receptionists and out on to New Fetter Lane. The fresh air – or at least as fresh as London air ever got – was welcome after their morning in the little room, which had become muggy with coffee, human heat and recycled air.

There was also an unescapable underlying tension in there. She and Dan were both on best behaviour, trying not to fight and bicker in front of the lawyers and the moderator, clinging desperately to civility. The disagreement about the flat was about as bad as it had been so far. But there was so much left to discuss that could make things very bad, very quickly.

At the root of it, to her mind, was a three-way tussle. They both wanted it done with. They both wanted it to be fair. They both wanted to avoid being screwed over. It was a game of Scrabble in which all parties were playing by the rules for now, but were apt to make up a new word any minute.

Anya started up towards Holborn. This little part of the city was busy with workers on a lunchtime dash. Hire bikes interrupted the pavement like unwanted street art and cars gummed up the roads. She crossed to Hatton Garden without waiting for the lights to change, and tried to ignore the display cases full of wedding and engagement rings, and the buyers at the opposite end of their marriage journey to her and Dan.

A little alleyway called Ely Court led her under an archway and down to a small courtyard and a pub called Ye Old Mitre. She'd been there a few times – meeting her friend Joanne who worked in the inns of court down the road – on busy summer evenings when the pub would bustle with a meld of the jewellers, lawyers and advertising creatives that inhabited Holborn and Farringdon. All of them thinking it a hidden gem because it was so out of the way, ignoring the fact that the presence of crowds made it anything but, and failing to realise that no such thing really existed in the capital anyway.

It was probably too early for a drink. And she would have to remember to buy a pack of mints on her way back so that nobody would know. But desperate times and all that. She opened the door and there, stood at the bar with a pint of what she assumed was Fuller's ESB, was Dan.

He stopped mid first sip when he saw her there, very nearly dropping the heavy glass mug he was holding by the handle. Anya briefly considered running, pretending that she'd gone in by mistake or had got the wrong place.

Instead, they stood in front of each other, metres apart, for a few seconds. As though they were about to draw pistols. The only other drinker in the place looked on, the tension distracting him from his bag of Mini Cheddars and pint of Guinness.

Then Dan turned back to the bar, where a young girl of around twenty was still standing, and said, 'Sorry, could I have a gin and tonic as well? And a bag of dry roasted.'

* * *

It had started raining and was far too cold to stand outside. So they took a small, round wooden table by the door and sat down as the strains of 'Don't Go Breaking My Heart' played out from the radio behind the bar.

'Bit late for that,' Dan said.

'Hilarious,' Anya said, taking a sip from a half-pint glass with a slice of lime floating in the top. This wasn't the type of pub to serve gin in those fashionable big fishbowl glasses. 'Look, should we even be doing this?'

'Why not?'

'Well, Dan, I'm not sure if you'd noticed but we're currently in the middle of getting a divorce and now we seem to have nipped off to the pub together.'

'I'm sure it's fine. I don't think there's any rule against it. Anyway, we came separately. It's a coincidence.'

They both took a few peanuts from the bag split open on the table, tilting their heads back to drop them into their mouths.

'How are you anyway?' Dan said, thinking how strange it was to be asking that of his wife.

'Fine. Busy.'

'Good. Busy's good.'

'Well, fine-ish, I suppose. Given the circumstances,' she said, going back for more peanuts.

'Good.'

'Did I tell you that concept of mine is going into production? Looks like it anyway.'

'Oh, great. That's brilliant. What was it again?'

'Animation. A monkey with a magic ukulele.'

'Of course,' Dan said, still unable to understand how children's television producers settled on which ideas to put money behind and which were just plain mad. Where was the line?

As the two of them drifted into silence, across from one another in a small, quiet pub, it occurred to Dan that this could have been any day in the course of their fifteen years together.

Back when they were first going out, there might have been a Sunday newspaper between them, pulled apart into its constituent sections that they'd share over a couple of mid-afternoon drinks. She would start with the magazine and news supplements, him sport and arts. Then they'd do the crossword together, Dan holding the pen because Anya's handwriting was so appallingly unreadable.

A few years later, there would be a baby or toddler asleep in a pram or pushchair – Dan and Anya using the golden hour of the nap to slip back into their old skin for a while. More recently, they'd be joined by two kids, mollified with either crisps or screens while their parents had a quiet drink and scrolled through their phones.

It was all very familiar. And the lack of discomfort he felt with Anya today was... unsettling. Where was the antagonism, the conflict, the cruelty?

'How did you know I wanted a gin anyway?'

'Well, beer makes you tired if you drink it during the day.

Wine goes straight to your head. And it's too cold for cider. So a process of elimination really.'

'Hmm.'

'I was right, though, wasn't I? Like, if I wasn't in here when you turned up, you'd have ordered a gin.'

'Maybe,' Anya said with a smile as Dan checked his watch. 'How long have we got?'

'Half-hour. Twenty minutes if you want to get something to eat on the way back. Another?' he said, gesturing to her almost empty glass.

'Shit. We shouldn't, should we? I mean, they'll be able to tell.'

'The way I see it, we're paying all of those people. So if we want to come back ten minutes late and a bit pissed, that's our business.'

'We'd become a story they all tell, though, wouldn't we? The couple that went to the pub together halfway through their divorce.'

'I'm all right with that.'

'Is it a good idea, though?' Anya said. And for a moment, they stopped and looked at each other. She swallowed nervously. 'The drink, I mean.'

'Probably,' Dan said, still staring at her.

'Fuck it,' she said, draining her glass, the lime wedge and shrunken ice cubes knocking against her teeth.

* * *

As Dan went to the bar, Anya opened her phone and checked her WhatsApp messages. There were four of them...

Mum: Having fun here!

With a photo of her dad, Martha and Edie in front of a hippo at the zoo. It was annoying that this thing happened during their half-term. But Margot was busy and hard to book, so they had to take what they could get and enlist her parents to babysit. She closed the message and went to the next one down.

Nila: Thinking of you. Hope it's working out xx

She had been in Anya's ear about the mediation process ever since she found out that Anya and Dan were going to try it, clearly believing their decision to be based on her own positive experience with Luke. As though she'd recommended a holiday cottage rather than a method of divorce.

But the final messages made Anya's heart stop for a second.

Kelvin: I hope you're okay today. And I am sorry for the part I played in this.

Kelvin: xx

Anya deleted both his messages immediately, and checked around to see that Dan wasn't looking at her.

She'd come close to blocking Kelvin's number twice. The first time was when she had ended things between them the week they were found out, over a Starbucks coffee in a busy, noisy branch near the BBC building on Portland Place. He had taken the break-up (if she could call it that) reasonably well, accepting that the chances of their affair evolving into a permanent relationship had been at best twenty per cent – and would have required Anya to fall in love with him, which was unlikely while he was still, in essence, a professional clown. He reacted far worse when Anya resigned from his show, citing the need to freshen up her career (which absolutely no one on the production staff believed).

What was he after now?

It had been months since they'd last been in touch (and the second time she'd come close to blocking). When Kelvin was drunk and back in Belfast, he had sent a photo of the hotel where they'd first slept together. Then the next morning followed up with a lengthy apology, including a half-arsed excuse about thinking it might've been funny. She knew that what had really happened was that he'd checked his messages in a hung-over haze, realised he was only ever one sex scandal away from the end of his career as Captain Funtastic, and sought to mitigate any offence.

Now, it could be anything. A power play. A tentative move to rekindle their relationship when she was out of the marriage. Maybe it was even a genuine attempt at kindness.

'What's up?' Dan said, surprising her as he sat down again, placing her second drink on a damp, torn cardboard coaster.

'Nothing... nothing. Just checking my messages. The girls are having fun,' she said, going back to the text from her mum to show Dan the photo of them and his soon-to-be ex-father-in-law.

For a second, she thought about telling him that Kelvin had messaged her. But knew the reaction it would get. Dan would pretend not to care for a bit, but would refuse to let it go. Soon there'd be accusations and denial, spite, and Dan calling him 'Captain Fucktastic'. Better to keep things civil, she decided.

'I have a question,' he said. 'Is it bad if I ask how you're finding it?'

'Which is the question? If it's bad to ask, or how I'm finding it?'

'Both,' he said, taking more peanuts. 'Fuck it, just tell me.'

Anya didn't reply.

'Well?'

'I'm thinking,' Anya said. They both drank, a little faster now that they didn't have long before they would have to be back. 'I mean, it's okay,' she continued. 'So far, I mean. There was only that one little... you know. That one thing that we...'

'Yeah... yeah. I agree. And the one thing was fine, I suppose?'

'As long as you think so.'

'Mmhmm.'

'Good.'

Dan drank again, a long draw from his pint.

'She asks a lot of questions, though, doesn't she?' Anya said. 'Margot, I mean.'

Dan laughed.

'I know it's her job and everything. But Christ. The sex stuff. I mean, is it relevant or is she just being nosey?'

Two men in suits came into the pub and went to the bar to order pints of ale and bags of crisps. The fella who'd been there all along with the Mini Cheddars and Guinness took an abandoned copy of the *Metro* newspaper and turned to the back page.

'I'm glad it's okay, though,' Dan said, after a moment. 'Like, not awful.'

'Me, too.'

'It's weird, though, isn't it? Like, actually doing it.'

'Yeah,' Anya said, staring into her glass.

'I was just thinking, when I was at the bar… what if—'

'Dan,' Anya said, stopping him short. She knew that tone in his voice. Where he was going. *Not now*, she thought. 'We should probably.'

'Yeah,' Dan said. He checked his watch. It was five to. Just long enough to get back across to the office in time for the resumption of play. 'Sure. Sorry. Let's…' he said, trailing off.

They drained their drinks and Dan took their glasses to the bar while Anya put on her coat. Outside, it was still raining, grey overhead and cold.

* * *

Anya and Dan hurried through Ely Court and on to Hatton Garden. Then back across Holborn to New Fetter Lane. They walked closer to one another than strangers, further apart than lovers. And as they approached Melrose and White, Dan stopped.

'What?' Anya said, turning back to face him.

'We probably shouldn't go in together, should we?'

'Oh yeah. Sure. You're probably right.'

'You can go first. I'll be the late one.'

'Thanks.'

'Oh,' he said, just as she turned away from him again.

'What, Dan?'

'Mint?' he said, pulling a packet out of his bag and holding it in her direction. She smiled and took one, then walked towards the building.

* * *

When he arrived back in the room, Dan was greeted with slightly irritated stares from everyone, including Anya, which he thought was a bit much. The counter behind Margot had been replenished with new jugs of water (this time with lemon wedges and mint floating among the ice cubes), two urns reading *Hot Water* and *Coffee*, and a plate of miniature cakes kept beneath cling film.

'A little pick-me-up for later,' Matt said, catching Dan eyeing them up, unaware that neither he nor Anya had eaten lunch and so would likely both spend the next hour at least wondering when he might let them at the little squares of chocolate brownie and Bakewell tart.

'Lovely,' Dan said with a slightly sarcastic smile. 'Sorry I'm a bit late. Got completely lost. Every floor in this place looks exactly the fucking same.'

'Wouldn't say that,' Matt said. 'Actually, the architects gave each floor its own unique character.'

'Well,' Dan said. 'You must be better at telling the difference between glass walls and pot plants than me.'

Matt took a sip of his espresso. Dan wondered if the man ever stopped drinking small coffees.

'Nice lunch?' Charlotte said quietly to Dan, finishing a Pret ginger beer.

'Fine,' Dan said, looking at Anya. 'Great.'

And for the briefest moment, she looked back at him in a way that he recognised, but hadn't seen for a while. Kind and hopeful. Like she used to when she was proud of him, or pleased to be back home after a work trip away. Something told him there was affection there, and a sense that, given the choice of everyone in the world, she would most want to be around him.

'Right, then,' Margot said, calling the four of them to order and snatching Anya's attention away from him and back to the front of the room. 'I think we've made some excellent progress today. We might even be able to give you a little of your afternoon back,' she added, with a look at Charlotte, who would no doubt be grateful for a little extra sightseeing. 'And with your property assets agreed upon, I would like to move on to the remainder of your financial and personal assets. Which I believe, Matthew, is on page…'

'Five,' Matt offered.

'Ah, yes. Page five of our documents.'

And five of them flicked through the bound little books Matt had made like students turning exam papers.

MONEY

NOW

The details alone made Dan feel anxious. Names of accounts with figures next to them, grids of living expenses explaining how much it cost to keep a family going, projections of future earnings (Anya's far more concrete and believable than his own). Every aspect of their borrowing, buying and spending laid out in a way that made him realise how complicated one couple can make their life together.

It was everything he hated about applying for a mortgage and checking his credit score rolled into one.

Dan was one of those people who could never be confident when withdrawing money from an ATM at the end of a month, for all he was too old to run his current account down to less than a tenner. Money was stress and confusion. Regardless of how much or little of it he earned, he was very rarely certain that he had enough to pay for what he needed or owed. So trawling over his financial history and possible future was his worst nightmare.

They had been going through the accounts for an hour so far. Taking care of the simple stuff. Cars, credit cards, valuables they each owned and had no intention of contesting. And then they were on to the complicated bit. How much each of them paid into a family that would soon no longer exist.

'Now,' Margot said. 'I'm going to encourage the two of you

to not get bogged down in the weeds of this part of our process. It's very easy to start thinking about who pays for what, who earns what, who spends what. And while that can be fair, it does tend to add an amount of friction to these things.'

'Sure,' Dan said, wondering if they might call it a fifty-fifty split and get past this bit quickly. He was certain that settling on cash and assets was the main reason people avoided divorce at all costs. At least losing custody of kids resulted in a few more lie-ins on the weekends.

'Far better is when we focus on outcomes,' Margot said with one of her slightly simpering smiles. 'Because while I know you in particular have some concerns, Anya, everything here took place during your marriage – when you were a partnership.'

Dan shifted uncomfortably. He knew what her concerns were.

'Look, I've said from the outset that I don't want any claim to Anya's pension. We can remove that from what we talk about,' he said.

This was a short-term view. Dan had no pension of his own, just whatever the state would bestow on him in his old age. Anya had always been far better at planning in that respect – contributing to a pot when she was employed by a production house, continuing it on her own when freelance.

'Fine. But you know that's not what I'm thinking about.'

'I want that money back, Dan. It was a loan, not a handout.'

'Anya,' Margot said. 'In the eyes of any court, it's very hard to justify a loan within the bounds of marriage.'

'Yeah, but that's what it was.'

'She's right,' Dan said. The awful conversation when they had agreed on it rushed back to him. One night in their living room in Queen's Park, long after the shop had closed.

There had been one or two arguments about household finances – Dan holding back on paying for a food shop or asking to pay a little less of the mortgage. He had stopped taking money from the savings but didn't have enough work coming in to support the life he had when the shop was open. At the same time, his reliance on credit cards had grown and grown, to the extent that two of them were maxed out and a third was well on the way.

It all came out at once in a horrible admission. Dan was embarrassed and felt sick from the hiding and lying, not dissimilar to how he felt after confessing his infidelity. Also similar were the behaviours he had entered into that were specific to the secretly indebted. From always being the first to the morning's post, hoping to catch any paper correspondence she might open accidentally, to holding back on buying anything that might require a credit check.

After her anger subsided, Anya suggested she lend him some money from her personal savings to pay off one card, then that they take out a bigger mortgage to take care of the other. It was bad, but she knew that whatever financial trouble he got himself into, she would feel the results of it, too. Better to take care of it quickly and decisively than let it rumble on.

But her relief was a loan. Not a gift. And now it was time to pay it back.

'I always said I'd give Anya the money when business got better and I started earning more. But over time, I started working less, while Anya did more. Then we moved.'

'You can't put this on me, Dan. You borrowed the money, you said you'd pay it back.'

'And us getting a divorce doesn't mean I can find five grand somewhere, does it?'

'You've got the flat.'

'My home,' he shot back. 'I live there again now, remember?'

He was surprised at how quickly she had turned into an adversary after the pub. Again, he blamed Matt. He was the type to have a game plan, to have trained her on what to say, what tone to take, when to hold firm and when to yield. 'I'm not selling my home for the sake of five grand, Anya.'

'Anya, as much as I understand,' Margot said. 'You can't simply demand—'

'We have suggested a settlement,' Matt said, referring back to the paperwork he had created for everyone. 'A goodwill gesture as part of Dan's maintenance payments for the family. An additional two hundred and fifty pounds a month. That will see the debt cleared within twenty-one months. Which I feel is more than reasonable.'

For a moment, Dan was stunned. He already knew that the maintenance for the kids would be a stretch. Seven-fifty a month to cover a share of food, the bills on their former home. But now the sums were there in print. A little grid detailing precise amounts for how much he would contribute to various elements of the life his family would lead without him.

Alongside it was the income and expenses form he had filled out with Charlotte. Far more imprecise. His projected earnings were based on a bit of guesswork and a lot of hope. And his outgoings were generally underestimated. All in all, it created a muddy picture of what he could call disposable income. Eight hundred pounds in theory. Probably more like four hundred in practice. Add on the additional two-fifty she wanted and he was living on less than seventy quid a week.

In all the things he had thought about before they started on divorce proceedings, his ability to afford life afterwards was well down the list. They had lived comfortably, if not extravagantly. There was never any trouble buying or paying for anything. But neither was there ever the sense that they had sufficient cash to throw at foreign holidays or wholly unnecessary purchases.

But within that was the reality that Anya earned more and paid for more. Particularly since his shop closed. When they were getting along, or at least peacefully coexisting, that was fine. Being pushed on his own exposed Dan to the gap between the lifestyle he had established and his inability to sustain it.

He looked at the new maintenance costs again. The fact was no paperwork existed about the loan. It was money from an account in Anya's name, not their savings. She simply transferred it over to him and he paid off the card. He remembered showing her the proof, the statement reading £0.00.

'I trust you, Dan,' she had said, as he held the iPad in front of her. 'You don't have to show me.'

'Thank you, though. You didn't have to.'

'I did,' she'd said.

Of course, he hadn't been aware at the time that her need to help him out was only part based on maintaining the joint health of their finances. The other part was guilt.

'You never wanted the money back before this,' Dan said to Anya.

'We were married.'

'Come on, Anya. You know why you were so keen to help out.'

'Don't, Dan.'

'But it's true, isn't it?' he said.

'I knew we'd never be able to move house again if you had a load of debt and a shit credit record. The timing was nothing. I'd have given you it whatever.'

'She gave me the money when she was with Kelvin,' Dan said, turning his attention to Margot. 'What was it, six months in?'

'Dan.'

'Seven?'

'Fuck you,' she said, getting up from the little table and leaving the room.

For a moment, the remaining four of them sat together in silence, before Matt fixed Dan with a stare, gave a little disapproving shake of the head, like he was a father admonishing his daughter's boyfriend who'd delivered her home drunk, and followed Anya out.

* * *

Knowing that Matt would be following her, Anya went directly to the bathrooms down the hall. She hurried past a woman who was checking her phone in front of the washbasins, and into an empty cubicle, where she was annoyed to discover it was one of those without any toilet lid to close and perch on.

'Fucking hell,' she said quietly to herself. 'What a dick.'

She hated Dan for bringing the affair up again now. The money was money. It was part of the deal of marriage, wasn't it? Shared possessions, what's mine is yours. Even if, at the time she lent it, they were struggling under some pretty heavy weather.

She also hated that she knew that there was some truth in what he had said. If the circumstances had been different, if she hadn't been spending half her time working out how to arrange secret meetings with another man, had his business not so recently collapsed, then maybe she wouldn't have given him the money.

Back then, Dan was verging on pathetic. Unrecognisable from the man of a year earlier, who'd not only believed himself to be attractive enough to flirt with other women, but had actually followed it through with one of them. So yes, the money was to help him and repair their finances. And it was also a way to assuage her guilt while she was doing further damage to the precarious bond between the two of them.

Now what was he going to be like, she wondered. Anya knew that he couldn't afford what she was asking for. But at the same time she couldn't accept letting him have the money forever. It wasn't right.

She took out her phone and tapped *Mum* in her recently dialled numbers. Before it could connect, she hung up. What would she tell her? *Dan's being difficult over five grand he owes me.*

Her parents were already so disappointed. So dismayed at the idea of her and Dan getting a divorce that telling them they were now squabbling over money wouldn't elicit much sympathy. Her dad, in particular, would be upset.

This Anya – the one standing in the toilet of a lawyer's office angry because she couldn't get an extra two hundred and fifty pounds a month out of her soon-to-be ex-husband – wasn't the woman he had raised. This Anya had none of the empathy, warmth and kindness he had taken such care to instill.

Her dad had always been protective of Dan. As a former policeman, he'd seen enough instances of young lads in his circumstances starting with a bad lot and making it worse over time. The fact that he'd made something of himself, kept out of trouble and become a good father despite having no example to follow put him on a pedestal.

Anya thought back to their wedding day. They hadn't gone for sides of the aisle, knowing Dan's would be so much emptier than hers. In fact, it was a small do all told. Short ceremony, then drinks in a Hampstead pub. More catered to Dan's small circle than her wide one.

'He's a good man, coming from all that,' her dad had said, watching Dan on the dance floor with his grandmother. 'Plenty who've gone through what he has wouldn't get this far in life.'

'I know.'

'You be good to him.'

'I will,' she said, watching him spin the old woman around, the two of them joyous that they were here, that he had made it this far into a happy life.

Of course, she wasn't being good to him now. But that was a wedding and this a divorce. Less about being good, more about being fair.

She was being fair, wasn't she?

Anya leant against the thin wall of the cubicle. The main door to the bathroom creaked as it opened. Anya heard a tap run then someone in the stall next to her.

She opened the photos app on her phone. Mostly pictures of the girls, plus a few items of furniture she was planning to sell on eBay. Whenever she felt uncertain or hesitant about her and Dan, about how things were progressing, she would find a photo of a happier time. As if to remind herself that there was once something better. That it hadn't always been like this.

This time she found a picture taken just over two years ago. A holiday in Majorca. A selfie on the beach with Edie and Martha and their big, gap-toothed smiles.

Two hundred and fifty quid, she thought.

Five grand, though.

Anya locked her phone and put it back in her jacket pocket. Then needlessly flushed the toilet she hadn't used and left.

On the way back to the room, she passed a vending machine that took contactless payments and bought a Twix, which she yammed one finger of before arriving back at Serenity, where everyone except for Matt was sitting around the little table. The cling film had been removed from the little plates of cakes now. Margot was eating a square of Bakewell slice, and had a lurid green macaron lined up next.

'Ah. Anya. We're not quite sure where Matt has gone. Would you like to—'

'Look,' she said, cutting her off. 'That was my money. And you know you said you'd pay it back, Dan. You know that.'

'I know. I—'

'Let me continue,' she said. 'Maybe, you know, I was a bit wrong. Putting it down on paper and all that. And I know, well, your money situation and all that.'

'Anya,' Margot said. 'I really do think we should wait for Matt.'

'Bollocks to Matt,' she replied, just as he walked in the door to hear it. 'I'm happy to take it out of this arrangement. But I want… something. Like I need something somewhere that acknowledges it.'

'The car,' Dan said, looking down at some paperwork spread across the table.

'What?'

'You can have my car.'

'Jesus, Dan. I don't want your car,' Anya said, going back to the table. 'I mean, is it even worth five grand?'

'Come on,' he said, defensive about his dented 2013 Ford Focus, with stained seats, a floor that was at least thirty per cent Wotsit crumbs, and a particular, unplaceable smell. 'Look, everything on here is split fifty-fifty,' he continued, looking at their list of significant assets – not much, except for vehicles, some of the new kitchenware, and two pieces of expensive art they had bought in a rash moment. 'The car's the only thing.'

* * *

Shared possessions. It was the only way out of this. Charlotte had recommended it a minute ago, almost as angry with him as Anya herself was after he'd brought up the affair again. It wasn't in their game plan. Not the way either of them wanted to do it. He felt bad.

'And you need it.'

'Not in London. I'll be fine.'

'And the girls?' Anya said. 'How are you going to get them back to yours every week?'

'They can get the train into town.'

'Seriously?'

'Fine. I'll rent one.'

'Every week?'

'I don't know, Anya,' he said, exasperated by the ordeal. 'I just… I can't be doing with arguing about fucking money.'

'And we can't leave it up to fate, Dan. I know you hate it. But we have to do this.'

Growing up, money had only ever been a source of frustration and negativity for him. Always defined by the lack of it or what to do with the little they had. Living with his grandparents meant watching his gran go back to working at the chip shop a few evenings a week to keep him in shoes.

Every gift of new football boots, on-trend clothing or toys was tempered by his understanding of how it was paid for.

He grew up with a far greater understanding of household finances than any kid should. And in the background of it all was his mum, the knowledge that she could turn up again at any point, in need of a bed or a few hundred quid. There would always be some for that, stashed away somewhere, or in banknotes under the bed. His grandparents were never quite able to fully cut adrift the daughter whose addictions they had first tried to treat, then tolerate, before finally accepting that they could do little about them, and so took Dan into their care – knowing also that his father was quite probably a one-night stand or dodgy acquaintance unlikely to be aware of his son's existence.

The result of his difficult relationship with family finance was that his and Anya's conversations about money were strictly on a needs-must basis. Like when they were getting a mortgage on a new house or buying a car. Everything else, all the monthly bills and day-to-day expenses, was seldom mentioned. Dan gave Anya some money every month (he always contributed less than she did) and she handled it. Beyond that, their finances were separate, with Dan only speaking to his wife about cash flow when it was desperate and he was unemployed.

Even the failure of the shop was handled mostly privately. She didn't know about the terrible decisions he had made about marketing that had cost a fortune. The daft decision to buy a load of collectors' item stock that he knew it would be tricky to sell. Or giving Barney a raise when the company was on its arse, purely because he couldn't stand the sight of him turning up every day for years on end, knowing his prospects would be no better at the end of his time with String Theory than they were on his first day.

No. Money was misery. Talking about it never did any good. Regardless of what the experts said.

'What do you suggest, then?' he asked Margot.

'I can't tell you that. I want you to be content with the decision you both arrive at.'

'Brilliant.'

'Dan!'

'Well,' he said, gesturing at Margot.

'Dan. What is clear to me is that making these additional payments to Anya would cause you significant financial hardship. And I should remind you that there is *no* obligation to agree to this,' Margot said, with what he thought was a look at Matt. Although Dan was prepared to consider anything a slight on him. 'The question is, are you prepared to look at your employment status and your earnings to make the payments? Or do you have another suggestion?'

He thought of the next few months. Cutting his cloth. He could live on cheap noodles and yellow-stickered stuff from the reduced aisle. Maybe get a job in a pub. He liked pubs and hadn't pulled pints since he had moved to London years ago. Immediately, he imagined himself applying, being interviewed and trained.

So why do you want to work here at The Pig and Whistle?

Paying off my ex-wife.

And where do you see yourself in five years?

On the other side of the bar, hopefully.

He wasn't sure if he could do it.

'You don't have—'

'I want to,' he said, interrupting Anya. 'You're right. It was a loan. I should pay it back. Christ, Anya, you paid more than me our entire marriage.'

'It's not like that, though.'

'And you could've earned more if it wasn't for that… shop,' he said, narrowly avoiding swearing.

'Dan.'

'Did you…' Matt said quietly. 'Because it's not down here. If you paid—'

'I didn't,' Anya said quietly.

'Then—'

124

'She got offered a job,' Dan intervened, both wanting to stop the hushed, frustrated questioning and prove to Matt that there were still things he knew about Anya that others didn't. 'In New York. She didn't take it because of me. Christ, I owe you the five grand for that if nothing else.'

'Didn't know that,' Matt said, picking up a piece of brownie and dropping it into his mouth. He had taken his jacket off now and was lounging on his chair.

'Listen,' Margot said. 'It's now almost five. And if we think more time might be helpful, we do have tomorrow booked. So I'm happy to push this to the morning if you are.'

* * *

Outside, the sun was beginning to set. The sky turning from rainy slate-grey to evening granite, albeit blended with that yellowy, foggy glow unique to London's light-polluted nights. Neighbouring buildings would be mostly emptying out for the evening, those staying late visible behind glass that allowed a view into open-plan offices, rows of tidy desks and ergonomic chairs running the length of the building.

Anya looked out, past Charlotte and Dan. She couldn't help but miss London. Even the mundane, workaday bits of it like the nondescript office blocks, and featureless areas where work was the hero rather than landmarks. She loved the urgency poured into every task and journey in the city. The way the energy of the place ramped up at certain times of day, from morning rush hour to lunchtime to home to last orders.

The countryside was nice. Quiet. But there was never any sense that a bigger life was going on around her.

London had presented a new side of itself for every stage of her life. A modular collection of buildings, streets and neighbourhoods that would reconfigure according to her age, immediate needs and bank balance. Starting with the excitement of discovering Camden and Soho in her early twenties, then becoming the setting to the nascent stages of her life with Dan, and finally her long-term home as they found the more grownup, steady side to the city full of people who'd decided to stay. Before, of course, she left them behind.

In many ways, it still felt like home. She breathed easier here than anywhere else in the world, despite the terrible air.

Part of her envied Dan for being back, and wondered what London might offer her today. Could this place – so linked to the young, the bold, the energetic – give anything to a forty-year-old divorcee who could barely remember the last time she wasn't bone-tired?

A cough from Matt brought her back into Serenity. Where the five of them sat there quietly, each with their own reasons for being desperate to get out of the little room.

She would head out to St Albans to spend the evening with the kids. Dan would go back home, maybe grab a pint in between the bus stop and the flat. Charlotte had sightseeing to be getting on with. And Matt, well, probably the gym or something. Margot, who knew? Maybe a dinner with a friend to discuss the gory details of their mediation.

'Tomorrow,' Anya said. 'Sure. I'm happy with that if you are.'

She was reaching for her bag when Dan spoke up.

'How about the flat?'

'What do you mean the flat? Your flat?'

'Yeah.'

'I don't understand.'

'I mean, that could be the way we settle it. The loan.'

'Dan, you said earlier you're not selling the place to settle five grand. Don't be ridiculous. Look, let's just—'

'No. I mean,' he said, addressing Margot, 'is there a way we can put an agreement in or something? When I sell it—'

'When you sell it, I'm already getting thirty per cent,' she said, making to get up. 'Look, I'm exhausted. Can we not just—'

'This is a two-second thing. Thirty per cent. Plus five grand.'

'As easy as that, is it?' Anya said, first looking to Dan. Then to Margot.

'Well, if you want, I can make a note of it.'

'Do.'

'Dan.'

'What?'

'Just… not now,' she said. 'We can sort it. Tomorrow.'

Without another word, Charlotte, Dan, Anya, Matt and Margot began to pack up their bags, take last sips of water and put their coats on.

* * *

Margot was first out the door, hurrying away to the lift while looking at a phone Dan only just realised she had dutifully ignored all day. Then Anya and Matt, who went to his desk for a moment to check over some paperwork that Dan couldn't be bothered to wonder about, leaving just him and Charlotte.

'Going all right, you think?' he said, as they ambled down the hall to the lift. The building smelled slightly stale now – coffee, people, food maybe. Dan assumed that a team of cleaners would come in overnight to deal with all that and ensure the solicitors and clients arrived tomorrow to seven sterile floors.

'Fine. No great dramas. One or two things to iron out. But no… fine.'

'Good,' Dan said, allowing Charlotte into the lift first. He had a question burning, but didn't know how appropriate it would be to ask it. *Fuck it*, he thought. 'Is this… like our one… is it normal?'

'Normal?'

'Yeah. Normal,' Dan said, as they began to descend. 'I mean, in comparison to other, you know… other divorces.'

'Oh. Sorry,' she said. They had arrived at ground level and the doors opened. The two receptionists had been replaced since Dan last passed through at lunchtime. This new pair looked broadly similar, however. 'Well… well, I…'

'You don't have to say.'

'No. No, it's fine. I mean, I must say that I've never encountered this whole "holistic" thing before.'

'Right. Will it work? Do you think?'

'Well, we'll see, I suppose. It seems fine, though. Fairly straightforward. I mean, my experience generally with mediation is that either we lawyers aren't there, or if we are, it's all a bit more formal. Official. Less chat.'

'Chat?'

'You know. Discussion. Context, I suppose.'

'Yeah,' Dan said. 'That's her thing, apparently. Margot, I mean. Anya found her. Holistic divorce or some bullshit.'

'Hmm.'

'And it's Matt's fault, by the way. That you had to be here. We were planning to do it without legal people in the room. But he got in her ear. Thinks I'm out for her money.'

'Well, that's as maybe.'

'I'm not, though,' he said quickly. 'After her money, I mean.'

'I know, Dan,' Charlotte said, repositioning her backpack as though she was about to start the Three Peaks Challenge. 'Anyway. The process is fine. Nice. I feel like I'm getting to know the two of you as a couple.'

'Probably a bit late for all that.'

'Well, you never—'

Charlotte stopped before she could complete her sentence and began looking around the reception to find something to look at that wasn't Dan.

'You never what?'

'Nothing. Sorry… no. Nothing. I shouldn't have…' she stuttered. 'Anyway. I'd better,' she said, looking out of the revolving doors and waving at a man wearing an orange cagoule, jeans and walking boots. 'My boyfriend.'

'Right. Sure.'

'Well, have a good evening, Dan,' Charlotte said, shaking his hand.

'You too. *Aladdin,* isn't it?'

'Yes. Well. M&M world. Then *Aladdin.*'

'Lovely,' Dan said, recalling having almost the same day out with Martha last year.

And then Charlotte was gone.

Aware that the security guard was looking at him, Dan made for the double doors. Outside, a fine drizzle was floating through the cold air. He found a sheltered spot at the corner of the Melrose and White building. After a minute of puffing while looking at football gossip on his phone, he became aware of Anya, standing a few feet away, arm in the air, trying to get a cab.

'South of the river,' he yelled, mimicking a cockney cabbie. 'This time of night? You must be mad.'

'Piss off,' Anya said through a half-smile. 'I forgot how much of a nightmare it is trying to get a cab at rush hour,' she added, only briefly turning to look at him. 'Who the fuck is taking taxis home anyway?'

'Important people. The ones with proper jobs,' he said. This was how they always referred to their friends who worked in law or finance. Serious. Proper. They didn't spend their days messing around with guitars or writing telly for kids.

'Fuck's sake,' Anya said, ignored by four more cars. 'Well, I've missed the quarter past, then.'

Dan checked his watch. It was five thirty, and a dark, cold evening. At least the drizzle had stopped for a minute.

'You know the girls will be fine,' he said, approaching her. 'They prefer their grandparents to us anyway.'

'I just want to get back. Have a bath. Get an early night. It's been… well, you know, don't you?'

'Quite a day.'

'Exactly.'

A bus stopped in front of them to let on a queue of people who boarded while half looking at their phones, or reading folded-over copies of the *Evening Standard*. Dan didn't want to tell her that searching for a cab in the busiest bit of Holborn, stood at a bus stop, might not yield the best results.

'When's the next one?'

Anya started scrolling through her phone now. As she did, Dan noticed a panicked look cross her face.

'What?'

'Fucking hell.'

'Is everything all right? Is it the g—'

'It says cancelled,' Anya said, horrified.

'Which one?'

'All of them. They all say it.'

'They can't all be—'

She put the phone in front of his face.

1831 Kings Cross > St Albans
CANCELLED

1852 Kings Cross > St Albans
CANCELLED

1905 Kings Cross > St Albans
CANCELLED

1921 Kings Cross > St Albans
CANCELLED

Dan began to look up the travel information as well, as if he might get different results.

'Fucking hell,' she said, the *fucking* sounding more like *focking*. Anya had a habit of becoming a bit more Irish when she was angry and frustrated. Particularly if she had been spending time with her parents.

They were both affixed to screens: Anya looking for an alternative way to get out of London and back to the kids for the evening; Dan trying to figure out why all the trains were down and if there might be someone to blame – incompetence in high office or something that he could uselessly complain about on social media.

'Shit,' he said, finding the rail company's Twitter page.

'What?'

'"We are sorry to inform you that all trains from London Kings Cross are subject to cancellation until further notice. This is due to a minor derailment of a freight train in the Radlett area."'

'A minor derailment?'

'Yeah. Like, one wheel off and one wheel on.'

'Dan,' she said, smirking. 'No jokes.'

Another bus arrived. Another queue got on. Dan imagined what the station would look like now. Thousands of people milling about on the platform. The pubs and bars packed with erstwhile homebound workers taking the opportunity to sink a few Thursday night pints and grab a Burger King.

'How the fuck am I going to get back?'

'Look, don't worry. They'll be fine.'

'Me, Dan. I'm worried about me. The girls'll be having a grand time.'

'I don't know. Uber?'

'Surge pricing. A hundred and thirty-seven quid,' she said, holding her phone up to him, where an hour-and-a-half ride in André's Volkswagen Passat was offered for roughly the same price as a European minibreak.

'Bastards.'

'Never waste a good crisis.'

'Bus?'

Anya's look told him that hours on a rail replacement coach wasn't an option.

'Well, look. Why don't we just grab a drink somewhere? Give it an hour. It'll sort itself out.'

'I don't think it's a good idea, Dan.'

'Why?'

'You know why.'

'Honestly, Anya, I really don't. You're stuck for a bit. We're in London. I can either leave you here and bugger off home. Or we could go and sit in a pub, perfectly nicely like we did earlier.'

'Earlier was a mistake,' she said.

The words were like a slap on a cold day.

Dan had thought it was okay. Maybe a portrait of their life after all this was all done. Amicable, relaxed, separate.

'We can't go around acting like best friends halfway through our divorce,' she added, attracting the attention of a few passers-by with the D-word. 'Anyway. It'll take more than an hour to put a train back on the track, won't it? I don't know. I'll find another way. There's trains out of London from other stations and then I can get a cab. It'll be fine.'

'It'll be a pain.'

'Well, obviously.'

She returned to her phone, looking for alternatives – maybe one of the mainline trains that branched out of the city and into the commuter towns that encircled London, where so many of their friends now lived, having swapped small flats and houses for big gardens, clearer air and expensive season tickets. Only a train from Euston would land Anya anywhere near her parents' house. The rest would take her further away.

Meanwhile, the rain was getting worse. Cold droplets landing on the screen of her phone, obscuring the view and making it hard to scroll.

'Jesus,' she muttered.

'We don't even have to talk,' Dan said, almost pleading. 'You could do some work. I could read a book. We'd just be there, sheltering from the rain, sharing a table.'

'And how do you rate our chances of finding a table in a pub at six o'clock on a Thursday night?'

'Well, we'll have to hurry, then.'

The streets were busy with people pushing past and around each other in the steady rain. Dan could tell Anya was thinking about it. The next hour would be a search for a taxi to get her out of London. The small talk with the driver. Arriving late enough to have missed dinner, early enough to have to sit there quietly while her mum watched *Coronation Street*.

'Fine,' she said. 'Where?'

* * *

Anya waited at a high table while Dan bought their drinks. Guinness for him, glass of Rioja for her. The pub was busy. But she got the sense of a place that would empty out before nine or ten. It was an office workers' sort of place. So everyone here would've been on it since at least half-five. One table in the corner was already on shots, choreographing the raise of the wrist and tip down the throat. Afterwards half of them groaned. Half of them suggested another. *Leaving do*, she thought.

Even now that she was here, Anya felt unsure about it. Was this mad? Earlier, things had been comfortable. Too much so, perhaps. If they'd argued over lunch, or carried some of the bitterness from the meeting room with them, it might have been easier, if not better. She simultaneously coveted and wanted to avoid the rancour of a divorcing couple. Pleasantries made her uncertain. She couldn't be doing with the buyer's remorse.

'That's a large one,' she said, as Dan put a bucket of red wine down on the table, as well as his pint and a china bowl full of wasabi peas.

'They ran out of small glasses,' he said with a grin.

'Dan. I don't want a hangover tomorrow.'

'You'll be fine.'

'What, will I just drink the equivalent of a small glass?'

'See how you go,' he said, as he pulled a book out of his bag. *Our Man in Havana* by Graham Greene.

'You're really going to read?'

'I said, didn't I? We don't have to talk. You can work. I can read. Just seemed daft to spend all that time you were waiting for the train alone. I know we're… you know. But isn't the whole point of this about being civil?'

'Yes.'

'And what's more civil than a quiet drink and reading a book?'

* * *

He noticed Anya smile. Even as the words came out, Dan couldn't believe what he was doing. Flirting. Actually flirting with his soon-to-be ex-wife midway through their divorce proceedings. *To what end*, he wondered.

'You don't have to read,' she said. 'Although, I am interested to see that you listened to me after how many years of recommending him?'

'Well, you said he was one of your favourite writers on our first date. So, what, fifteen years?'

'The entire lifespan of our relationship. And you take my advice now. A therapist would probably have a lot to say about that.'

'Now. Tomorrow is not the end of our relationship. Think about what Margot would say.'

'The secondary phasing of your... connection,' Anya said, mimicking Margot's soft tone and the way she paused at unnatural points between sentences.

'Exactly. Anyway. We tried the therapy thing, didn't we? My choice of books didn't make the agenda.'

Dan wished he hadn't mentioned the T-word. Anya seemed sad at the very thought of it. Those pointless hours they had spent on the leather sofa of a counsellor in Highgate, the bits of his legs not covered by shorts sticking to it on warm days.

The therapist's counselling room was at the bottom of the garden, in a little purpose-built office with big bifold doors that looked out on to her pristine lawn and big house. It meant that to get to their appointments, Dan and Anya had to walk past a living portrait of domestic harmony and lifestyle porn. It was sort of a reminder of everything they wanted and were drifting further away from, as they argued through torturous extended examinations of their collective cruelty, dishonesty and philandering.

They had managed four sessions before they jointly agreed not to go back, even sacrificing the two remaining hours after the therapist had insisted on upfront payment for six. *Perhaps*, Dan had thought at the time, *her line of work sees a lot of people doing just one, either to kick the tyres and see if they have a saveable marriage, or to give a healthy partnership the occasional tune-up.*

'I've not read much of it anyway,' Dan said, putting the book away as Anya looked at her phone. 'Anything?'

'Nothing. Think I'm in for the long haul.'

'Bugger.'

'It'll be fine,' she said, forcing a smile. 'Anyway. Enough about trains. I want to know what living in the flat again is like? Have you had George round yet? For old time's sake.'

'It's fine,' Dan said. 'I mean, it feels like I've regressed about ten years. And you forget how cold the place can get.'

'I'll never forget how cold it can get. I remember my first night there. I genuinely thought I couldn't date you unless you bought a thicker duvet or a fan heater.'

'And yet here we are.'

Another silence. Another half-smile from Anya. It felt like every time they got going with a friendly conversation, something to laugh about, they were stopped by some memory of their happier past.

Was it that the context and history were killing their ability to talk? Or just that an evening without arguing or being distracted by the television was so alien to them?

'What about you, though? How's h—' Dan caught himself before he said 'home'. Because it wasn't any more. 'Suffolk,' he said. 'How's Westleton?'

'The same. I mean, given that the place has barely changed in fifty years, it's unlikely much happened in the past couple of months, is it?'

'No. What about the neighbours? Have they been noseying around?'

'Well, of course Mrs Bligh has noticed you're not there,' she said, referring to the interfering but generally kind widow who lived two doors down. 'The others. I dunno. They either haven't said anything or couldn't give a shit. I always thought a village would be a bit gossipy. Everyone into everyone else's business. But really they're no different to people in London.'

Dan almost added, 'And the girls?' But again, he stopped himself. That – the asking after kids he should know inside out – was the stuff of Sunday dads and absent parents. People who caught up with their children rather than lived alongside them. He didn't consider himself to be that man yet. He couldn't.

Instead, he asked, 'How's Nila?' Knowing that gossip was easy conversation that could sustain them for the next half-hour or so with no major bumps or breakdowns along the way.

* * *

By the time that Dan and Anya were on their third drinks, the pub had thinned out a bit. The once big group with the shots in the corner was now just five people around a little table. On the next was what looked like a first date that had run dry of conversation.

The two of them, however, were still going. Talking about their mutual friends with those little affectionate character assassinations people do when discussing those closest to them.

'Shit,' Anya said, during a lull after she'd told Dan about Luke's new girlfriend, over a decade his junior, and his increasingly futile attempts to keep up with a lifestyle he was a decade out of shape for. 'It's gone eight. I'd better.' She tapped away at her phone.

Dan mimed the 'drink?' gesture, to which she responded

with a shake of the head, then doubled back with, 'Actually, no, I will. But a small one. And I mean it. Small.'

'And we should eat, shouldn't we?' he said, climbing down from the chair.

'Dan.'

'What? It's getting late. Neither of us want to be wrecked for tomorrow. Come on, there's plenty of places round here.'

'Burger King at the station,' she said. 'I've already set my heart on a Double Whopper.'

'Trains running, then?'

She showed him the phone. A similar story to earlier. Everything cancelled. A gala night for the pubs around Kings Cross and the taxi drivers willing to drive miles out of town.

'Sorry.'

'It's fine,' she said, dropping her phone back in her bag. 'Look, don't worry about another. It's probably best if I just get a hotel or something.'

'Here?'

'Well. Somewhere around here. I've had enough to drink and I need an early night. There'll be rooms available.'

'What about a cab? I'll pay half,' Dan said, although he almost certainly could not afford to pay so much as a quarter.

'Thanks. But I really can't be arsed with an hour or so driving out of London to go straight to bed and come back in again tomorrow. I'll just get a Travelodge or something.'

'Don't be silly,' Dan said. And before he could stop himself, added, 'Stay at mine.'

For a moment, it felt like time stopped. And the next few words Dan uttered would more than likely change the course of his life – if not forever, then certainly for the next day or so.

'Ours, I mean. The flat. The spare room.'

Anya, for her part, looked as though he had just dropped to one knee and proposed.

'You're not serious?' she said.

'Well…'

'Dan. Come on. I'm not staying at yours.'

'Why the fuck not? Until two months ago we stayed in the same house every night.'

'Because we were *married*.'

'Still are. Just about.'

'I'll get a hotel,' she said, collecting her things and picking up her coat.

'No. Just… just listen. I'm not… you know… suggesting. I'm just saying. There's a flat a few miles from here. It's free. You know it. There's a spare room. There's… linen.'

'We're not staying in the same flat, Dan. What would Matt say?'

'Fuck Matt. Dickhead,' he said. 'Anyway. It's not like we'll go broadcasting it. My point is, there's no sense in spending… I don't know how much on a hotel. When the flat is just there. Empty.'

'Except for you.'

'Look. We'll go back. Get a curry. You can have a bath and go to bed. Done. Easy.'

* * *

Anya knew that finding and paying over the odds for a hotel wouldn't be too hard. Neither would getting some food delivered and having an early night.

But she also knew that she wasn't going to do that. Some combination of drink and nostalgia was compelling her to go back to the old flat, to get a takeaway from one of the places she and Dan used when they were younger and happier, to spend the evening – their last under the same roof as a married couple – *together*.

'Well, then?' Dan said. He showed her his phone, thumb hovering over the button to book an Uber to Crouch End. The map displayed the little snaking path to what still, in some small and confusing way, felt like home.

'Fine,' Anya said with a smile. And Dan hit the button.

* * *

The journey felt like an open-top bus tour of her past. Their past, really. The route followed her old commute, taken either by bike or on the lower deck of W7. Every half-mile or so, another little landmark reminded her of some piece of recent, but oh-so distant, history. Shops, pubs, restaurants. The corner where she had slipped on a patch of ice cycling to work one January morning, breaking her arm. The bush she had once vomited into after getting off the night bus at four in the morning.

Then they were into Crouch End itself. It was a funny thing, seeing this little enclave of London again. She had spent years immersing herself into the community here. Getting to know the names of shop and café owners, experiencing that little bit of warmth that came with visiting a market stall and having the seller know precisely what she was after. It was a vague community of people who weren't friends, but were a tangential part of her life. They saw her through her first pregnancy, the bump emerging, growing and eventually disappearing to be replaced by Martha. They knew when Anya was on holiday because of her absence, and asked about it when she got back. They came to know a family – the Moorcrofts – without ever setting foot over the threshold of their flat. All of it through minor interactions and transactions throughout the weeks, months and years.

Like millions of others, Anya had assumed that London was transient. Everyone was just passing through. It shocked her a little when she learnt that wasn't the case, for her at least. And leaving, when it happened, was a wrench she hadn't anticipated.

'Just here,' Dan said, and the driver pulled over to the side of the road, attracting the blaring horn of the car behind.

Anya peered out of the rain-spattered window at the curry house. 'Jesus. It hasn't changed at all,' she said, opening the car door and getting out, looking up at the gold, black and red sign for The Viceroy of India. 'Is it the same people working there?'

'His son runs it now. They've done it up inside.'

She followed Dan in. Sure enough, what was once a restaurant decorated with dusty fake plastic trees, a floral carpet and a mural of the Taj Mahal, now resembled a wine bar. All pink neon lights, parquet floors, chrome and glass. A waiter she vaguely recognised stood behind the bar, pouring a gin and tonic for the one couple who were in there eating.

'Order for Dan?' he said, noticing them.

'That's the one.'

'Two minutes. Beer while you wait?'

'Oh... nah,' Dan said with a look back at Anya. 'Not this time.'

The waiter looked up and said, 'I see. I see, I see,' with a knowing grin that both misunderstood the situation and assumed that, if Dan was taking a woman back to his flat, he would stop to grab a curry on the way.

'Oh. No. Not like that,' he said, as the two of them awkwardly milled around until another waiter she knew by sight appeared with a large purple bag with *DAN* daubed on it in white marker pen.

Something like muscle memory led the two of them out of the curry house, left up the hill and on to their old flat. But for a few minor changes in shopfronts and road markings, Anya felt like she had been thrown a decade or so into the past, arriving back home slightly pissed and with a takeaway in hand.

But it was also those minor adaptations that reminded her of how much had changed and who she was now.

Like how Sicily Joe's had rebranded to Amalfi, and was dominated by a vast stone pizza oven rather than a grubby counter and a chicken fryer. Now it advertised *wood-fired pizzas* and *sourdough bases* instead of its *Famous Kebab*

Meat Stuffed Crust! Everything was still cooked and served by Mehmet, mind.

Like how the betting shop a few doors down had closed and been taken over by a competitor.

Like how the front door that led up to the flat had been repainted blue instead of the chipped, turgid green of before.

Like how String Theory was now an interiors shop called Fika. How the guitars and amplifiers had been replaced by houseplants, cushions, a nice armchair and what looked like incredibly expensive mugs. And how the old pink neon sign above the shop had become silver lettering, all in lower case, against natural wood panelling.

It was almost heartbreaking to see it like this. To know how much of his life had been wrapped up in String Theory, and now there was nothing except this shrine to overpriced soft furnishings. Not that she had anything against soft furnishings, of course, but they felt less significant and noble to Anya than musical instruments.

'It does quite well, you know,' Dan said, noticing her looking through the window.

'I'd expect so round here.'

'They sell a tea towel for nine quid.'

'Nine quid?' Anya said. 'Fucking hell.'

'They're nice, though. The people that run it.'

'You've been in, then?'

'Once or twice. Birthday presents and that.'

'As long as it's not the tea towels,' she said. 'Do they know what it was? The shop, I mean.'

'I told them once.'

'And?'

'They couldn't care less. Didn't even give me a discount,' he said, with a sad smile. 'Anyway. You ready?' Dan looked up into the sky, as though he was surprised that it was raining again. She could never understand how anyone described the London night as inky. It was more like looking into a puddle.

'Sure,' she said, putting her misgivings about this evening

to one side and following Dan through the blue door, up the still worn and torn stairwell, and into her one-time home.

'Shit,' she said, on stepping inside. 'It's…'

'The same?'

'Like, exactly the same.'

Right down to the posters that Dan had rehung on the wall since moving back in, which had spent the last couple of years in his workshop, instead of on general display. The most prominent, of course, was his prized CBGB print, bought alongside a T-shirt on a visit to the legendary venue in New York, shortly before it closed down. Once again, it was above the television, as if he'd never left in the first place.

She also noticed posters for gigs that had happened before he was born. A collage of tickets for things he had been to. And his beloved framed Newcastle United shirt, signed by Alan Shearer.

And there, by the TV, was a small stack of *Q* back issues, a few DVDs, that book about economics she knew he'd never finish, and an ashtray.

While Dan set about finding plates and opening a couple of beers, Anya gingerly looked around the hallway and living room, as if she was a viewer rather than a part owner of the place. She was every bit as uncertain and curious as she had been the first time she came here fifteen years ago, trying to discern what the furnishings, decorations and bookshelves could tell her about this man.

Had Dan regressed since moving out of the family home? Or was this just him when unadorned by family? Dan in his purest state. Music. Football. Cigarettes.

More than likely, it was comfort. The next best thing to the life they had built together. Seeing it all made her equally heartbroken and happy.

This flat was where it had begun. Was it going to end here as well?

'Right, ready,' he called from the kitchen, where two plates piled high with curries, rice, sides and bread were on the small round table they'd eaten their meals at for so many years. A bottle of Birra Moretti was next to each plate, and a paper bag full of poppadoms in the middle.

Anya took a seat opposite him, pulled a chunk of chewy, just-about-warm naan away from the lump on her plate and dipped it in that yellowy yoghurty thing decent curry houses give out for free.

'You know, you never asked me what I wanted,' she said. 'From the takeaway, I mean.'

'Chicken dhansak, pilau rice, saag bhaji, half a Peshwari naan.'

'So confident.'

'Well, I'm hardly going to forget, am I? It's the kind of thing you just know about someone.'

Anya smiled. 'I suppose,' she said. 'What if I'd changed, though?'

'No one ever changes. Once every so often, you have a tandoori chicken. But only if—'

'Yes. If I'm on a diet or something.'

'I bet you can remember mine,' Dan said through a mouthful of bread and lime pickle.

'Lamb bhuna, share the rice, saag aloo – despite the unnecessary extra carbs. And two onion bhajis.'

'Spot on. It's intimate knowledge, isn't it? You'd never know that about your friends or your parents. And you never deliberately commit it to memory. It just sort of gets in there over time.'

'Is this your insight on relationships? If you can remember their curry order, they really matter.'

Anya pushed down on the bag of poppadoms, feeling the satisfying crack as all four of them shattered at once.

'I bet you can remember exactly what your exes used to order from a takeaway,' Dan said.

'I'm pretty sure Jake had a korma.'

'Well, I can see why it didn't last.'

'Hey! Jake was nice.'

'Yeah. But you never stay with a korma, do you?'

'A korma isn't a personality trait, Dan.'

'Except it kind of is.'

'Who's Mister Korma, then?'

'You know. Dependable but a bit boring. Won't take risks. Always on top of his paperwork.'

'He sounds delightfully unstressful.'

'And yet so dull.'

'Well, what about yours, then? Exes and curries.'

'Hannah, no idea. Too long ago. Sarah, chicken tikka masala. Every time.'

'Shit.'

'I know.'

'Jen?'

'Vegetarian. She had a few starters and sides.'

'Awkward.'

'Exactly,' Dan said. He was feeling good. A little drunk. Not too bad, but certainly more than he should be, given the circumstances.

'Fine. Let's say you're right. If you'd date a korma and avoid a tikka masala, what would you do with a vindaloo?'

'Shag a vindaloo.'

'Of course. Marry?'

'Marry, I don't know, something in between. Like a madras or a jalfrezi.'

'Well, I married the bhuna,' Anya said with a smile.

'And look how that turned out,' Dan said, before he could stop himself. 'Maybe you should've gone for something else?'

The smile fell from Anya's face immediately. The little game was over. Dan castigated himself for the bad joke, as she pushed bits of chicken around the thick dark red sauce on her plate, and sipped her beer.

'Sorry. I…'

'It's fine.'

'Misplaced joke.'

'Well, comedy equals tragedy plus time,' she said.

'I suppose we need the time?'

Anya smiled politely. It had been fun, talking to him like that. Joking, doing a bit. That's how it always was.

She always used to marvel when people told her about how hard they had worked at marriages and relationships. To her mind, it was a sign that they'd married the wrong person and had nothing in common. Creative or artistic friends had settled down with accountants and quantity surveyors, then complained about how hard it was to find shared interests. Visits to museums felt like dragging a sullen teenager around, and they could never find a film to agree on. Every time, she felt like asking, *Well, what did you expect?* As if she had got it so right with Dan. Because that fun and comfort came so easily.

Turned out that it takes more than a mutual fondness for Hockney exhibitions and Noah Baumbach films to make a marriage.

Even so. That chat, the evening itself, was a little taste of it. Then his reminder of why they were here, in their old kitchen, eating together, cut right through it.

Dan clipped off a piece of poppadom. She wondered if he would put the uneaten shards in the bread bin like they always used to, left there to go soft and chewy, and thrown out for good a day later (if not eaten before breakfast).

'You know, I always did think it'd be forever. Us, I mean,' she said, still looking down at her plate.

'Me, too.'

'Were we stupid, though?' she said, putting her cutlery down. 'Like, we just assumed it'd be fine. Should we not have tried a bit harder?'

'We did try.'

'We think we tried. What if that wasn't what trying is? What if you really have to suffer before it gets any better?'

'Is this your Catholic side coming out again?'

'You know what I mean,' she said. 'Did we get complacent? We always carried on through thinking we would be fine.'

'I don't think we can blame ourselves for being complacent. Marriage *is* complacent, isn't it? You'd never sit around in your worst joggers with someone when you start going out. Two years in, you can barely be arsed to wear trousers.'

'It's more than that, though, isn't it?'

'I'm just saying you can't be on your toes all the time. We always loved each other. We always made an effort.'

'So how did we fuck it up, then?' Anya said.

* * *

Dan had asked himself the same question so often recently. On those lonely, long evenings in the flat that had once been home to his small family.

How had they gone from the couple that was so in love they were set for life within just six weeks of meeting each other to separate beds, and separate lives? How had they invested so much effort into having a family, nurturing and growing it, only to pull it apart in a series of micro-transactions agreed on in a lawyer's office?

They'd seen people they knew divorce and winced at their shared lives becoming shrapnel. Over time their circle of friends had changed as people close to them left to be gradually replaced by new partners, most of whom carried their own war wounds and issues. All the while, Dan had thought, *Not us*. Whatever the argument, the problem, the concern, they'd get over it. None of these things were big enough to break them. But put enough of them together, and that's what happened.

A few sexless months and low self-esteem led to Dan having an affair. Their inability to deal with it led to Anya having a longer one of her own. Maybe it was done after that, he thought. That was the end. But still they had struggled on, like an injured runner dragging a lame leg, determined to finish the race.

He was so disappointed in himself. Having come from a

busted-up family, he had refused to see the same happen to his own. And yet…

'I don't know,' Dan answered after a while. He placed his hand on the table. Anya put hers into it. 'I don't know how we fucked it up. But I always thought we'd get further than this.'

'Me, too,' she said, trying to keep hold of her voice.

'I still—'

'Don't,' she said quickly. 'I know what you mean. But don't.'

'Sorry,' Dan said, taking his hand back.

Anya looked above Dan's head, into the kitchen, where tinfoil takeaway boxes were piled together next to the bag the curry had come in. Then over at the spare room door. Where she'd spend her final night in this flat.

'It's late,' she said. 'I might just have a bath and get to bed.'

Dan checked his watch. Just turned ten.

'No. Of course. I'll set up the room. Put some sheets on and all that.'

'Thanks,' Anya said, getting up from the table, and leaving Dan alone.

* * *

An hour later, Anya was in the single bed in what had variously been their office, a spare room and Martha's bedroom. A place she'd only slept in either when Dan was snoring so loudly rest was impossible, or her daughter needed a mother's comfort. The sheets were clean but creased from months spent in a cupboard. And they smelled of her home in Suffolk, from where Dan had taken them when he'd left. The pillow was lumpy and worn, one of the old ones that had moved house with them for no good reason other than it felt odd to throw a pillow in the bin.

Above her, a bare bulb hung without a shade; behind, a damp-spotted blind blocked out maybe half the light from the street outside. A tumbler of water, a lip balm and her phone sat atop three cardboard boxes, labelled *Books*, *Dan summer clothes* and *Misc*.

Anya was restless. So much of tonight felt like a mistake. But then so much didn't. It felt comfortingly plain and normal. Like this was how things were meant to be. That this was her life as it should be lived. Squaring that with what was going to happen tomorrow was hard. She knew the next twenty-four hours would be much easier had she never come here at all.

Dan was still out there in the living room. She could hear his old slippers slap-slap-slapping between the laminate floor and the soles of his feet. And the occasional click of a light switch being turned off, a door being locked. Then, finally, came the creak of him getting into their old bed.

She picked up her phone and turned the camera on to selfie mode. There were a few more lines on her face than there had been the last time she was here. Her mouth looked like it was drooping a little, too. She wondered if that was the result of so much unhappy frowning over the past couple of years.

Anya nodded to herself, locked the phone and got out of bed. She had expected to feel butterflies or some sort of nervous energy about what she was going to do. But there was none of it. Besides, she didn't want to self-examine too much. Not now.

She didn't even pause outside Dan's room, knowing that any break in momentum could scupper her impulse. And she didn't ask to get into bed beside him, somehow understanding that he wanted this every bit as much as she did.

'Hey,' he said, turning to face her. She could just about make out his features in the dark. But she didn't need to see them. They were as familiar as the backs of her eyelids.

'Hey.'

'You know this might be a bad idea?'

'I don't care,' she said.

'Neither do I,' he said.

And they kissed.

DAY TWO

NOW

Dan took the first bus to the Melrose and White offices, Anya saying she would wait ten minutes, then get on the next. To complete the illusion, she would then send Matt a message to tell him that she was running late, blaming a delayed train on her way into London.

Charlotte was already outside when Dan got there, holding two cardboard coffee cups, one the size of a pint glass and the other the size of, well, a normal coffee.

'Morning!' she said brightly, looking up from her phone. 'I got you one with an extra shot,' she said, handing him the enormous cup. It would take him at least an hour to get through that much espresso and frothy milk. 'I know some people don't sleep too well while these things are going on. Might perk you up a bit. You know, if you need perking up.'

Dan looked at himself in the window of the office building, wondering if he looked overly tired or downbeat. Not really. His hair was slightly untidy and his shirt a little creased, both a result of a bit of a rushed morning with two of them needing to use the bathroom. Also, a lack of alternatives meant he was wearing the same jacket and trousers as yesterday, feeling a bit like a *Great British Bake Off* contestant as a result. But beyond that, he didn't look any more dishevelled than normal.

'Cheers,' he said, taking a sip of the cappuccino, getting mostly milk and a bit of chocolate powder forced through the little hole at the top of the cup.

'Good evening?' Charlotte asked, leading him into the reception and signing them both in.

'No,' Dan said quickly. 'I mean, like, not bad. But not good either. You know. Weird one.'

'I can understand that.'

'Just a curry and bed, really. Early one. Want to keep my head, you know. Focus,' he said, unable to stop speaking.

'Absolutely.'

'What about you?' Dan said, noticing that the two original receptionists from yesterday had been charged up and were back behind the desk. Charlotte handed him a visitor lanyard and sat down on a firm red sofa.

'Oh! Wonderful. Great, yeah. It's really good, that *Aladdin*. Have you been?'

'No. Not yet,' Dan said, unsure of why he added *yet*, realising that might suggest some intention of going one day.

'Well, you should. It's just...' Charlotte began, then stopped short. 'Oh! Think they're here.'

Dan didn't want to look round. To see Anya there, dressed in the jacquard trousers and white shirt from yesterday, that he'd last seen at the bus stop forty-five minutes ago. To say hello and start the discussions that would end their marriage, only nine hours after they'd last had sex. To be formal and professional, so soon after she'd swerved his attempted kiss goodbye.

'Dan,' Charlotte said. 'I said—'

'Sorry. I know.'

Then he heard her voice behind him. That soft Irish accent that had said, 'No, sorry,' before he boarded the 91 towards Holloway Road.

Dan stood up to face her. Anya was serious and straight, looking right past him to the lifts, holding her overcoat across her forearm. He noticed that she was wearing a black wool jumper over the top of her shirt. No doubt she had worried that someone might clock that she hadn't changed since yesterday and found an early-opening branch of M&S on her way in.

Matt was stood next to her. A dark grey suit this time, with a clean, pressed white shirt and a purple tie.

'You both all right?' Matt said.

'Great!' Charlotte said cheerfully.

'Fine.'

'Good.'

'How was your evening?' Charlotte asked. Dan looked at Anya, but she was still staring straight ahead.

'Not bad. Gym. Dinner. Bed,' Matt said.

'Anya?'

'Sorry?'

'Oh. Nothing. I was asking if you'd had a nice evening. It doesn't—'

'Sorry. Fine… thanks. Just had a curry and an early night.'

'Ha! Funny.'

'What?' Matt said.

'Curry and an early night. Same as you, Dan. Maybe you've got more in common than you thought,' Charlotte said to deathly silence.

'Right. Well shall we get on with it, then?' Matt said, leading them towards the lifts in their pairs, where they once again went up three floors, down a short corridor and arrived at the room called Serenity, with Margot waiting inside, her notebook at the ready.

* * *

'Good morning, all,' Margot said. Anya noticed that she was wearing different glasses today, swapping the bold pink frames for thin wire ones and dark purple lipstick to make up for the lack of colour. Maybe, she thought, this was part of Margot's personal brand. She had once worked with a man who put a picture of the baker-boy-style hat he wore on his business cards, as if to suggest that headwear marked him out as somehow interesting. Was this her equivalent?

The four of them took the same seats as yesterday, like jurors returning after an adjourned trial. Matt didn't bother talking them through the tea and coffee options this time, instead making himself one while ignoring the rest of them. Charlotte poured five glasses of water from the jugs on the table, which today had lime wedges and cucumber slices floating among the ice cubes.

Anya could tell that Dan was trying to catch her eye. In the same way he had across dining tables at meals with friends, back when they were younger and happier and less tired and it was easy for him to tell her that he thought she was the prettiest woman in the room with little more than a shared half-second glance.

She wouldn't meet his eyes, though. It was too easy for other people to pick up on little cues like that, to read too much into it. Although, in this case, there was a fair amount to read into it, of course.

But what did he want?

The morning had been awkward. In a depressing, cracked mirror image of their first night in that flat, he'd left early to get coffees and pastries. When he got back, their conversation was stilted and raw.

They weren't going off into their separate young London lives to tell people about the great date last night, and how it had ended up in some pretty decent sex, considering it was the first time and that first times were usually a bit clumsy, unfamiliar and laborious. Instead, they were going to a little room in a big lawyer's office to talk about how they would divide up their kids' time after their divorce, all the while clinging to civility and trying to keep a lid on the timbre of their voices.

One shag, or rather two, didn't change that. It sure as hell complicated it. But it was too late to make any meaningful difference. Last night was a flourish, not a reinvigoration.

'Everybody settled?' Margot asked, as everyone muttered their agreement and Matt took the elastic strap off his notebook with an exaggerated ping. 'Good. Now, before we begin today, I'm quite aware that the next couple of hours will be the most difficult point in this process for both of you. When people have children, they very rarely do so expecting that they will have to negotiate the custody of them at some point.'

Margot turned a page of her own notebook. Dan noticed her write *KIDS* at the top of the page in scruffy, all-capitals handwriting.

'So my preference is to make this child-centred,' she said, softening her voice at the end of the sentence. 'We must all be guided by what's best for them. So, with that in mind, I like to begin this part of the process by asking you to tell me a little more about your children. Dan, you might like to begin.'

'Me?' he said, surprised to be called on.

'Yes.'

'Tell you about the kids?'

'If you could, Dan. Some people like to start with when they became parents.'

'Right,' he said, wondering where to start.

FAMILY

EIGHT YEARS AND FOUR MONTHS AGO

They were at a set of traffic lights, barely moving as cars crept through the perpetual bottleneck of rush hour London. Roadworks around Gospel Oak meant their route home was taking them up past Hampstead Heath, where trees glowed yellow and orange against a bright pink late October dusky sunset. A rare one, as it turned out, in a mostly soggy and grey autumn.

Dan looked out of the window as dog walkers and runners enjoyed the last few minutes of half-daylight before night fell over the only part of the city that felt like it knew true darkness. Occasionally, a cyclist would bumble past, up the middle of East Heath Road, incredibly slow but still much faster than the cars.

The radio was quiet but playing away. A drive time show where the DJ took requests from listeners, ensuring a playlist that was akin to a wedding band's repertoire. All 'Summer of '69', 'Don't Stop Me Now' and 'Come on Eileen'. Easy enough to ignore.

'You all good there?' Anya said from the back.

'Fine.'

'Thousand-yard stare.'

'Just tired,' he said, realising as he did how true that was.

'Should probably get used to that.'

Dan laughed and said, 'How is she?' He turned around to face his wife and daughter, sat there in a car seat that he couldn't imagine she would ever fill, sleeping quietly, bundled under waffle blankets and wearing a little white cotton hat bearing a picture of Elmer the Elephant. She'd been here for just eight hours. And even in that small space of time had made the previous thirty years of his life feel like little more than a run-up to her arrival.

'Fine,' Anya said. 'Sleeping. I mean, I guess that means she's fine.'

A pair of flashing lights from behind reminded him to move three or four metres up the road. Ten seconds closer to home.

'What'll we do when we get in?' Anya said.

'What, you mean like food?'

'Well, I more meant her.'

'Oh,' he said. 'Sure.'

Dan wanted to suggest something. But if he was honest, he didn't know. What did people do with a new baby when they first got home? For all the parenting classes taken, books and blogs read, unsolicited advice listened to, that bit didn't really come up. He knew they weren't supposed to leave her alone in a room. So did that mean she would just stay in the living room with them? Or did they go into the bedroom with her?

Normally, when something big and new and exciting arrived in the flat, it would sit there in its box for a couple of days until they decided where it would go, and what they would do with the thing that was in that place already. But Martha wasn't a fridge or a TV stand. She was, well, she was sort of everything, already.

Almost everything else had become totally insignificant very quickly. Mundane concerns from their old life before she happened and demanded one hundred per cent of their attention, even when she wasn't actually doing anything, slipped away.

Could they pick up with the box set of *Mad Men* they were watching? Order a pizza? Check their phones?

'Show her around, I suppose?' Dan offered, as the traffic moved again.

* * *

Night had more or less fallen by the time they got back. Purple replacing the pink in the sky. The runners now home.

Having practised the installation and removal of a car seat perhaps a hundred times over the past week, Dan took Martha out of the back of their little Renault Clio. The pram was already in the hallway before the stairs up to the flat, both of them knowing that lugging the thing up and down every day might result in talks about a house move within weeks.

'You all right with the stairs?'

'Think so,' Anya said, holding on to the bannister, as though a little uncertain about whether she would make it up to the door, or if her legs would give way and she'd collapse onto the dull, stained green carpet.

'I can do two trips.'

'It's fine.'

'Well, you go first. I'll be right behind if you need me.'

'No. You're carrying her. You go.'

'Sure?'

'I'll be fine,' she said with a weak smile. One that took her last vestiges of strength and energy after sixteen hours in labour, and twenty-one without sleep.

With Martha still sleeping in the seat hanging in the crook of his arm, Dan climbed up to the flat and took their daughter into her home for the first time.

The place looked the same as when they had left it. But was somehow completely different. The Moses basket in the living room, bottle machine and steriliser in the kitchen and extensive collection of coloured muslins on the couch no longer represented preparation – runners in their blocks waiting to be put into action. They were suddenly in use, as much a part of domestic life as the kettle, toaster and microwave.

The once spare room, now decorated with woodland-scene wallpaper, was actually owned by the little person it had been done up for. Specifically, Martha's room, not generally the baby room.

And beyond all the aesthetics and gadgets and wall coverings, the fundamental purpose of the flat had changed. The simple act of carrying Martha through the front door meant this was now a family home rather than a young couple's flat. Just as it had transformed from a bachelor pad when Anya moved in.

'She still sleeping?' Anya said, taking off the big maternity coat she had worn to the hospital, beneath which she was wearing one of Dan's jumpers and a pair of black jogging bottoms.

'Yeah,' he said, putting Martha down in the living room. 'She's all right,' he added, inwardly acknowledging that he had no idea whether or not a baby was all right, having had very little working knowledge of them until this exact point.

'I might have a nap, then. Get me up if she needs feeding.'

'Shall I take her out?'

'Give her a minute,' Anya said, standing by Dan's side and taking his hand. He kissed her on the forehead. 'I can't believe she's here,' Anya said. 'And that she's a she.' The two of them had convinced themselves and most of the people around them that they were having a boy, based on spurious gut feelings and old wives' nonsense like train-track heartbeats and how high the bump sat.

'I know,' Dan said. 'It's...'

And he realised then that he didn't know what it was. He had been told what to expect, and how his feelings would change. But there was no overwhelming bolt of love that rendered him sick and scared and thrilled like he thought love would. Instead, there was a new urge to protect. To make sure this little thing, there on the patterned IKEA rug in front of the telly, which was too big for the room, got through her days safely and happily.

A new kind of love maybe, built less on passion, more on protection. It would take him a while to understand it.

'I'll see you in a bit,' Anya said with a squeeze of his hand. And they were alone in the living room. Dan and his daughter.

* * *

He waited until their bedroom door closed, then turned off the big light and, with the ball of his foot, pressed down on the floor switch of their big, arched chrome lamp.

The room had been in stasis from when they left in the early hours of the morning for the hospital. Two mugs still sat on the coffee table, rings of dried tea on the white porcelain, next to a small library of old newspaper supplements and free supermarket magazines, chaotically stacked and cherry-topped with some unopened post. The wrapper of the LoveFilm DVD they had watched half of was in front of the telly. He wondered if or when they might see the rest of *Beasts of the Southern Wild*, though didn't really care either way.

With all the lightness of a ballerina, Dan crouched down on the floor in front of Martha, and carefully pressed the little red button that would unclip her padded seat belt. He waited for a second, as if he'd snipped a wire on a bomb, before pulling her bulky, cardigan-padded arms out, and moving Martha from the car seat on to the little U-shaped pillow on the couch. He sat next to her, looking down on the still-sleeping little girl.

'Hello, then,' Dan said. He'd always worried that it would feel odd, talking to a child. That he might struggle to meaningfully opt into it. Or that he wouldn't be able to do the 'voice'. But it was there. A kitbag for parenting he never knew he had. 'Your mum's just having a bit of a nap. So it's only the two of us for a bit,' he continued, stopping as she wriggled like a worm out of soil, but didn't wake up.

'I know you probably can't understand all this. But… well. I just want to say that I'll always… *always*… be here. Whenever you need me. And I'm going to try so so so hard not to fuck this up, okay? I will. I'll also try to stop the swearing. Especially when you can understand it. Because it might be funny, but I don't want to be the dad who has to apologise for his kid telling someone to "get off the fucking swing".

'Anyway. That's me. Dad. I promise I'm going to try. But I'll make mistakes. I really will. Even if you don't realise I'm making them. But it's important that you know that now. Because...' he said, feeling more vulnerable about making this admission than he ever had before, even though his audience couldn't really understand him. 'Because I don't really have any good examples to go on for all this dad stuff. I don't come from much of a family, really. It was just me and my gran growing up. My mum, your nan, I suppose... She sort of came and went. Got into some bad stuff. And I never knew my dad. Still don't.'

Dan could feel something welling inside him. He pushed it down, knowing that he would have this same conversation with Martha a few times, so needed to get used to it.

'And I don't want that to be you, okay? I want you to always know your dad. Even when I cock it up. Which, to confirm, I will. Even though I won't mean it. But this is an absolute promise... I'm going to try so hard to give you a good family, Martha. And if you can look back when you're my age and know that your parents loved you, and loved each other, and everybody made everybody else happy, then for me, that'll be job done. I'll be all right.'

Dan stopped when Martha squirmed, then kissed her on the forehead and said, 'I love you, little girl.'

And for the next fifteen minutes, father and daughter sat quietly together. One watching the other – who was oblivious to the fact that she was being watched – until she breathed in deeply and let out a small, high-pitched cry.

Dan lifted her out of the pillow and held her against his chest, Martha's head resting on his neck, under his chin, like that space had always been waiting for her. She continued to cry, needily and quietly, as he went into his and Anya's bedroom, where the Moses basket was set up on her side of the bed, along with another stack of muslin cloths, and a little white speaker for the monitor.

'She need feeding?' Anya said, just about managing to lift her head off the pillow.

'Think so.'

'How long did I have?'

'Not as long as you hoped.'

'An hour?'

'Not quite.'

'Fucking hell,' she said, holding her arms out to receive Martha, then pulling down her nursing top.

'Sorry.'

'It's fine.'

'Tea?'

'Sure.'

When Dan returned with the mug, Anya was against the headboard, Martha on her breast.

'Doing all right?'

'I think so,' she said. 'Hard to know if I'm any good at it.'

'Of course you are.'

'Thanks. I mean we'd better hope so.'

Dan sat down next to Anya and took her free hand.

'We'll be okay at this, won't we?' she said. 'I worry that we won't be.'

'We'll get there,' Dan said with a smile. 'I hope.'

SIX YEARS AND SIX MONTHS AGO

Parking at the Royal Free was as nightmarish as ever. As Dan searched for a space, Anya thought back to four months earlier, when their late arrival and a rather more swift labour than Martha's had very nearly resulted in Edie being delivered in the car park. As it was, a wheelchair and a hastily vacated room gave them an hour in the hospital before their second daughter made her entry into the world.

And it was around a month after that Anya began to notice how things were different compared to Martha. Not a comfortable different, either. Edie didn't respond in the ways that their first daughter did. Even so early on, the world around her seemed to make less of an impact.

Initially, Anya brushed her concerns away. And Dan, whether because he felt the same or wanted to placate, agreed. Edie still learnt to smile and grinned at her parents and family as they gurned at her. She laughed when her feet were tickled or when Martha hid behind her hands and played peek-a-boo.

Still, though. Anya worried. She googled symptoms and showed the results to Dan, worrying about glue ear, hearing loss or a learning disability. All the while hoping to God that nothing was wrong with her daughter, then hating herself for considering that something could be *wrong* at all. She promised to love her and value her in the exact same way she would if everything was all right, and felt sick at the notion of rightness in a child. Whatever the problem was (if it was anything) was part of Edie. Like blue eyes, a little crop of dark hair and noticeably big feet were part of Edie.

'There!' Anya called, pointing to where a four-by-four Porsche was reversing out of a space.

Dan slammed down the accelerator, and with its customary underwhelming level of oomph, their shabby blue Citroen Picasso lurched forward and nabbed the space before a black BMW could get there first.

'Calm down. Lewis Hamilton.'

'Well, you said.'

'I didn't say it was a race.'

Dan let the comment pass and looked round into the back, where Martha and Edie had both been lulled to sleep by the short car journey.

'What shall we do? Wake her up?'

'She needs her nap,' Anya said. 'She was up at five.'

'You can't take Edie on your own.'

'Of course I can. If you hadn't noticed, I spend most days with her on my own,' Anya said, which Dan thought a little harsh, given that he rarely started work before nine and was always home well before six.

'I mean I want to go with you.'

'We'll be fine. It's a check-up, isn't it? I'll text you where we are. Just let her sleep as long as she needs.'

'They said they'd give us some results.'

'I'll call you if there's anything you need to know. Don't wake her up.'

With that, Anya got out of the car into the hot August day. It was due to hit thirty at some point that week, which meant all sorts of trouble as she and Dan would have to monitor and adjust the temperature in their bedroom with scientific rigour, removing and adding fans, layers of clothing and blankets according to a thermometer that glowed an angry red when it deemed the room too warm. Before having kids, Anya had loved the hot weather. But now she found herself longing for grey skies and fifteen degrees. Safe for the baby. Easy for Martha.

Today, she felt that almost Mediterranean stillness in the air. The London plane trees were bright green and barely moved by an almost imperceptible wind. Beneath her feet, the asphalt verged on soft, and radiated heat up through her sandals. The sky was the kind of cloudless blue that ushered thousands of young Londoners onto Hampstead Heath, or spurred them to take trains to the nearest coasts in Southend or Kent.

'Come on, then,' she said, lifting Edie out of the car, laying her in the pram and covering her with the canopy and a hastily bought add-on parasol.

It was a lot of faff. Anya had always wanted to avoid having a baby in the summer. Or at least having to care for a newborn during June, July and August. Britain wasn't kitted out for heat of this kind. There was no impetus to install air conditioning or swimming pools for the three or four weeks a year when it was hot enough to warrant their use.

But then Edie wasn't exactly planned in a way that meant they could strategically target or swerve specific months or seasons. She wasn't *unplanned*, as such. But was more brought about by the absence of prevention rather than proactive trying. In short, seasonality hadn't been a concern in her conception.

For all the surprise when they found out, it was good news. She and Dan had always wanted two (maybe, but probably not, three). Although there were so many things Anya wanted to sort out before that happened. A couple more holidays with Martha, maybe. And she had ideas on buying or renting a camper van for a trip around Europe.

The main thing, of course, was their flat.

It was too small for a family of three, let alone four. And she wanted to think more about *where* they lived in terms of location as well as property. Even though she knew that convincing Dan to leave behind the cheap mortgage payments and emotional tie to the place Eddie had left him would be a wrench. London itself had been an almost automatic choice for them both. They had met in the city, and rarely paid any thought to why or if they should stay.

In the end, the move had been rushed. The unexpected but not unwelcome pregnancy and the idea of two kids tearing around three rooms convinced Dan to remortgage, put the flat up for rent and look for a new place elsewhere.

Instead of visiting satellite suburban towns where green space was more plentiful and properties larger, they took friends' advice on decent enough places to raise kids in North London and spent three weekends attending mass viewings that felt like school open days. All the while, her growing bump and expanding list of pregnancy symptoms added urgency to their search.

Even when they celebrated an accepted offer Anya knew that the place in Queen's Park was a good house, but not their perfect house. She hated herself a little for being seduced by ideas of forever homes. Where notches in a bannister would chart the steady growth of their kids, the lounge would have a chair and blanket covered in more hair than the dog who sat in it. Where they'd stay long enough to plant trees in the garden and watch them grow.

'It's called a property ladder for a reason,' Dan had said, unsympathetically but correctly, when trying to talk her down from the ledge of abandoning the purchase and making for the Chiltern Hills because they'd been to a barbecue there and it all seemed quite nice. 'We'll get there.'

There was now firmly on the longer-term to-do list. The kind that never gets looked at as living day to day takes precedence.

Anya pushed the pram into the hospital reception and made an immediate right for the paediatric department.

'This way,' she said to Edie, the two of them gliding swiftly along the lino floor.

In her bag was a letter, instructing her on where to go, who to ask for, where they'd be. But already, she felt lost and disorientated. The hospital was stifling in the heat. That smell of soup and disinfectant all the more pervading, making the air thick and hard to get into her lungs.

After a couple of wrong turns, she finally found the desk she was looking for. Much the same as the one in the main reception, albeit with a large rainbow painted across the front, along with a sheep, a cow and a chicken.

'Hi. Edie Moorcroft,' she said. 'Here to see…' Anya took out the crumpled piece of paper, like a map rather than a missive. 'Doctor Asgheddi.'

'And you are?' the receptionist said, not looking up at her.

'Anya. Her mum.'

'Take a seat,' she said, and Anya pushed Edie over to a little waiting area, decorated with more cows, more rainbows and an approximate drawing of Mickey Mouse that she was sure Disney lawyers would request the removal of if they knew it was there.

She checked in the pram, where her daughter was asleep. Things were running late. And the forty-minute wait was at once frustrating and a blissful break as the baby slept. Before an elderly male Asian doctor put his head out of a small consultancy room and called her name out.

* * *

The words, when she heard them, could've caused her to collapse. It made complete sense and no sense at the same time.

'Hearing loss,' he said. One of the many things she had diagnosed Edie with and later discounted, shooing away her parental paranoia.

She assumed she'd replied. Probably with something banal and inoffensive. Like, 'Right, then,' or, 'I see.'

But Anya didn't really take in anything beyond that initial diagnosis. And didn't feel entirely in the room. Instead, while

Doctor Asgheddi explained the background, the prognosis, the next steps. Anya's mind jumped forward to the age Martha was, picking up language and speech from everything and everyone around her. Then forward to school, and whether Edie would have to go somewhere different and specialist. She thought of how they would have to learn to communicate with her in different ways, and create a distinct, wobbly path through the world that Edie would be able to walk down, veering away from her sister's.

Anya wanted to ask whom to speak to about this, and what they planned to do to correct it.

This wasn't a diagnosis. It was a rearrangement of the life she'd imagined for Edie – and a reminder not to plan anything.

'How?' Anya eventually said, cutting the doctor off midway through a spiel about early years solutions and advancing technology or some bollocks.

'Sorry?'

'How did it happen?'

'Well, it could be a number of reasons,' Doctor Asgheddi said, with a slightly frustrated look that told Anya that he'd already been over this once and she hadn't been listening. 'Possibly an infection we didn't see. Or an issue in the womb or during birth.'

'So it could be my fault?' she said, holding Edie on her knee, only just realising that none of this conversation would be making its way through to her. Just as none of the funny noises, little comments, declarations of love she and Dan had made over the past weeks and months had got through.

'Mrs Moorcroft, I really do encourage you not to think of it like that. In many cases, half I would say, we never know the actual cause. Our energies – *your* energies – are better focused on what's to come for little Elsa here.'

'Edie.'

'Sorry.'

Anya felt a brief surge of anger. At this doctor who

couldn't get her daughter's name right. She was just another ticket from the counter.

It passed with a deep breath and the acceptance that he must see hundreds of kids every week, most of them in varying states of temporary or permanent unwellness. He was only a few letters out, after all.

Instead, she turned the lens back on herself and the things that might've contributed to this. Was it because she had been more relaxed with this pregnancy? Enough to allow herself the very occasional half-glass of wine and a Prosecco at a wedding. Maybe it was the weekly exercise classes she had kept up until the bump was big enough to make gentle squats and sprints horribly uncomfortable, if not quite impossible.

What could she have sacrificed that would've avoided this? As Doctor Asgheddi spoke about new referrals, further assessments, options for treatment, Anya wondered inwardly if a simple thing to improve her life had been the cause of the defining characteristic of her daughter's.

'Okay,' she said. 'So… now?'

'You'll receive a letter for the referral to the audiologist. That shouldn't take too long. A week, two at most. In the meantime, keep playing and interacting with your daughter just as you would,' he said, stopping short of adding: *if she could hear you*. Or so Anya assumed.

'Right. And is there… I don't know… Any help anywhere?'

'Absolutely. I recommend you look at the National Deaf Children's Society website. They have plenty of information and resources that you'll find useful.'

'Okay.'

'And before you go,' he said, ushering her out in the gentlest way possible. 'Is there anything else I can do for you?'

'No,' Anya said, checking her watch. She had only been in the consultancy room for ten minutes. That was all it had taken to get the test results back and deliver the news. 'Thank you,' she added, gathering up the changing bag and the BBC Worldwide branded tote she'd been using as a handbag recently.

Doctor Asgheddi stopped her just as she was about to walk out.

'Mrs Moorcroft,' he said. 'If I may. I know this will all come as something of a shock. But I can tell you that there is every chance that your daughter will lead a full, happy life. There is so much support now, and the technology they have today is really quite remarkable.'

Anya offered a weak, conciliatory smile in return. He was a kind man, trying to offer a mother some hope. But she did not want Edie to grow up reliant on support and technological advances.

She hated herself for it, but she wanted normal.

* * *

Two months later

The last time Dan had been in a classroom was sixteen years, and half his life, ago. That was his final French class before a GCSE exam he would go on to scrape a D in. Afterwards, he and some friends bought multipack cans of Fosters from an off-licence run by a man who put profits before police attention, and went into Newcastle city centre.

Today, it was a level one course in British Sign Language. And afterwards, he would meet Anya and Edie at a café around the corner.

He had enrolled the evening they returned from the hospital. Looking back, he recognised that he had been unable to deal with the hurt Anya felt and the confusion around what had happened. Instead of talking about it, he had reached for the nearest solutions to hand. In that case, a course that might help him communicate better with his second daughter. He had also applied to run the marathon on behalf of the charity that helped deaf children.

Now here, about to begin his learning, Dan felt nervous and unsure of himself. There were eight others in the room. He couldn't tell by looking at them whether they were fellow parents, social workers, teachers or just the curious and helpful.

He checked his phone. On the screen was a photo of Martha holding Edie on their couch. Both girls were smiling. Since he'd finally succumbed to Anya's pleas and bought a smartphone a year ago, he had come to realise that this – the home screen – was the new photo in the wallet. Today, it was a little reminder of why he was here. The point of doing this, uncomfortable as he was.

The lesson was due to begin in two minutes. No sign of the teacher (did they call him/her a teacher?) yet. He typed out a message.

Dan: Feeling a bit daft x

Anya: What you're doing is brilliant. I'm proud of you x

Dan: Thanks x

Anya: We'll be in The Black Penny when you come out. I'll buy you a cake x

Dan then heard the door open, and put his phone back inside his jacket pocket.

* * *

An hour and ten minutes later, he walked out on to Keeley Street into a pleasant autumn day. One of his classmates pushed past him, placing a set of headphones on as she went, then stopped a few seconds later to mess around with her iPod. His head still in the class, Dan continued to the café where Anya and Edie would be waiting for him.

Covent Garden was busy with office and retail workers

dodging tourists and scowling at them for having the gall to stop and look at something interesting in the city they'd paid to visit. He narrowly avoided walking into a man carrying a cello and a satchel full of music books, who Dan assumed was off to busk in the market down the road.

It was Edie he noticed first, sat on Anya's lap at the back of the café. They were reading a book together, Anya pointing at pictures, talking to her as she had been told to, knowing most of it stood little chance of being heard.

The first few weeks after that appointment at the Royal Free had been intense and difficult. They adhered to the advice, went to the follow-ups with the specialists and learnt new things about how to raise their daughter. They explained what was happening to Martha, who barely understood herself. And it was both heartbreaking and frustrating to watch her efforts to get through to her sister, whether it was talking very loudly, drawing scribbled pictures of what she was talking about, or carrying on exactly as before.

'This was meant to be the easy one,' Dan had joked one night. 'We were supposed to know what we're doing.'

Anya struggled more than he did. She found it hard to shake the notion that there was fault, rather than foul luck, at play. Every few nights, she would spend an hour or so in tears about it while he reassured her that Edie would be okay, whatever happened.

'All right,' he said, sitting down at the table and kissing Anya and Edie. A coffee was already waiting for him. As was a piece of chocolate cake that looked like it should appeal more to a five-year-old than an adult.

Edie looked at him, and Dan put his hand against his head, and took it away again. As though saluting rather than greeting her.

'And that's?'

'"Hello",' he said, taking a sip of his coffee. 'Day one. Lesson one.'

The sign rocked Anya a little. The fact that they were already underway with this, accepting how they would have to communicate with their daughter in years to come. Signs, lip-reading, hopefully some speech if the aids eventually worked.

'And how was it?'

'Fine,' Dan said with a forced smile that pushed down every worry he had about the whole thing. 'We'll be fine.'

NOW

Anya reached forwards and picked up her glass of water. It had been so long since they'd told anybody new the first stories of Martha and Edie. Back in the days of NCT classes and the newness of parenting, they were like folk tales, repeated and retold over and again. Now so much had passed since that it felt almost like another lifetime ago. Her life – their life – was in two halves: before and after their kids. Now it was about to be halved again.

'Tell me,' Margot said, looking at her over the top of her glasses. 'How is Edie now? Does she…'

'Talk?' Anya said. She was used to this. The first thing anyone ever wanted to know after hearing about Edie's start in life, her difficulties, was how she fared now. Generally, the closer to normality, the better they felt about it. It's so much easier to hear about a little girl who had improved upon her prognosis than one who'd broadly followed the course they'd assumed was set out before her.

'I suppose so, yes.'

'She can. And she can hear most of what we say. The aids they've given her are… well, they're pretty amazing.'

'That's good to hear.'

'Well, it's not the same,' Anya said. 'When Edie hears, she doesn't hear like you or me. The sounds are… different.'

'Okay.'

For a second, Anya wanted to expand on this and clarify. But what, really, was the point? Nobody wanted to know about how the type of sound her daughter heard was that much different. Or how technology made hearing possible for Edie, but only when a certain set of conditions were met – from the ambient noise in a room to the need to see lips move. People didn't want to know that she and Dan had spent years filling TV hard drives with sign-language equivalents of her favourite TV shows. Or how he was still often her primary source of access to communication, having learnt sign language to a much higher standard than anyone else in the family.

People wanted to be told that Edie was mostly fine. That she had overcome something. It was easier than knowing the reality that her life would never be simple in many respects. Easier than letting a child with a disability into their lives.

'She's grand,' Anya said with a smile and another sip of water. 'She's a happy little girl.' Which was true. That much was always true.

'Good,' Margot said, confirming what Anya thought. 'Now, the reason that I ask the two of you to start this part of the process by talking about your children is so we can focus on *them*. I doubt that either of you expected to have to spend much time apart from either Martha or Edie when you had them. But a lot has changed since then. And what we'll agree today will in all likelihood make spending nights, maybe even weeks, apart a legal requirement.'

As Margot spoke, more rain began to tap against the big floor-to-ceiling glass window of the meeting room. Dan allowed himself to be distracted by it for a moment, slightly unable to believe the gearshift that had taken place over the past two hours. They had started the day under the same duvet, legs intertwined like plaited dough, stale breath ignored as they bid each other quiet 'good morning's. And now, barely an hour after breakfast, they were on opposite sides of a table, about to talk about divvying up their kids' lives.

A step had been missed somewhere.

'Now,' Margot continued. 'My first question is whether you've spoken about this already. And what arrangements are already in place.'

'Weekends,' Dan said quickly, noticing that Anya was about to talk. 'I have the girls on weekends.'

'Good. And that involves you travelling up to Suffolk, I assume?'

'No. Well, sometimes,' he said. 'Most of the time we meet in a service station. Near Colchester. It's about halfway.'

'Right,' Margot said, taking a note, her first of the day.

'I drive them down after school on a Friday. Dan meets me there. He gets them a McDonald's and they go on to London,' Anya said. 'Junction twenty-eight. In case you were wondering. Near the football stadium.'

Matt looked at her quizzically.

'Colchester United,' Anya said, and Matt nodded.

'And how do you find the arrangement?'

'Fine,' Dan said. At the same time that Anya said, 'Not ideal.'

'Tell me more,' Margot said.

'Well. Every Friday, I have to pack the girls' bags, pick them up from school, drive an hour to the services, and an hour back home. Then on Sunday, we do it again.'

'And you, Dan?'

'Well, the same. But I don't mind it as much. And it's an hour and a half for me.'

'I'm thinking of the girls, Dan. Two and a half hours twice every weekend. You remember the reason we moved up to Suffolk was so they could live in the countryside. Enjoy the outdoors. And they spend every weekend back in London.'

'It's fine,' he said. Although, inwardly, he accepted that it wasn't completely fine. There had been times when finding a route out of London seemed to require a cabbie's knowledge. Martha had been sick in the car three times already that year (as far as Anya knew, it was only once). That was leaving aside how spending every Friday evening driving from Colchester to London, then vice versa on a Sunday, with the *Moana* soundtrack on loop, was beginning to feel like some unique form of torture. Singing along with Martha while Edie played on her iPad had been cute the first time, but the novelty had been quick to wear off.

'My question is whether it's an arrangement you'd be happy to continue with?' Margot said, as Charlotte began scribbling notes next to him. Dan sensed that this was when things were about to get serious. Or nasty. Or both.

'Sure. I mean,' he said, trying to catch Anya's attention, aware that she was trying to avoid it. 'I don't mind getting a B&B up there every so often. Or a hotel. So the girls can… you know… enjoy the countryside. And there's less travel or whatever.'

'And what about you, Anya?'

It was her pause that told Dan that things had changed, that something was up. Just a second or two. But in response to a yes or no question, it said a lot. He saw Anya and Matt look at one another conspiratorially, like parents about to announce the cancellation of a trip to Disneyland.

'Now?' she said. Matt nodded, and both of them fixed on Dan. This was a tactic, he knew. Somewhere in Matt's desk was a playbook for this sort of thing, notes from a coach to players on how to surprise their opponent and make a decisive move they weren't prepared for.

'What?' Dan said. 'What's going on?'

'I just want you to hear me out, okay? Before you say anything, let me finish.'

Instead of answering Anya, Dan looked at Charlotte. 'It's fine,' she said. 'We can talk about it.'

'Okay?' Anya said.

'Okay.'

'Right,' she said, shifting in her seat. 'Look, I've been thinking about taking the girls to Ireland.'

'Anya,' Matt said.

'Fine… sorry… I mean I *want* to take the girls to Ireland.'

'No,' Dan said quickly. He was shocked and confused. Like he'd been punched and mugged and had to put up some resistance. It was the only word he could muster.

'You said you'd hear me out, Dan.'

'And I heard enough. No. I'm not letting my kids live in Ireland.'

Anya rubbed her forehead and spoke quietly to Matt. 'I knew he'd be like this.'

'It's okay,' he said, almost at a whisper. 'Carry on.'

'Like what?' Dan said, loudly. They both looked up. 'You knew I'd be like what? Annoyed that the pair of you have come up with some plan to move my kids to another country.'

'It wasn't the *two* of us, Dan,' Matt snapped, briefly cracking the professional veneer he'd worked from beneath so far. 'It's something Anya wants. How many… times,' he said, redacting the *bloody* or *fucking* that would have otherwise emphasised his words.

'And that's true, is it?' Dan said. 'You want to move them to Ireland.'

'Not all year. Jesus. I asked you if you'd let me finish. I can explain it all.'

Dan looked at Charlotte again. She gave a brief, private nod. He could see that her notepad was now covered in ink. Scrawls and memos that told Dan the process had become contentious, that yesterday had been fairly straightforward as these things went.

'Fine,' Dan said.

* * *

Anya collected herself and looked Dan in the eyes again. This was what Matt had told her to do. Be rational, be calm, be clear. Don't get drawn into arguments and personal squabbles about it. State her case, discuss it, prepare to compromise, but not too much.

It embarrassed her a little, but they had role-played it last week. Anya had taken the train down to London and visited Matt's house in Willesden, where they sat at the kitchen table and acted out how the conversation might proceed while Emma plied them with tea, snacks and, later, wine. They had gone through three possible versions of the conversation, in which Dan variously accepted her plans, disagreed but discussed, and flat-out refused. The whole process had taken four hours, interrupted by occasional interventions from Matt's children, and Emma bemoaning her plan to move to Ireland as much as she worried Dan might.

Now, it felt like they were some way between versions two and three of the scenarios. Anya felt like an improv actor trying to remember how to respond to a cue line.

'My mum and dad are moving back there. Dad's…' she said, something catching in her throat. 'He's not well.'

She saw the look of concern on Dan's face. They had separated. But their families and lives were still connected.

'Parkinson's,' she said.

'I – I'm… sorry.'

'You weren't to know.'

She felt bad for not telling him until now. A text message would've sufficed. Now did all this look tactical?

'Look,' she continued. 'It won't be the whole time. Like, not the entire year. My suggestion is that term time, we live in Ireland. I can help Mum out. Then in the holidays, here. Or I can stay and the girls will live with you. We can work that bit out.'

'What, so you get the easy school days while I have to figure out what to do with them for six weeks every summer?'

'I'm not finished, Dan. Anyway, I said we can work it out. That's why we're here, right?'

'It's why I'm here,' he said. She ignored it, trying to keep in mind Matt's guidance. 'Dad and Mum have decided to go back home. To Cork. They'll need some support over the next couple of years, and the girls have never spent any time there, have they?'

'Holidays,' Dan said. 'Every year.'

'I mean proper time, Dan. Look, I don't want this to become a whole thing, but I always told you that some day I wanted to go home.'

'I thought this was home.'

'You know what I mean, Dan. I loved London. Suffolk is… I mean, it's fine. But it's not really worked out the way we planned.'

'You said you'd be staying there. Yesterday. When we talked about the house. You said you'd be staying.'

'I said for the time being.'

'Ha!'

'What?'

'Well, he's taught you all the tricks, hasn't he?' Dan said.

Anya almost bit back. But, really, he was right. Some of the ways she had phrased things had been pre-planned and prepared. They had used the quirks of language to be clear and honest without being specific. She couldn't escape the feeling that they had also taken advantage of how Dan had entered into the process in a slightly more benevolent spirit than she had.

'I know how you must feel about it.'

'It's just funny how you haven't mentioned it before,' Dan said pointedly. 'Until now, I mean.'

'Come on. Now, you know that's not true.'

He almost responded with another volley. The truth was she had mentioned Ireland before. Every couple of years, they had a conversation about moving to Cork. Holidays there had given Dan a glimpse of the life they might have. Near the coast, plenty of space, decent schools, family close by. And he had been vaguely receptive. But always in a 'sure, some day' kind of way that didn't require them to put their house on the market and begin talking to the girls about leaving for another country and saying goodbye to their friends. Even when they left London, Ireland hadn't been a serious consideration. Their jobs, lives and connections weren't trees that could be uprooted, transported and expected to thrive equally well somewhere new.

But they both knew what Dan meant about not mentioning it before.

He wasn't talking about this conversation in the little room with the silly name. He was talking about when they had a drink together yesterday lunchtime. When they ate together in the evening. After they'd had sex and slept in the same bed and he had gone out early to buy pastries and coffee in a ghostly, heart-rending parallel of their first night in the flat over fifteen years ago.

And now Anya was wrong-footed a little. Off balance. She had been so sure and certain about this plan when she came into the process. The months apart from Dan had done much to solidify her view that he was the problem in their marriage, that she was justified in taking the kids to Ireland. It would be a better life, she had told herself.

Better than what, though?

Better than relative solitude in a small village where they still knew so few people. With a single mother, increasingly over-reliant on babysitters, and weekends spent handing over their kids at a service station on the A12, like they were contraband.

Perhaps.

But better than a life with their dad properly in it? One without the questions that would inevitably come with his continued absence. A life in which he didn't become distant from them, and their hugs goodbye at airports after summer breaks became that bit tighter every year.

Perhaps not.

Anya looked over at Dan. The only time she'd seen him so obviously bereft was after a call from his aunt to say that his grandmother had died.

'Do the girls know?' he said.

'Not yet.'

'When were you going to tell them?'

'I… I was going to talk to you about it. After this. I thought we could do it together.'

He laughed. Scoffed, really.

'Dan.'

'Come on, Anya. "Daddy thinks it'll be a great idea if he doesn't see you for most of the year."'

'So what, then, you'll tell them it's a terrible idea. That it's Mummy's plan or something. Christ, Dan. The reason we're doing this is to *avoid* them having therapy in ten years' time.'

'Anya,' he snapped. 'I'm open to talking about anything. But if you think I'm going to be happy with you moving to another country with my kids, well, you're dreaming. What about schools? What about their friends? What about Edie?'

'She's getting better with lip-reading.'

'Anya, she's miles away. She needs the signing. And you know as well as I do that—'

'Don't you dare,' she said, before he could drop it in. The ace card he always held if they argued about the kids.

She could do the signing. Just not as well as he could. Anya hadn't started learning in earnest until Edie was two.

There were mitigating factors. Dan always had more time, for one. And she had been so rocked in those first couple of years about having a child with hearing problems that actively learning to work with them felt like admitting some sort of failure on her part. Edie's issues were her issues. After all, they had shared a body for a while. No matter how much Dan tried to talk her down, Anya was staunch in her view.

'I'm not, Anya. But you know it as well as I do,' he said, bringing about a brief hiatus.

In the silence, Anya looked around the room, into the face of her husband, their solicitors, Margot. There was no support that she could see. Nothing to suggest that any of them sympathised with her position. Maybe Matt. Although he was a dad, too. And was possibly thinking how he might feel were the same to happen, even though he had encouraged her to do it.

'I don't know what you want me to say, Anya,' Dan said, calmer now, passion and tension giving way to reasoning. 'I'm never going to be okay with this. Jesus, I'm not going to be one of those idiots who chains himself to Downing Street dressed as Spider-Man. But I'll fight it.'

'And what if it's what the girls want, then? My mum and dad are moving back this year. They'll miss them.'

'More than me?'

'It's different, Dan.'

'You haven't even asked them!'

'Well—' Anya began. But a raised hand from Margot stopped her. Like a linesman holding up a flag.

'We're not making progress here,' she said bluntly. It was the most severe she had been since they'd started. Even the tactical little smile afterwards didn't soften it. 'I'm always open to hearing the background to your situation. As you know, my belief is that understanding the history of a relationship makes us more able to determine its future. However, I think we were getting a little too close to trading blows.'

Anya sat back in her chair. She wanted to say that Dan had started it. Good sense kept her from opening her mouth.

'I'd like to understand this a little more from your daughters' perspective. Whatever decision we come to today will have to be in their interests. Not only your own.'

'Well, I can tell you—' Dan said. But the raised hand – the flag – cut him short.

'How did they react when you told them?' Margot said.

'About the divorce?'

'Yes.'

'Sad,' Dan said. 'Upset. I don't know, they were confused.'

'They didn't know anything was wrong,' Anya added.

'Well…'

'Fine,' she added, with a look at Dan, clearly summoning to mind those pictures of the family (and the dog they never owned) that the girls had drawn. And the pleas for the two of them to stop fighting. 'They could see that we weren't getting on. But they didn't think we'd split up. Kids never think that, do they?'

Margot made a note, then looked up.

'You tell me.'

THREE AND A HALF MONTHS AGO

Westleton, Suffolk

Two days had passed since the night spent at the kitchen table. Agreeing to end the marriage had brought greater peace with each other. But only in the same way that the world seemed quiet after a bomb had dropped.

Day one was mostly passed avoiding each other in the house. Each of them listening for floorboard creaks to know who was in what room, and so where was out of bounds for the time being. The move to a quiet village made it worse somehow. At least if they were still in the city there'd be some ambient noise, a shop to pop to for no reason. The stillness made them all the more aware of each other's presence.

They had agreed to tell the girls right away. It seemed only fair. But that plan was nixed at breakfast, when the girls had an argument over whether to eat boiled eggs or fruit toast. Martha stormed off and it was generally agreed that it wasn't the right time.

'Tomorrow?' Anya had said to Dan during an unavoidable meeting at the kettle.

'Think so. Need to prepare.'

But then tomorrow came and they were no more ready than they had been yesterday. Instead, they had a relatively normal Sunday. Bacon sandwiches, a short drive to the coast and a walk on the beach, roast chicken and a showing of their current Disney film of choice (*Ratatouille*).

It was towards the end of the film, when the grumpy food critic takes a mouthful of the film's eponymous dish, that Dan (who was cuddled up with Edie) looked at Anya (who was cuddled up with Martha). They nodded to each other, and effectively set in motion a process that would ensure no more family cuddling up of any sort ever again.

'Girls,' Anya said when the film ended and the credits rolled, shifting out from beneath Martha. Dan followed her lead, picking up Edie and facing her towards him. Her ability to hear was always much better if she could face the speaker. And this was something she needed to hear. 'Your dad and me need to talk to you for a minute.'

'Can I have a marshmallow first?' Martha said, the bag they were collectively munching through still open on the table.

'Okay. But…'

She took one, then Edie did the same. Then Martha took another, so that each cheek was puffed out with whipped sugar and gelatine, and she resembled a hamster storing food for later. Again, Edie followed on while Anya waited. She wanted their full attention, and she didn't want to have this discussion with two children who were distracted by sweets.

'Finished?' she said, when the girls swallowed.

'One more—'

'Not yet,' Anya said, firmly but kindly. Dan got up and went to sit next to her. He felt sick with nerves. The only thing he could compare it to was when he'd gone to break up with an old girlfriend while her parents were downstairs. He was there to deliver bad news only. Hating himself for what he was about to do.

Despite the promise to prepare, they hadn't rehearsed this, or planned what they were going to say. They hadn't been around each other for long enough to do it. So now, their audience waiting, Dan realised they really should have done. The answers for the inevitable questions weren't there for them to reel off like politicians spinning a line. Likewise, the right words of comfort, the reassurances, the there-theres and now-nows.

There were surely blogs about this sort of thing. *Five Things to Say When Telling Your Kids Their Family is Ending.* For a second, he thought about excusing himself to nip to the loo to read one of them.

But he felt Anya's thigh nudge his.

This was it, then. She'd thrown him out on stage. All he needed was for the prompt to throw him his line. Annoying that the only example of this conversation he could think of was from *Mrs Doubtfire.*

'Your mum and I,' he began. 'We… well, we… We've decided to spend some time apart from each other, okay? It's—'

'How much time?' Martha said.

'What did she say?' Edie said.

'She asked how much time. Well, I suppose that's the difficult thing,' Dan continued. 'All the time, really. It's not been easy to decide that. But we think that we both would probably be a lot happier if we were on our own now. And…' Dan said. But no. He couldn't think of what to say next. Martha and Edie's gaped mouths and vacant expressions suggested that they needed something. Clarity, context, reasons, a clear explanation of what this would mean for them. Which, in that moment, he had none of to hand.

This time he nudged Anya's thigh to tell her to take over. Divorce-announcement tennis.

'Right,' she said, suddenly now trying to organise her own thoughts. 'Look, the important thing is that you know that we both love you,' Anya said, hating herself for reaching straight for cliché. 'The thing is that your dad and I… well… I suppose we just—'

'Don't love each other?' Martha said.

'No. We do,' Anya said, looking at Dan to confirm this was still the case, while inwardly thinking if this might make it even more confusing for them. Why split up if you still love somebody? 'It's that we haven't been very happy together for a little while now. You've heard us arguing a bit. And we don't like that any more than you do. So, we thought about it for a very long time and decided that all of us would be happier if we had some time apart.'

The girls seemed to take this bit in. Edie was the first to broach it.

'Just for a bit, then?' she said, loudly. She always spoke loudly.

'Well,' Dan said, picking up the conversation. It was more like a relay than tennis, really. 'No. Not for a bit. We think... actually, we've decided that it's going to be forever.'

And this, finally, was the statement that put the severity of what was happening into focus.

Lips started to wobble. Martha's eyes began to flick between the two of them. She'd had friends in London whose parents had divorced. The notion of it wasn't unfamiliar. Although she always spoke with surprise when telling them that so-and-so's mummy and daddy didn't live in the same house, as though any subversion of the nuclear family unit she was used to was a curiosity.

'Soon I'll be going away for a bit. To London. And you two will stay here with your mum. Nothing will change about school, or your friends, or your house. It's only that I won't be living here any more,' Dan said, feeling his own hold on his emotions weaken. This was the first time he'd said it out loud, too. Previously his departure from the family home had been a notion – an idea. And here he was confirming it. 'But I'll still see you,' he added quickly. 'Every weekend. I'll come up here. Or you two can come and stay with me. So... well, there's that.'

The second he stopped talking, Martha threw herself into Anya's arms and Edie did the same to him. Both girls immediately started crying, and the consoling began. The promises that it would be okay. That they were still both loved. That it was nobody's fault and 'just one of those things'. Dan and Anya answered everything they could, each listening to what the other was saying, so that there was a united front, so that the information was consistent.

And both of them were so busy thinking about the girls that they didn't really realise that this was the end of something. That half-hour on the couch would be the last time they sat together as a family of four. It was the last film on a Sunday afternoon, after the last lunch, after the last walk, after the last breakfast. There would be no more Sunday lunches, no more teas with the girls in their bathrobes before bed. And no shared bedtime stories, with all of them in the same room.

Steady habits were ending just as Dan recognised the value of them.

Raising children often felt like a never-ending series of firsts and lasts. Each one heartbreaking, hopeful, satisfying and sad in varying measures. The thing was that they were always dictated by the kids rather than the parents. When Edie stopped crawling, it was because she'd learned to walk. When they grew out of one toy, or TV show or phase, it was to make room for another.

This time, he and Anya were making the change. Tomorrow Dan would start packing bags and possessions. Ready to move back to London. Within days he would be gone. It all felt easier than it should be.

As Edie cried, Dan leant in close, kissed her head and quietly said, 'I'm sorry.' Then looked over at Anya, whose face was also wet with tears.

Something had died that afternoon. They had killed it.

NOW

Everyone had been taken to that living room in a cottage in Suffolk, lit by a dim lamp and a television paused on the end credits of a Disney film. Charlotte, Matt and Margot formed their own individual mental pictures of this little family, this unit, huddled on a sofa, together, understanding it was the beginning of the end.

Dan looked over at Margot. She saw this stuff all the time, of course. He and Anya weren't special or unique. Just like thousands of others, they'd taken their eyes off their marriage, carried on through life with the misplaced belief that they would be okay, sustained by evenings in front of television series, weekends when there was too much going on to think, the occasional holiday. There were sufficient distractions to keep the obvious at bay as they drifted through with an unknown overconfidence in their ability to get past the years of relentless focus on children, mortgage, work and home, still signed up to their partnership, still with a love that made a relationship viable.

Every so often, in moments like these, he took himself back to the moment he decided to have an affair. And that was the thing, it *was* a decision. People always tried to excuse things as slip-ups, errors of judgment, mistakes. Clipping a wing mirror was a mistake. Having that sixth pint was an error of judgment. Sex rarely was – there was always enough chances to temper impulse with reason.

Before he had gone over to Eleanor's house – before he'd touched her, kissed her, fucked her – no part of him acknowledged that what he was doing would remove the cornerstone he'd built his family on. His head was full of justifications, some of which he had relayed to Anya in the weeks afterwards, as they'd sat at either ends of their sofa in Queen's Park, TV off, talking it through.

'We weren't sleeping together.'

'The affection had gone.'

'You were doing so well with work, I felt like a failure.'

'She made me feel wanted.'

All of them pathetic, undeniably. And Anya had her own set of excuses, too, after she ended things with Kelvin. She blamed Dan's extended pity party after the shop had closed. The simple salve of revenge. And she was a little more brutal in telling him that she found Kelvin attractive at a time that Dan was giving up on himself.

Maybe if he'd stopped outside Eleanor's door and considered what that might've led to, he'd have acted differently. If there was the inkling that a short, unnecessary affair would've ended with his kids moving to a different country, maybe it could've all been avoided.

Of course, he remembered what their marriage counsellor had said, during the short series of appointments they'd bothered going to.

'Infidelity is a symptom. Not a cause.'

If that was true, well, he still had no idea what the root of the problem was. Was his marriage to Anya always destined to end here, in a lawyer's office? Rather than one of them finding the other dead on an armchair well into their nineties? Because that was the ticket he'd bought. Now he was about to exchange it, Dan wasn't sure that he wanted to.

'Thank you,' Margot said finally. She looked at Dan, then Anya. Then back again. As if she was about to cross the road. 'I know talking about that can be very difficult. So, I'm going to suggest that we take a short break now. And when we come back perhaps we can think about how we can resolve some of these issues around childcare and move on?'

Everyone nodded and started to get up to leave.

Dan, however, remained for a short while. He knew 'resolve' meant him getting used to Anya's plan, accepting it as a best version of the worst case. The distance between them on this was unbridgeable – more than about what house to live in, how many weekends he might have, and how they would split payment for the girls' clothes, food, leisure activities and holidays. Margot knew it, too. Despite everything that was nicer and kinder about her mediation, there was likely no possible outcome in which Dan ended up with their children, while Anya moved to Ireland alone.

'Everything all right?' Charlotte said, when Matt and Anya had left with Margot.

'Yeah,' Dan said, looking down at his scuffed black shoes. 'Well, no, I suppose.'

'This is the hardest bit.'

'Tell me about it,' he said, then looked up. 'Are they even allowed to do that? Pull something like that out without telling us.'

'I'm afraid so.'

'Well, what can I do, then?'

Charlotte paused for a second.

'It's probably best that you know that anything you do to try and stop this or frustrate the process will almost certainly push the matter towards the courts. The whole idea of mediation is that you resolve these issues between yourselves. And if it's Anya's wish that your children live with her in Ireland then—'

'I'm fucked?'

'Well... Look, the courts very rarely award primary custody to the father.'

'I'm not asking for that. I'm just asking that she doesn't move to bloody Ireland.'

'And that's not really something you can enforce. At least not without a legal battle.'

Dan said nothing. He stood up and collected his coat. Maybe a walk around the block would be good. Clear his head. Maybe find a way forward.

'Look,' Charlotte said, before she left the room. 'It's probably not my place to say. But you two seem to get along quite well for a couple that don't want to be together any more. If I were you, I'd try not to let this end up in a protracted legal argument.'

'Shorthand for "let my kids move abroad".'

'I know it's not an easy thing to accept.'

'I didn't have a proper family growing up. No dad. Barely saw my mum. I promised myself I'd do better,' Dan said. He couldn't miss Charlotte's look of mild terror. Having been brought into this process essentially for administrative reasons, she was now unwittingly becoming a bit of a sounding board. Like when you ask how someone is and instead of saying 'Oh, fine' they actually tell you.

'I…'

'Sorry. I know it's not your place. I just sometimes wonder if I'm fucking it up because I never had an example for doing it right.'

'You're not… messing it up,' she said, swerving the swearing. 'Millions of people go through this. All the time. It doesn't make them bad people. Sometimes things don't work out. Even when it feels like they're meant to.'

Charlotte turned away towards the door.

'Wait,' Dan said. 'Is that what you think? That things were meant to work out? Between Anya and me, I mean.'

'It's really not my place to—'

'Fine. But in the couples you've met. The people you've done this for. Do we seem like… you know, all right?'

Charlotte seemed to hesitate. Dan wasn't sure of what the

professional boundaries were here. Fine, she was a solicitor. Here to represent him. But she was also a human. And more than anything right now, he needed some advice. Some sense of a sliding scale from the worst, most messy and unhappy divorce to a couple who possibly had enough residual affection to mount a resurgence.

Because if this whole thing might be a mistake, then there wasn't much time left to stop it happening.

'Dan.'

'Please. For the next thirty seconds, don't be my solicitor. Just be… I don't know… a friend.'

'I barely know—'

'Whatever. All I want to know is—'

'You seem to like each other,' she said, finally. 'The couples I normally deal with doing this… I don't know. They don't have the spark left. They could be strangers. You two look at each other differently.'

'Okay,' Dan said, standing up to leave the room.

'Look, I don't know you. That could just be how you are. So, please don't do anything off the back of what I think.'

'I won't,' Dan said. 'Thanks.'

He waited for Charlotte to leave the room, then checked the clock on his phone. Ten minutes until they were due back.

* * *

As soon as she saw Dan, Anya edged backwards until she was flush against the glass wall of Melrose and White. It wasn't as if she was hiding, as such. More that she just didn't want to be seen.

By anyone.

She'd come outside for some 'air'. Which meant smoking half of a cigarette from the emergency pack of ten she'd bought on the way in that morning. Ostensibly, she had given up smoking years ago, when they were trying for what became Martha. But every so often, mostly in times of deep stress, she would find herself in a newsagent, as conspicuous and shifty as a teenage boy buying porn, asking for a pack of ten Marlboro Lights.

Usually, she'd smoke one. Two at the most. And then the rest would be stored away somewhere she knew Dan wouldn't look for maybe two or three months before being binned.

Over the years, she had tried to self-analyse why she had these lapses. Variously, they had been attributed to a need to revisit her youth, to have some necessary rebellion in a life full of responsibility, or to keep a secret from Dan. But as she gained bigger secrets and became more irresponsible, those excuses fell away. Maybe she just liked smoking when she was up against it?

'Fuck,' she said, as Dan turned in her direction. She flicked the butt away and fished around in her bag for a mint (an essential purchase alongside the cigarettes) and spritzed herself with perfume.

He was practically running towards her. His movement ungainly and without purpose as ever. Like he was jogging to a parked car in the rain.

'Dan,' she said, a warning note in her voice. 'We can't—'

'No. Not that.'

She waited a second as he caught his breath. He had run, what, twenty metres? Exhausted already, even though he had run a marathon only a few years ago. The amount he drank and ate, she was always stunned that his paunch hadn't grown into a gut, or even a belly, over the years. During the good times, she had worried about him pegging out early and leaving her alone – winning that losing game of who dies first, and who gets left as the widow.

'Last night,' he said, standing up, hands on hips like he'd just received a finisher's medal.

'No.'

'Come on.'

'Dan. It was… I mean, I don't know what it was,' Anya said, which was true enough. She hadn't worked it out herself yet.

Mistake felt too strong. Also, disingenuous. In her past, the pre-Dan days, the awareness that she shouldn't have slept with somebody didn't so much creep up on her as quite literally wake up in her bed the next morning. She hadn't felt that shocking, guilty realisation when she groggily opened her eyes next to Dan, in a bedroom she'd last slept in another lifetime ago.

But neither had it been the right thing to do. Nothing fit. The timing, the situation – Christ, even the preamble of curry and beer wasn't conducive to sex. So while she could never say she regretted it, she probably wouldn't do it again if she could go back.

'A sign. A fucking sign is what it was.'

A well-dressed businesswoman walked past, holding a cup of coffee. She looked at Anya in an 'Are you all right?' sort of a way, to which she nodded in the most imperceptible fashion possible.

'We're not meant to be doing this, Anya. We're not.'

'Dan—'

'No. I'm telling you. There's something there. I know it. Last night wouldn't have happened if not. We got on, Anya. It was like how it was. Before... everything.'

'Before the affairs and the arguments and the separate bedrooms and the fact that we could barely hold a conversation?'

'It's solvable. It's all solvable.'

'We tried, Dan. We did the counselling. I tried to be more understanding. You said you'd make more of an effort.'

'Yeah?'

'And neither of us fucking did it.'

'But—'

'Dan, please. I hate this,' she said, considering another cigarette. Why not? What was there to lose? 'We tried. We tried so hard. You're only doing this because of the girls, and it's not enough. They deserve more than parents who can't stand to be in the same room. A marriage of convenience.'

'And that's the point, isn't it? We *can* be in the same room.

We're spending two days in the same room. We spent lunchtime in the same room. We spent the night in the same room.'

'Shhhhhhh,' Anya said, looking around for Matt. She was sure he suspected something. Or maybe that was just his general legal shiftiness.

'We're good together, Anya,' Dan said, the passion in his voice replaced by a sort of imploring earnestness. 'Everyone said it.'

'And we ran our course. You know I still love you, Dan. But it hasn't been enough, has it? And last night,' she said, still unsure of how to categorise it. 'Maybe it was the right way to end it. But it's not a new beginning.'

For a second, he looked defeated. In the same way he had when he got home that day the shop closed, drunk and wobbly after the post-mortem in a pub and a curry house with Barney. Dan had a way of bringing all the hardship he'd endured with him into every one of his life's defeats. Another sadness piled on top of a lifetime of them. But there he was, still standing. Here was another one.

'I wore this today,' he said, unbuttoning his shirt to reveal a T-shirt depicting two silhouettes – Bruce Springsteen and Clarence Clemons. From the reunion tour in 1999. It was a sweet gesture. The type of thing he used to do all the time, theming his band T-shirt with an occasion. It was also the type of thing he'd stopped doing when the fun and joy had leaked out of their marriage.

'Bands break up,' Anya said.

'And they get back together.'

'Sometimes they shouldn't, though. We'd only be doing it for the money,' she said, trying to raise a smile. 'Sort of.'

A taxi pulled up in front of them and two men got out, neither of them thanking the driver. Anya looked up, above Dan's head. It was going to rain again soon.

'We're late getting back.'

'Before you go,' he said. She stopped and turned to face him again. 'If we do, you know, do it. What next?'

'What do you mean what next?'

'Like, will you find someone else?'

'Dan. For fuck's sake. I haven't even thought about that yet,' she lied. Of course she had. 'Come on,' Anya said after a moment, as the first droplets of new rain hit his cheeks. 'We should be getting back.'

And with that, she turned and left Dan with his last-minute plea in rags at his feet.

* * *

The four of them – Margot, Charlotte, Anya and Matt – looked up as Dan entered the room. As though they were pupils waiting for their teacher to arrive.

He was a few minutes over the fifteen Margot had given them, and she seemed keen to get started again, notebook open on her lap, pen resting like a loaded gun. Maybe she was after wrapping things up, he thought. Had another job to go to after this.

'Okay, then,' she said, as Dan took his seat. 'We've all had some time to think. So I hope we can find a resolution to this reasonably—'

'She can take them,' Dan said, staring down at the coffee table, where Charlotte had refilled his water.

He had decided on his way up in the lift. Although maybe decided was the wrong word. Dan could oppose his children moving to Ireland in the same way a turkey opposes the slaughterhouse at Christmas. Whatever he did to block and evade would only frustrate the inevitable.

If he dug his heels in, Anya would do the same. They would end up in court and the judge would rule in her favour. Edie didn't need sign language as much as she once had. So his practical use was becoming limited. He was also the lower earner, the one without a steady and defined income, the one who had moved out when the marriage fell apart, who only had a small, drafty two-bedroom flat in Crouch End to offer.

By any acceptable measure, Dan was the less useful parent. There was really no decision to make.

'I'm not taking them,' Anya said. 'You're still their dad. Things are just going to be different.'

'Too different.'

'We knew life would be different after this. Things had to change, Dan.'

* * *

Anya could tell what he was thinking as she spoke. *They didn't.* They didn't have to be different if she didn't want them to be. He had made that clear – given her the option of stopping this now and working on whatever still existed between them.

Bullshit, she thought. If he thought that – really thought that – then why wait until now? Three-quarters of the way into mediation, rather than months ago when he left the family home, or on one of those horrendous handovers on the A12 near Colchester.

But then, Anya wondered, why did none of this feel quite right?

It had been playing on her mind yesterday morning. Until now, the process had been too easy, too friendly. It was like she was leaving a job on good terms, behaving like they'd see each other again for a catch-up pint in a few weeks from now.

She'd put it down to the confusing, disorientating unfamiliarity of it. Maybe it was Margot's disarmingly therapeutic nature, the fact Matt was there, or that Dan had done something so typical in appointing the firm who did their conveyancing to represent him, because he couldn't be bothered to research other solicitors.

It had been her intention to think it over at the pub yesterday during lunch, until Dan had turned up. Then again in the evening, while relaxing in the bath until… well…

And that was another thing, wasn't it?

She had replayed yesterday evening over and again

since she'd left the flat that morning. Dan was right. The conversation had been easy. It had been comfortable. She had instigated sex, despite feeling full after a curry, which in any normal circumstance would've been a useful reason not to.

None of it should've felt as simple as it did. And yet.

'Anyway,' she said. 'I meant it. Every summer. Easter as well. They'll visit you and I'll—'

'That's actually my only condition,' he interrupted. 'I want to visit. I'll come over, maybe once every two months. But I won't be able to afford the flight and the hotel every time.'

'Seriously?' she said, suddenly ready to withdraw all the affection that had been clouding her judgment.

'If you want to move them there—'

'Then I have to pay for you to fly over every other weekend?'

'Every two months, I said. And,' Dan said, looking away from her. Ever uncomfortable about talking money. 'I'm not saying you pay. Like, as in get your credit card out. But those months, I don't know, maybe we work something out.'

'And you pay less?'

'I was thinking the loan. If we call that the payments?'

She was frustrated. Yes, she would be losing a bit financially. But wouldn't it be worth it? And the loan thing was dodgy. She knew that.

'Anya,' he pleaded. 'I'm trying to find a way that I don't oppose this and it turns into... you know. All I'm saying is that instead of forty per cent of the childcare costs I pay thirty. Just for those months.'

She felt a nudge on her arm. Matt was leaning over.

'You don't have to agree to this,' he whispered, his breath sweet and stale with too many small, strong coffees. 'He hasn't got a leg to—'

'Fine,' Anya said, shifting forward, away from Matt who slumped back into his chair. 'Why don't we call the payments thirty-five per cent all year round? You put the rest into a savings account and use it for flights and hotels.'

For a moment, Dan looked stunned. Then he smiled, and

for a split second, Anya didn't see the man she'd spent the last year arguing with and almost coming to detest. She didn't see the man who'd cheated on her, because he was so desperate to boost his own self-esteem that he couldn't see how he was destroying hers. She didn't see the man she'd found so pitiful that she had managed to justify her own affair as necessary self-kindness rather than cruelty and infidelity.

Instead, she saw the man who had cradled his daughters in hospital delivery rooms. Who'd helped teach them to talk, walk, and in Edie's case, experience the noise of the world in an entirely different way. She saw a dad. A good dad, who now accepted that he wouldn't be able to keep his family together, and so only wanted to limit the amount of time they were apart.

And things became more confusing still.

'Oh,' Dan said. 'Right. Well… I mean, if you're sure.'

'And if you're sure?'

'Yeah. I am. That's great. Really great,' he said, knowing deep down that he had gone from seeing Edie and Martha daily, to weekly, and now bimonthly. But in comparison to the alternative, yes, it was great.

'And you're both content with the financial arrangement?' Margot said. 'Thirty-five per cent of all childcare costs to be paid by Mr Moorcroft year round?'

They both mumbled yes.

'Well. I'll say that's agreed, then. I'm always pleased when couples come to these arrangements themselves,' she said. 'This is usually the part when it gets very messy.'

She then made one more note and closed her book.

'Sorry,' Anya said, stopping Margot who seemed to be wrapping up. 'There's one more thing. A family matter, I suppose,' she said, looking at Dan. 'It's not massive. But it matters. I'd like to talk it through.'

Then she looked at Dan, who nodded, cleared his throat, and began to speak.

FOUR YEARS AND TWO MONTHS AGO

Crouch End, London

He ignored the phone buzzing away on his desk, as he always did when he didn't know the number. Usually, it was an insurance company trying to encourage him to take out more cover for the shop. Or maybe one of the music memorabilia dealers he'd been in contact with over the years to gauge his interest in a particularly rare or interesting band T-shirt, the scarcity, condition and provenance of which might mark it out as something a collector like him could spend several hundred pounds on. Though he never admitted it, at least not to the wider subcommunity of collectors, the older Dan got and the more time and money he spent on and with family, the less he had for what increasingly seemed like a bit of a juvenile hobby.

Out on the shop floor, Barney was talking to a customer about a particular amplifier that had been stuck with them for years now, occasionally turned on only to check that it hadn't given up through lack of use. Dan was about to join him when the phone went again.

One text and a voicemail. Both from the same person.

He read the message first.

Hi Dan. Could you please call me on this number?
I know we've not spoken in years. It's important.
Gemma Short.

Immediately, Dan felt prickles all over his back. A little sweat broke out on his forehead.

The name was enough to do that.

He had last seen Gemma Short around nineteen years ago. It would've been midsummer, after his final year of school. They'd arranged to meet in the playing fields round the back of his nan's house. There was a corner of it obscured by a couple of trees, making it a popular spot for teenage smoking and drinking, so much so that the mud around the old roots was constantly decorated with fag ends and ring pulls.

After he'd told Gemma that he was breaking up with her – after 'four months and six fucking shags' (her words) – he'd gone back to his nan's house, watched a bit of telly and by teatime was more or less over it.

That was it for them, he had assumed. Until now. And he strongly suspected why she was getting in touch before he even returned her call.

They hadn't been careful back then. Not remotely. Their relationship had played out at a series of house parties, drunken nights on the field, and one group camping trip into Northumberland, where the quantity of alcohol and weed dwarfed that of common sense. There were no dates, meals with each other's families, evenings out in restaurants or nights in front of the television. Nothing that either cost money or involved too many people above the age of eighteen who weren't up for buying them cheap cider.

They'd lived by the mantra that it'd 'be okay'. And even if it wasn't, what kind of life would it be stopping? No amount of informal school sex education, administered by spotty, nervous and probably virginal sixth-formers, could convince them otherwise.

'Fuck,' Dan whispered to himself. His stomach lurched.

Edie had not long ago turned two. Martha was just four.

There would be no easy way to explain it to either of them.

A sibling.

A brother or sister.

What would they be now, eighteen and a bit? The right time to find out a little more about themselves, to get some proper answers to some long-held questions. No surprise that their mysterious, absent, unknowing dad might be top of the list.

Then there was Anya. How would she react?

Surely, he thought, she couldn't be mad. It wasn't his fault (while being absolutely one hundred per cent his fault). But she would be... what? Upset, maybe. Shocked for sure. Maybe angry at that early version of Dan. The one who hadn't enough respect for Gemma and for himself to think of the consequences of what they were doing. For whom present-day Dan's only defence could be that his sixteen-year-old self lived with the element of nihilism common to people who felt like theirs would never be an easy life.

He felt sick. Every part of him was hoping there might be another reason for Gemma Short to get in touch. But there wasn't. They had shared so little of life and there were no lingering connections from each to the other. She couldn't be calling to tell him about a mutual friend passing, because Dan had effectively severed all those ties when he left and didn't go back. There was no residual knowledge of their respective families or homes.

No. There was only one reason for her to call. One thing binding them together.

Give me five minutes.

Dan sent the message. Then made a list of everything he might need or want to know.

Boy or girl, of course. Actually, man or woman, given their age. And name.

He'd need to know if they were okay. Or if the call was to give him some unexpected news, then some bad news.

On which, what about care? Had someone else been the father figure for all these years? While he was leaving the north-east, setting up his life in London, working, making friends, starting a family and becoming *this* version of Dan Moorcroft, probably the only one he'd ever been vaguely happy with.

And money. If that was why she was calling he would understand. Just four years of parenting had shown him how much raising a kid cost. Even if there was no relationship to be had, then he would still feel the need to put some things right.

He looked at the list in front of him.

Sex

Name

How are they?

Dad?

Money

He picked up his phone and tapped the little phone icon on Gemma's message. Before he put it to his ear, he added one more thing.

What happens now?

It rang twice before she answered. And on the other end of the line was a voice that took him back to a separate life, and a Dan Moorcroft who spent that life in Adidas trackies and Reebok Classics paid for by his paper round. Who was rarely without a football at his feet and a ten pack of Sovereigns in his pocket.

'Hello?'

'Hey,' he said. 'It's Dan.'

A few seconds went by. He heard footsteps and a door close.

'Thanks for calling,' she said. 'I wasn't sure that you would.'

THREE WEEKS LATER

Yorkshire Moors

The doors from the vestibule into the train carriage opened and Anya emerged, carrying two takeaway cups. She walked sideways down the aisle, where Dan was sitting, waiting and staring out the window at the English countryside rolling past.

'Oi,' she said, moving his attention away from the endless green fields and sheep that stretched away to the hills of the Moors National Park.

'Sorry,' he said, taking the cups so that she could sit down. 'Miles away.'

'As usual.'

Dan smiled thinly, feeling that his recent discovery of a son, not long turned eighteen, was reason enough for him to be distant and pensive. He'd been like it all through Christmas – active and excited around the girls, but away with himself in any moment when it was him or just the two of them on their own. If he could've helped it, he would've.

'How long to go?' she asked.

'Hour. Maybe less,' he said, taking a sip and recoiling from the hot coffee. And then he went back to the window.

* * *

'You'll be fine, you know. He's probably every bit as nervous as you are.'

'He's eighteen. Of course he's nervous. I don't think I've got as much of a right to be.'

'Dan,' she said, slightly frustrated, slightly weary at a conversation it felt like they'd had a thousand times since he came home from work three weeks ago and Rhys Wallace first entered her life. 'You deal with it how you need. No one's expecting anything from you. Not today.'

He didn't reply to this. Instead he went to his phone, where he had three photos of the boy that Gemma had sent a fortnight ago. Rhys was tall, with short dark hair. Behind his glasses, he was unmistakably Dan – the same eyes and nose, similar face shape and bone structure. One of those people who, had Anya seen him in the street, would've made a point of telling Dan about. *I saw a kid that looked the dead spit of you today.* In each of the photos, he was wearing a Newcastle United shirt over tracksuit bottoms and bright white trainers.

Since that first call, there had been two others. The initial contact, it turned out, was for Gemma to see if Dan was open to meeting Rhys. The boy had been asking questions about his real dad. Gemma's ex-husband Gareth had picked up the father-figure mantle (and given Rhys his surname), but was clear he wouldn't officially take on the role. Now Rhys wanted a proper answer.

'She said she wanted him to wait until he was eighteen. If he still wanted to know about me then, he could,' Dan had explained the evening he told Anya. Albeit half an hour after her shock had subsided, anger cooled.

Gemma, apparently, had kept tabs on Dan ever since social media allowed her to learn a little bit about his life. It was easy enough to find his mobile number through the String Theory website (*For out of hours queries, call Dan on…*). Facebook, Twitter and later Instagram did the rest.

The next time he spoke to Gemma, Dan was able to ask more questions. Meanwhile, she was keen to make him understand how disruptive his presence would be in her son's life, regardless of how much he wanted answers. Then, two days before Christmas, she opened the door and allowed father and son to talk for the first time.

Anya remembered listening in to the FaceTime call, hearing his side of it. His tone and the way he looked down into his lap brought to mind a teenage boy, full of nerves and naivety. Rather than a grown man, who had his own family, business, wife, life.

'Yeah. Dan. Daniel. Daniel Moorcroft.'

'Near Elswick. That's where I met Gemma... your mum.'

'I have, yeah. Two girls. Martha and Edie.'

'Anya.'

It was when he was off the phone that Dan spoke the words that Anya had been simultaneously hoping for and dreading.

'He wants to meet me.'

'And?' she had said, unable to think of anything other than how the girls might react, and the worries and fears they would almost inevitably have as soon as the novelty of a big brother wore off.

'I'd like to,' he said, seeming to fear her reaction, no doubt remembering how angry and hurt she had been when he told her at first. 'You don't have to come. Or the girls. But I need to. That's okay, isn't it?'

'Of course,' she said after a few seconds during which she imagined saying no, closing down that little interruption to their lives and forcing Dan to put a pin in it for now. Before quickly understanding that there would be no going back from this. That Rhys was not something or someone that could be placed back in a box and moved on from. 'And I'll come,' she added. 'You shouldn't do it alone. He should meet both of us.'

* * *

Now, Anya looked over at Dan's phone, where the photo of Rhys smiling was still open in front of him.

'I wonder if he still looks like that?' Anya said.

'I know. Maybe he'll wear the shirt to the station. So we can recognise him.'

'What about her? Do you remember what she looks like?'

'Ish.'

This was another thing that gnawed away at Anya. Though she hated herself for admitting it, some part of her felt strange about meeting Gemma. She was Dan's ex, even if that had been half his life ago. And she was the mother of his child – like Anya herself.

It had all added to her initial reaction, given an extra edge to that anger and frustration. In no logical way did Rhys demean her position in his life, but she couldn't shake the feeling that he had.

Even as she had shouted at Dan, cried at what it meant for her, for them, for the family, she had known that there was nowhere productive to direct her feelings. Except, maybe, at the teenage version of her husband, who had so little respect for himself, his girlfriend and his future to wear a fucking condom. Everything she was raging against was about a Dan who had ceased to exist a long time ago, and who had matured into as decent a man as anyone knew.

'He must be excited,' Anya said.

'Probably more confused.'

'Dan, you've got to remember that he wanted this. He asked to find you. And it turns out his dad knows what he's doing. It could be worse for him.'

'That's just it, though, isn't it?'

'What?'

'Like, I know what I'm doing as a dad. And I couldn't do it for him.'

'He can't blame you, though. If you'd known—'

'It's not about him blaming me. It's me blaming me,'

Dan said, shifting in his seat to face her. 'With the girls, it's sometimes the really little things I'm glad I'm there for.'

'Like what?'

'I don't know. Holding their hands when they can't get to sleep. Staying on the floor when they're ill. That sort of shit. People always go on about the big moments, don't they? When the kid learnt to walk or their first word. To be honest, I couldn't tell you when either of them walked. It was a gradual thing, wasn't it? Crawling, standing, walking. There was no one moment when Martha got up and waddled off. But I remember exactly where I was when she was sick for the first time. I know what happened when Edie had her first night in a big bed and fell out.'

'Rhys doesn't know you missed that. Christ, the girls won't remember it anyway.'

'It's me, though, isn't it?' Dan said, as though it were obvious. Which, actually, it was. 'I want to have had all that stuff.'

Immediately, how Dan felt made sense to Anya. It wasn't all about Rhys, and his upbringing. Instead, this was about how Dan viewed himself as a father – that constant worry of his she remembered from her first pregnancy, about how the lack of any paternal role model would mean he'd have nothing to base himself on.

The early months with Martha had convinced him that he *could* do it. Whether it was holding her in the right way so that her head was supported, changing nappies without covering himself with whatever was inside them, or taking her to classes and groups, often being the sole representative of fatherhood in the room. It had convinced him that parenting wasn't a skill you needed peer training on. You just did it.

Anya had assumed that the years of mostly efficient, steady fatherhood he'd managed since had washed away the big question mark he'd painted over himself. But it was still there, clearly. And she wondered how much doubt and uncertainty he lived with every day.

Did Rhys set him back to square one? Was he now the absentee dad that was a spectre across his own childhood? Or could he come to see it as a teenage mistake compounded by a mother who honestly thought she was doing the right thing by everyone by disregarding him?

'I know,' Anya said, placing her hand on Dan's. 'But you know that you can be a great dad to him. Whatever kind of dad he wants you to be.'

'It'll always be there, though, won't it? Every time someone mentions what he was like as a boy, they'll look at me and know I wasn't around.'

'You would've been. Had you known.'

Dan laughed.

'What?'

'That's the thing, I suppose. I probably wouldn't have. Gemma knew me well enough. She knew I was a difficult little prick. I'd have run away or moved to another country. Anything to avoid the responsibility.'

And this was the other thing Anya had struggled with. How much to blame Gemma.

During the last few weeks, she'd moved some of the anger she had felt at teenage Dan on to Gemma. How could a mother knowingly exclude the father of her child like that? Unless, of course, everyone would've been worse off had he been included.

Part of Anya had been suspicious about Gemma. How did she know it was Dan anyway? Could there have been others? She remembered herself as a sixteen-year-old in Cork. Not loose. But certainly not a paragon of fidelity. The Dan Gemma had chosen not to tell was by all accounts a bit of a dickhead, with few prospects. The current one owned a business, had a home in London. The example presented by his Facebook page seemed to show a man who'd turned it around.

'I asked,' Dan had explained when Anya had once

tentatively brought it up. 'She says she wasn't seeing anyone else at the time. And she's not asking for money or help or anything. So I don't see why she'd lie. They both want a test as well. Just to confirm it.'

Anya was satisfied with the reasoning. It was hopeful to think that Rhys wasn't Dan's. But one look at the boy told her it was more realistic to believe that he was.

But still.

'Well,' she said, as the train began to slow. 'I suppose it's all about doing the best job you can from now, then. You can't change the past, Dan. But whatever happened back then doesn't make you a bad dad now.'

* * *

Ten minutes later, the train pulled into Newcastle Central. Around them, solo travellers and small families put on their coats and collected their belongings. The temperature had dropped by three degrees as they'd travelled from London to Newcastle, and it was minus one outside, according to the app on Dan's phone. He felt the cold more than Anya, who had been conditioned to it by plenty of bracing walks on the southern Irish coast as a child, dragged along by outdoorsy parents.

'Right, then,' Dan said, getting up from his seat. Anya did the same.

They stepped off the train, onto a platform covered by a Victorian ceiling. The station harked back to the glory years of rail travel, when it was all grandeur and excitement rather than overpriced tickets and replacement bus services. The old clocks, ornate pillars and decorative arches butted up against modern advertising boards, digital displays and brightly coloured plastic signs for Upper Crust, WHSmith and M&S Simply Food.

The two of them were sharing one small suitcase for their overnight stay in a city centre Premier Inn. The girls were with Anya's parents, and perhaps the one aspect of the trip she was looking forward to was that it more or less guaranteed the decent night's sleep and reasonable lie-in that living with two small children prevented. Dan wheeled the suitcase towards the barriers, where he stopped suddenly, looking out on to the concourse.

'There,' he said, nodding and directing Anya towards a young man stood looking at his phone. He was wearing dark blue jeans, bulky trainers and a green and black North Face puffa jacket, under which was the Newcastle United shirt Dan had jokingly suggested he wear so they'd recognise him.

'Right,' Anya said. She tried to sound upbeat, but could easily throw up at any second. Up until now, Rhys had been theoretical. No more.

Dan had a son.

It was weird that Dan had a son.

Here is Dan's son.

* * *

Dan himself, meanwhile, enjoyed the few seconds that Rhys's attention was diverted. He felt nervous, but heartened by the fact that the boy had turned up when he could so easily and justifiably have bailed. And before he could stop himself, he started forwards, showing his ticket to the guard who let him through the gate for passengers with luggage, and into the busy melee of travellers, workers and a few pigeons shielding from the cold of the city. With Anya trailing behind him, he walked straight up to Rhys, his son, and stood before him.

The boy looked up.

'Rhys?' Dan said, holding out his hand. 'I'm Dan.'

NOW

'And what about today?' Margot said, looking at Dan. 'With the boy.'

'He's good. Really good. He joined the police earlier this year. We get along... well, I suppose.'

'More than well,' Anya said. Dan refused to look at her. 'He calls you Dad now. The girls know him. He's in our... your life.'

'I know.'

'So what is it the two of you feel you need to agree on with Rhys?'

'Two things,' Anya said. 'One is the girls. I know it's been a bit... you know for them. But he's their brother. So I don't want us splitting up to cut ties with them.'

'It won't,' Dan said.

'You say that now. But in a year from now. Two years. Especially when we're in—' Anya said, cutting herself short. There had been a resolution over the move to Ireland. But they were still a long way from Dan being happy with it rather than accepting it in the face of a lack of alternatives. She didn't want to say it.

'So what? We can't put an agreement in, can we?'

'Not everything has to be a binding agreement, Dan,' Margot said quietly. 'For some things it's simply important that you discuss them. So you know how things might work when the divorce is finalised,' she added.

Dan hadn't realised until now how little Margot actually said the D-word. So much so that she almost seemed uncomfortable with it. Like she was trying to speak while chewing a toffee.

'Well, can't we just say that, then? I'll make sure the girls still see Rhys. I mean, I barely see him myself now that he's on duty all the time. But yeah. We will.'

'And me, too,' she said, quietly.

'You?'

'He's my stepson, Dan. It's not like turning off a switch.'

'Okay.'

'I know I've no right to this. I mean, considering. But I don't want to cut him out. If we're trying to do this whole thing kindly, then, I don't know. Maybe?'

'Sure,' Dan said, uncertainly.

He hadn't really thought about his son throughout the past two days. Rhys was always part of another life really. One that had only recently interlocked with the one he shared with Anya. Now there was a Venn diagram, with Rhys on the one side, Anya and the girls on the other, Dan in the middle.

The idea that Anya was worried about losing her stepson was news to him. Even though it shouldn't have been.

It was Anya who had carried the conversation during that first meeting up in Newcastle, while Dan had been so overly careful about what he said that he barely spoke at all. When they went for a coffee in a branch of Costa near the station, he saw how she focused on making Rhys feel part of their unit, showing him photographs of his half-sisters when he asked about them. In a pub later that evening over dinner, she had talked to Rhys about his life plans and hopes. Then as he became more a part of their lives, she continued to reach out and put an arm around him – wherever Rhys found himself.

In the moments when he was jealous of her ability to

connect with him, or angry that he couldn't, Dan told himself that it was because she carried none of the emotional heft he did. In reality, it was clear that she was simply really good at that stuff.

'Do you still talk now?' Dan asked, worried that the answer might cast him in a bad light.

'Every so often. We text now and again. Look, Dan, I know this must all seem a bit weird—'

'It does,' he said, unable to detangle Anya's intentions for the girls, for Rhys, for himself. Her seeming desire to keep the family together while taking half of it overseas.

'I'm sorry. You can say no.'

'I'm not going to say no, Anya. Rhys loves you. You love Rhys. Besides, he's old enough now.'

'I mean I'd respect your wishes. If you wanted me to keep my distance, you know.'

'What kind of person does that, though?' he said. No one answered. Everyone knew the kind of person who did that. A petty, vengeful, small-minded man did that. That wasn't Dan. They had entered into this mediation to be kind and calm – to hopefully come out the other end not hating each other. And if it was going to happen, in spite of his better efforts, then that was the least he could hope for.

'I don't want you to change,' he said, finally. 'It's good that the two of you…' he said. But his mind was trailing off. Back to the phone call with Rhys when he had to tell him about the divorce. The boy had taken it well, if stoically, rarely answering with anything more than a 'right', 'yeah' or 'fine' as Dan went to great lengths to over-explain that the split had nothing to do with Rhys's entry into their life, and everything to do with how they'd effectively stopped paying attention to the things that kept their life together.

'Thanks,' Anya said quietly.

Margot made a note, then cleared her throat. They both looked over at her, each with a face that asked, *Is that it, done? Is the hard part over?*

'Good,' she said. 'Well, you'll be pleased to know that we're very nearly done here.'

Matt briefly disturbed everyone by placing a tray of chocolate digestives down on the middle of the little coffee table. Dan wondered if this was how it worked at Melrose and White. Cakes on day one, biscuits day two. What would happen if they ran into a third day? Would they all have to share a Kit Kat or something?

'All of the major things like property, money, children have been addressed,' Margot continued. 'I've written up my notes on the official matters like custody arrangements, financial settlements and property. As I said yesterday, these will become the Minutes of Agreement that Matt and Charlotte will lodge at court for you. I hope to have a version for you both to review and confirm by next Wednesday. And we all seem to be comfortable with how we'll address the legalities around the petition.'

Dan and Anya both nodded, neither minded to bring that up again and expose the discomfort they each felt with where the law had to see the reason for their divorce. Briefly, Dan did think about saying that he wasn't okay with everything. But it would only be a delaying tactic, something to avoid the finality of a destination he was increasingly certain was the wrong one. He'd played his hand there.

'Good,' Anya said, seemingly itching to get up.

'Now, as you know, there's one last thing that I recommend couples do as part of my method,' Margot said. 'Some choose not to. But... well, I believe it helps us to bring this process to a close in the right spirit for the future.'

'Okay,' Dan said, slightly confused, and once again caught out by the fact that he'd not read much of the material about Margot and her process before starting it.

'Obviously, we must talk about the future of your relationship. When you divorce it's very rarely the case that you can delete each other's phone numbers and carry on with your lives. Especially in your case when it seems like contact will be very frequent. So my view is that you should discuss that. Be open about how you want to communicate going forwards. The place you'll each play in the other's life. Also some boundaries that you'll each agree on,' Margot said, with a look at Anya that Dan felt was full of suspicion, from a woman who could tell that something had happened last night.

They both muttered a quiet 'okay'.

'But before that, I'd like to discuss the past.'

'Our past?' Dan said, mildly horrified.

'Yes. As you know, I believe in a more *holistic* form. More therapeutic.'

'Right.'

'In my experience, a reminder of your past selves has helped many divorcing couples to, in time, become friends. It asks you to remember why you became a couple in the first place. Because while your journey might feel like it ends here, it really doesn't.'

'Fine,' Dan said, uncertainly.

'So let's go back to the beginning,' Margot said with a smile. 'Anya. Tell me how you two met.'

US

FIFTEEN YEARS AND TWO MONTHS AGO

Borough, London

Sarah, Anya's flatmate, ambled into the living room and flopped down onto their worn-out blue sofa. She was wearing her customary evening jogging bottoms with an Abercrombie & Fitch hoodie, and had a towel wrapped around her head. As usual, Sarah brought with her the twin aromas of coconut bubble bath and nicotine, always of the opinion that the steam from the bath would carry her cigarette smoke outside with it. Theirs was a non-smoking flat.

Anya tried to reposition her white plastic MacBook so Sarah couldn't see what she was reading. The screen showed the reflection of their paltry Christmas decorations. A few fairy lights on the window, a small plastic tree, one string of tinsel draped along the curtain rail. Indicative of people who didn't want to ignore Christmas, but wouldn't be in this flat to celebrate it.

'More?'

'No. Working.'

'What work?'

'Writing to a production company.'

'A job?'

'Intern.'

'What about actual work?'

'I'll reduce my hours,' Anya said, knowing that cutting the

amount of time she spent making cappuccinos and toasting paninis at a nearby branch of Starbucks would also cut her ability to pay the rent on the cold, damp third-floor flat just off Borough High Street she and Sarah shared with two others.

Unlike Anya, Sarah's work was steady and with a clear future mapped out for her. She'd joined a recruitment programme at a consultancy firm a year ago and had already been rewarded with two pay rises and the responsibility of line management. Anya was certain that Sarah could quite easily find and afford a nicer flat in a better area of town. It was only her hesitance to live with 'randoms' that kept her in this little box.

'Whatever,' Sarah said. 'Anyway, bollocks are you doing work. Since when did applying for a job happen on Match?'

'It's not—'

'I've already seen.'

Anya blew on her hot tea, making waves across the top.

'Who is he?'

She turned again and tilted the screen down.

'Jesus, Anya. I'm not asking to approve him. I just want to know what he looks like.'

'I probably won't even meet him. The last three were all disasters. I didn't even recognise one of them from his picture.'

'I told you. They're all liars. The dregs of London's singles. I don't know why you're bothering.'

'I paid for a month.'

'Fucking hell,' Sarah scoffed. 'How much?'

'Tenner. I got an offer after the free trial.'

'You're worried about affording the rent but you're happy enough to throw a tenner away on internet fucking dating?'

'All right, mum.'

'Well, how many people do you know who've properly met someone decent on the internet? Like actually worth starting a relationship with.'

'Nila met that guy… what's his name?'

'Carlo?'

'Yeah.'

'Decent?'

'He was fine.'

'He was basically a con man. My point is, these websites are full of people who can't function in the ordinary world. That's their market. Give it a year and internet dating will be fucking dead in the water.'

'And that's your opinion as a… whatever you are, is it?'

'Innovation consultant. And no, it's my opinion as a reasonable human being. I mean, how do you know that these people you're talking to on there are even real? Or aren't psychopaths? I'm telling you, it's a fad,' Sarah said, taking a sip of red wine from a tumbler because all the other glasses were in their respective bedrooms. 'Anyway, what does he look like, then?'

'I thought from all that you'd not be interested.'

'Well, you've had his profile open for the last ten minutes, so you're clearly lying about not meeting up with him.'

Anya relented and turned the laptop round. On the screen was a photo of a slightly scruffy-looking man wearing a checked shirt over the top of a Ben Folds Five T-shirt. Brown hair down to just below his ears and a broad smile that suggested the photo was taken in a genuinely happy moment rather than a curated shot for the website.

'Dan,' Sarah said.

'Yeah.'

'What's he got to say for himself?' she said, leaning over to read the screen. '"Hey I'm Dan. I'm twenty-four and live and work in Crouch End. I repair musical instruments for a living, support Newcastle United and collect band and gig T-shirts.".'

The face Sarah was wearing suggested that Anya had described a forty-seven-year-old estate agent, whose hobbies were scrapyard diving and necromancy.

'What?'

'No.'

'Why?'

'Just no.'

'Sarah.'

'He's not for you.'

'Because?'

'Fixes guitars. Band T-shirt collection. Come on, Anya.'

'What?'

'He'll be that sort of guy. Full of fucking useless information. Thinks he knows everything about music and films and all that. Massive record collection, terrible in bed. You know exactly the guy.'

'That's a bit much.'

'Children wear T-shirts with their favourite things on them. Like bloody *Spider-Man* or something. Band T-shirt people are no different.'

'Children?'

'Exactly. Man-child.'

'And you're getting all of this from two sentences and a photo?'

'Isn't that the point of these things?' she said, as Anya took the laptop back and turned it to face her.

The truth was, she did know the guy Sarah was talking about. And had met more than a few of them at university, at work – more or less everywhere she went. But there was something about this guy that she liked the look of. A kind face maybe. A genuine smile. Besides, two hours ago Dan had sent her a message.

Hey. New to this. But I came across your profile and you look nice (is that okay to say? Seems a bit forward). Anyway. I thought maybe you'd like to meet somewhere? Just a drink. Let me know. Dan.

'What?' Sarah said. 'Please don't tell me you're thinking of it.'

'I'm not.'

'Good,' Sarah said, as Anya typed out her reply.

'Anyway. What's on this evening?' Anya said, turning on the television.

* * *

Six miles away, Dan was in The Flask pub in Highgate with his flatmate. George had been almost an hour late. He was still of the belief that he could work as a junior at an advertising agency and stick strictly to his contracted hours, despite six months of evidence to the contrary, and insisted on scheduling drinks with Dan at six-thirty, when his colleagues were all still hard sat it, and George's own to-do list was several lines longer than it had been at nine in the morning.

Anyway. The consequence of the lateness was that Dan was four pints in to George's one and they would almost certainly be staying for another couple.

'The thing is,' George said, gently sipping from a heavy glass tankard of Fuller's ESB. 'It's meaningless, isn't it? I mean, if I stay an extra three hours, what happens? More adverts. On the train. On the buses.'

'Telly?'

'They don't let me do the telly. They don't even let me do the radio.'

'What do they let you do?'

'Spreadsheets mostly. And booking lunch for people.'

'So you're a secretary.'

'Junior account executive.'

'In charge of lunch bookings and dry cleaning.'

'I only did that once. Anyway. It's pointless, isn't it? Ultimately. We're not saving anyone's life. We're just selling them shit.'

'So, what, you're going to quit, are you? Become a missionary or something?'

'Maybe,' George said, taking another drink. Pleasingly longer this time. Dan wanted to get home. It was unlike him, but he was keen to be back with his laptop. 'Charity or something. Where I can do something meaningful.'

'Hmm. You know it's all probably the same, don't you? You'll get just as annoyed working for a charity.'

George ignored him. He dipped a pork scratching into the top of Dan's beer and bit it in two. Likely this would be dinner.

'Anyway. You always wanted to be in advertising, didn't you?'

'Sometimes you shouldn't get what you wish for. Like, what did you want to be when you were at school?'

'Nothing,' Dan said, truthfully.

'No, I mean, like you must've wanted to do something. Be something.'

'I wanted to be a footballer until I was thirteen. Then I stopped wanting to be anything. Except sixteen, so I could leave school.'

'Not even—'

'George. Trust me when I say that no one at my school was thinking about how they could get into advertising when they were fourteen.'

Dan checked his phone. Getting towards half eight now. Two hours since he'd sent the message. The online dating thing hadn't been his most thought-out decision. During a slow day at the shop, there'd been a piece on the radio about its growing popularity among younger Londoners – people who were too busy with their careers and friends and social lives to mix and meet in the time-honoured ways of awkward conversations in crowded bars, escalating workplace flirtations, or through friends.

In truth, Dan was never too busy with friends. Besides George and occasionally Eddie, his London social circle was small. As for work, his job in the shop enabled him to keep reasonable hours, and even when Eddie was away, there was little need for him to spend anything longer than half an hour doing overtime.

No. Dan was not the focus of that segment on the radio.

But when the one-month free trial of the dating site arrived a day later, he couldn't see the harm. Because above all, Dan was lonely.

Since he'd arrived in London, he had felt loved and cared for by Eddie. When George moved in, he was lucky enough to gain a good friend immediately. But he still acutely felt like a visitor. Still believed that everybody apart from him had a wide social circle and felt no need to expand it to accommodate Dan Moorcroft. Still knew his was a small world in a big city.

Frankly, he had no idea of how he might meet someone, unless he fell in love with a customer who stuck around in the shop long enough to fall in love with him.

'Another?' George said.

Dan could see the desperation in him. The desire to stay out for one more. To make an evening of it.

'Half,' Dan said.

'Fuck off.'

'What?'

'Half.'

'I've had three more than you.'

'You're from the north-east. Aren't you supposed to handle it better?' George said with a smile. This was an ongoing joke between the two of them. When he was nine Dan had moved to Newcastle, although before that had been brought up near Peterborough (which explained his barely-even-faint Geordie accent). George, meanwhile, was from Surrey, with all the obvious rugby, grammar school education and life chances that entailed.

'And it's getting busy in here.'

'It's three weeks before Christmas and it's a London pub. What did you expect?'

'Quiet.'

'Don't be miserable,' George said. Dan thought how it was all right for him. His firm had a Christmas party next week in an old London music hall, where the drinks would be free, the food decent and entertainment provided by a stand-up comedian who'd found fame by searching the world for people who shared his name. Dan's Christmas do, meanwhile, would consist of a curry with Eddie and the two part-timers – Nigel and Jack. Then a few pints and hastily made excuses when Eddie suggested continuing the evening at a tawdry strip club in Holloway.

'I've got an early start.'

'You literally work downstairs from your bedroom. You're the one person in the world who could install a fucking slide to get to work.'

Some part of Dan knew that he wasn't going to get away with it. George would entice him to stay with the offer of a taxi back home, instead of the two buses it normally took to get to Crouch End plus a walk in the cold evening air. He'd maybe buy a packet of fags from the machine for them to share, or a bowl of chips. Dan was easily bought by any of these.

'Fine,' he said. 'One more. But then I'm off.'

'What is it?' George said, stopping before he went to the bar.

'Nothing. I'm just… I dunno… I'm not up for it.'

'Bollocks.'

'Serious.'

'Dan.'

He waited for a second. But knowing that he would tell George eventually (likely later) and emboldened by the drink, he went for it.

'I'm waiting on a message.'

And George looked baffled.

'Jesus,' Dan said to himself, in disbelief that he was having to explain it. 'From a girl. A woman,' he said. 'I sent her a message.'

'Your phone's there?' George said, confused.

'Not, like, a message message,' Dan explained. 'A message,' he added, air typing.

'You emailed her? Who the fuck asks someone out on email?'

'It's not email.'

The penny took a few seconds to drop, bounce, then settle. But when it did make sense to him, a broad smile took over his face.

'The internet?'

'Don't be a prick about it,' Dan said. 'Or I'm gone now.'

'I can't believe it.'

'George.'

'The internet,' he said again, still smiling. 'Well well well.'

'Last chance.'

'I'm saying nothing,' George said.

'Good,' Dan said.

And George went to the bar.

They ended up staying another hour, Dan itching all the while to get home until they got a cab back to the flat in Crouch End, where he practically ran up the stairs to open up his incredibly slow and clunky laptop.

When it did finally load up, and he got online, and remembered his password, the message was there.

Hey Dan. Sure thing. How's Thursday? I'm in Borough.

Full of courage and with a slightly spinning head, Dan began to type.

* * *

'Fuck!' Anya said, alerting Sarah, who'd almost fallen asleep during a recorded episode of *Frasier*. 'He's replied.'

'You didn't,' Sarah said.

'Thursday. He's coming here.'

For a second, Anya expected excitement. Not girlish screams and jumping up and down. But at least a little enthusiasm.

But no. Instead, Sarah paused the television, looked at her and said, 'You're fucking mad.' And went back to the TV.

NOW

Margot was smiling. Maybe, Anya thought, despite her job, she was one for a love story and enjoyed a meet-cute. Even if hers and Dan's was twenty-first century enough for the initial spark between them to have happened in two locations, across London and miles apart.

'It's funny,' Anya said, when Dan had finished talking about that first drink in the Market Porter in Borough. It was a couple of weeks before Christmas, and the two of them had to stand outside in the cold amidst groups of office workers and market traders who had finished for the day. 'I think I was the first of my friends to do internet dating. I almost didn't bother going.'

'Why's that?' Margot said.

'Well, you never knew with the internet stuff back then. I'd been on a few dates and they were all disasters. Part of me only went to prove my flatmate wrong.'

Anya looked over at Dan. She hadn't realised that she'd been playing with her rings as she spoke. She quickly moved her hands back down to her sides.

That was another thing. When to remove them? She'd tried it a couple of weeks ago, but found the little indentation on her ring finger almost as much of a distraction as the two loops of white gold. How long does that skin take to return to normal, she wondered? Would it ever, or did it stay like that – a permanent bodily reminder, like a tattoo or a scar?

'And did you prove her wrong?' Margot said.

'I suppose so,' Anya said with a little, sad smile.

No one moved for a second. Maybe because, like Anya, they were contemplating the impermanence of things, and if their failed attempt at marriage had been nonetheless worth making. Or because they thought that Margot's question was a little on the nose at this stage in proceedings.

'You'd be surprised at how many couples I work with who met on the internet,' Margot said, in the manner of a cabbie who thought you'd never believe who he had in the back last week. Anya thought about asking for more details. But held back.

There were two possible reasons why Margot's clientele might be skewing towards people whose initial contact was online. Either people in the earliest generation of internet daters were now reaching the point where their marriages were disintegrating. Or the sceptics – the people of Anya's parents' generation who refused to believe that meaningful connection could be achieved virtually – were right.

Whatever the truth, Anya didn't care. She and Dan were about to become a statistic. One of the fifty per cent or so that didn't make it as far as death do us part.

'And you were together how long before you got married?' Margot continued.

'Four years,' Anya said. 'Just about.'

'Just over fifteen years in total,' Dan added.

'Yes. Well, just over. We met in December. You know, I can never work out if fifteen years is a decent try, or a terrible failure.'

'Most divorces happen at around eight years.'

'Right. Better than average, then.'

'Go us,' Dan said with a smile. But Anya couldn't look him right now. This little sidetrack had taken her back all those years, reacquainting her with that young couple who'd been so confident in their fortitude as a unit.

For years they were sure that nothing could break them. Anya went into it with her parents as an example – people who'd lived through harder years than she and Dan would ever know, who had raised children and kept sufficiently in touch with each other to remain true when they got out the other side of those tiring, endlessly distracted years. Dan meanwhile arrived with no example and a fractured, dented family life, but with every motivation to break a trend rather than continue it.

Now, here they were. In the last throes, talking about their origin story if only to assuage a mediator who believed a more holistic approach to divorce might be a happier one. Or at least not quite so sad.

Anya wondered if Dan was thinking the same as her – *How did we fuck this up?*

As Matt, Margot and Charlotte made some notes and checked their phones, Anya thought about her conversations with friends when breaking the news.

'God. I know things weren't great. But you two always seemed so perfect together,' Nila had said.

'On paper,' Anya had replied.

If you two can't do it, what hope for the rest of us? Lucy, a longtime colleague who'd become a close friend, wrote in a WhatsApp after finding out.

Things haven't been good for a while, was Anya's excuse.

But those were just the things people said to divorcing couples, weren't they? No one ever responded to news of a split after eleven years of marriage with, 'Thank fuck, you two were a disaster from the get-go.'

No. The instinct was to reaffirm that decision to share a life they'd made years ago. Reinforce the idea that they were right to think it should've worked, despite evidence to the contrary. But the system wasn't wrong. The faults were inbuilt. There was no lifetime guarantee and promise that it could be fixed or replaced, like a Le Creuset casserole or a sturdy Volvo.

When she did finally look at Dan, he was staring down at the little space between his shoes. Like a defendant about to be sentenced. Was his little plea outside genuine, she wondered. Or a desperate lunge to stop the girls from moving away from him?

'Now,' Margot said, dragging Anya away from that train of thought. 'The reason I ask you to talk about those early days is to remind you that, once, you were different people. You were excited by the thought of each other. You were going to fall in love. And all the difficulties you've experienced over the past few years won't change that. And I hope that when you leave today, you'll leave with the many good times you spent together front of mind.'

Good luck, Anya thought.

'And with that in mind, it's time to talk about how the two of you will stay in each other's lives after your marriage has ended. Now, have either of you given any thought to that?'

They both shook their heads.

* * *

If Dan was honest, he hadn't allowed himself to think of it. Even during those days and nights alone in London, when he still believed this was the right thing to do, he hadn't thought of his life beyond the divorce, when he would again be a single man. In fact, he had barely given any thought to anything beyond a month from now.

Life, recently, had been lived in small units: hours into days, days into weeks. Time was easier to fill that way. Not so cluttered with awful little reminders that he was soon to become a middle-aged divorcee, a part-time father, a man in need of a restart when there could be no certainty that all his constituent parts were in working order.

'Well,' Margot said.

But she was stopped short by a blaring, whirring alarm. Then a loud voice proclaiming, 'THIS IS A FIRE ALARM. PLEASE MAKE YOUR WAY TO THE NEAREST EMERGENCY EXIT. THIS IS A FIRE ALARM. PLEASE MAKE YOUR WAY TO THE NEAREST EMERGENCY EXIT.'

And then the alarm again.

'Oh, fucking hell,' Matt shouted above the noise as he got up and grabbed his coat and bag. 'Not fucking now.'

The others followed his lead, trying to keep up as he stormed out of Serenity's glass door, and towards the seldom-used stairs next to the lift, where a stream of suited Melrose and White employees were hurrying down through the building, a line of ants marching away from a nest.

* * *

Outside, the company collected on the corner of Bartlett Court, a small, recently built mews of shops and offices, where a good number of people seemed to treat the fire drill as an opportunity to get takeaway coffees from the one small café. Meanwhile, the two severe women from the reception desk had donned high-vis jackets with *FIRE MARSHALL* emblazoned across the back, and armed themselves with clipboards.

Dan, Anya, Matt and Margot found themselves pushed to the edge of the crowd, most of whom were staring back at the office as though it were going to burst into flames any minute. Those who had forgotten to grab coats before leaving hugged their own bodies, or jogged on the spot to keep warm.

'How—'

'Christ knows,' Matt said, cutting Anya off. 'Last time it was fifteen minutes. The time before that an hour,' he continued, looking through emails on his phone. 'Usually, it's because some stupid bastard's burnt their toast. It's never an actual bloody fire.'

She checked her watch. Almost midday. *Too late for toast*, she thought. So maybe a fire was tearing the place apart as they watched on? Any minute now the windows would blow out, and the collected lawyers, paralegals, secretaries and solicitors would realise that their gym bags, cashmere coats, computers and shoes collected under desks were being burnt to ash. That would certainly teach the complacent lot who'd eschewed the fire register to stand in line for a flat white.

'Well, can we just take an early lunch, then?' Anya said. 'We can finish up this afternoon. When we go back in.'

'If you're happy to do that?' Margot said to Matt and Charlotte, who both nodded their assent.

And before Dan could properly react, Anya was away, walking towards Holborn.

* * *

Dan stood hesitantly for a moment. Surely, she couldn't be going back to the same place as yesterday, he thought. Before she disappeared off into the busy street, he set off after her, aware that Matt, Margot and Charlotte were watching on, likely confused by what the hell he was doing.

Unlike yesterday, though, Anya didn't cross the busy road on to Hatton Garden, then head down that little alleyway to the conveniently hidden pub. Instead, she turned right, walking away from him in the direction of St Paul's Cathedral.

He followed for a few metres, but Anya was walking fast. Soon a growing crowd of office workers, shoppers and early lunch breakers obscured her from view.

* * *

Anya stopped in the street for a few seconds and looked around, just as she was arriving at the cathedral. She wanted to be alone, and only found herself able to relax when surrounded by a crowd of tourists milling around to take photographs of (and selfies with) the monolithic white church, interrupted by lunching workers staring at their phones or chomping down Pret baguettes, showing a blasé ignorance of the history around them.

She took a seat midway up the steps, surrounded by tourists amidst the imposing pillars and towers, some of them now sheltering under umbrellas. In her bag was a bottle of water she'd nabbed from Serenity, and three biscuits, the edges of which had chipped away to become crumbs lingering among her purse, lip balm and a few loose tampons.

Space and time. That's what she needed. She had no idea who'd set off the fire alarm, but if she ever found out, she'd buy them a drink.

The morning had been… confusing. From Dan's declaration to the things they had to rake over.

Kids, custody, communication. Their rights and their preferences. The things that really mattered when a shared life was cleaved into two.

Right now, there was more cause for wobbles than confidence. It was that pang of uncertainty after turning down dessert at a restaurant. But times a million.

They'd done second chances, put in more effort, had breaks without the kids and eventually resorted to therapy. Session after session in which neither found the empathy to understand the other's position.

They had *tried*.

Perhaps not as hard as they might've. But the ease with which their efforts had failed was *surely* damning.

And then there was the world after their marriage. There would never be a life without Dan. Anya didn't want there to be. The problem was knowing exactly how much of him she did want in her life.

They had both lived with the adjustments of the past few months as though they wouldn't be permanent. Moving the kids back and forth was an inconvenience. Dan's living situation was temporary. The questions the girls still had would go away in time – either with answers or growing indifference. But all these things were slowly calcifying.

Workarounds would become best practice. Although none of it would necessarily get any easier.

She would lose access to second-hand friendships and relationships. As much as Dan promised to involve her in Rhys's life, how long would that realistically last when the boy had so little incentive for her to be there? He, surely, would soon become a Facebook friend at best, a memory at worst.

'Shit,' Anya said to herself, frustrated at her uncertainty. 'Shit, shit, fucking shit.' Which attracted a glare of a family group browsing a travel guide map a couple of metres away.

And then a new thought barged in. The one she had tried to resist thinking about, despite the almost-itch it had created since they agreed to split.

The prospect of starting again.

Maybe there would be a new partner. With him would come another family, new circles and that whole exciting/terrifying beginning bit again. People always say it was fun, but that was only ever in retrospect, when the relationship had worked. No one going through it in real time enjoyed it. There was too much hesitance and second-guessing, trying to glean the motivations and intentions of someone through the number of Xs at the end of a text and their choice of emoji.

Besides, what were the chances the next man she met would be right? Non-existent, really.

Nonetheless, he would meet her kids and she his. They would weave into each other's tapestry, only to be picked out again months later.

Anya knew that fear of a reset was no good reason to stay. But it wasn't exactly a bad reason either. And she and Dan would both be lying to themselves if they didn't admit that it mattered.

On that count, he was right. There might not be anyone better.

She checked her watch. Almost half past. She would have to be in the room again soon for the curtain call.

Anya worried at her engagement and wedding rings, eventually twisting them both off.

Each ring had a date inscribed inside.

17. 03. 2008 NYC

27. 06. 2009 LON

The engagement and the marriage. How they got here in the first place.

She knew she still loved Dan. Regardless of what happened, there could be no changing that. The question was if she still loved him enough to think that last night wasn't the mistake? And why they were even here in the first place?

She looked at the rings again.

ELEVEN YEARS AND ELEVEN MONTHS AGO

New York City

She had hoped to get a glimpse of the city skyline as they approached it in the air. But Anya was sat on the wrong side of the plane, and (as a steward told her) approaching JFK wasn't the best airport for that sort of thing. 'You need LaGuardia. But LaGuardia sucks,' he said quietly.

The plane rumbled and bumped as it descended. She took Dan's hand. He was a terrible flyer, full of nerves and always looking out for signs that they were going to crash. The slightest tilt of a wing, a change in tone from the engine or noticeable drop was enough to convince him that this was the end – that he would be one of the newsworthy few who died on impact in the choppy waters of the Atlantic. He didn't make it easier for himself by reading every report about aviation disasters before a flight, or refusing to sleep during, so by the time they came into land, he was an exhausted, erratic mess.

'The thing is,' he had once told her, 'even if you survive the crash then you're scarred, aren't you? And they'll probably make you fly home afterwards anyway.'

'You could take a boat,' Anya had said.

'I hate boats.'

He attributed his mistrust of planes (it was never a genuine fear) to a childhood of domestic holidays, travelled to in the back of the car or maybe at the most adventurous on the train.

Those impressionable early years had gone past without exposure to flight. So when he eventually had to do it any excitable novelty was tempered by the adult suspicion of anything new.

'What's the plan, then?' Anya said, distracting him from the window, where he was looking down at the inky black water, then across to the east coast of America, doubtless thinking that if the engines failed, maybe they could at least make it over there and find a field to land in. That would give them half a chance.

'Sorry?'

'I said what's the plan? When we get there.'

'I don't know. What time will it be?'

'Eight. Just past, maybe. By the time we get through baggage and the passport Stasi it'll be nine at least.'

'I don't know. Grab something to eat? Bed? I'm knackered.'

'You should've slept.'

'I can't sleep on these things,' he said, like they were on a roller coaster instead of a British Airways flight to New York.

'I'd like to see Times Square,' Anya said. 'I want to *feel* like I'm there, you know?'

'Sure,' Dan said. 'It's your trip. You make the rules.'

'Come on. Our trip.'

'Fine. But we wouldn't be coming to New York if it weren't for your—'

'Don't,' she said. 'I don't want to think about it now. It makes me nervous.'

'You'll be fine,' Dan said, taking her right hand and planting a kiss just below the knuckles.

Now Anya was the nervous one – reminded of everything that was riding on the next two days. She reached into her bag and pulled out the information she had printed out.

The idea of it was still mildly terrifying. Even the logistics of moving to America were mind-boggling. They would have to find a new place to live, settle into an area, pick a preferred grocery shop, figure out how travel worked. There would be visas and government hoops to jump through. All those little comforts in Crouch End would be gone and they'd have to find equivalents over here, like tourists who spend hours searching for English products in foreign supermarkets.

It would be especially hard for Dan, who would have to get a job himself. She hadn't even allowed herself to think about things like healthcare and insurance, which were unfathomable in America.

But, if not now, when?

As a couple, they were untethered. If things worked out for the long-term, as Anya hoped they would, that would never be the case again. Mortgages, kids, debt, work would all keep them wherever they were.

Right now, she had made the leap to move away from her family in Cork, who were already a plane journey from home. And while Dan might feel a pang about putting an ocean between himself and his grandmother, there were no other meaningful ties keeping him on English soil.

One change in any of that and this kind of move would be impossible.

Anya picked through the pile of papers to the email she had received a month ago. She must've read it four or five times a day since. It had come out of the blue one Wednesday afternoon while she was in a production house office in Soho, preparing some notes for a script meeting the following day with an up-and-coming children's television personality named Kelvin Fisher.

The sender's name, Janey Wiseman, was new to her. But she got a little jolt of nervous excitement when she saw the name of the company Janey worked for, and immediately tilted her laptop screen inwards to keep it from nosey colleagues.

There were little sentences that jumped out even as she read it again now.

We were extremely impressed with your work.

Ours is one of the most prestigious and successful writing programs for children and teen entertainment in the world.

We'd like to invite you to join a writers' room, meet with some of our series creators and discuss a possible role for you here.

Two telephone interviews had followed. One with Janey, who said she'd decided to get in touch after her sister-in-law in the UK had told her about a new show called *Monkey Magic*, which had been Anya's concept. Then another with Janey and someone from HR who asked a series of inane questions about corporate values that both Anya and Janey knew would count for nothing if a job offer was made.

Now here they were, descending into New York City to see if it might be a place where they could see themselves working, and living.

* * *

Dan rested on a concrete bollard, next to a set of crosswalk lights outside the Viacom building in Times Square. In front of him, a man dressed as Spider-Man posed with tourists in exchange for dollar bills while enthusiastic young promoters gave out flyers for comedy nights, gigs and shows nearby. What seemed like thousands of people walked by every second, talking into phones, listening to headphones, eating, drinking, dodging one another.

The scene wasn't exactly strange to him. He had lived in a city for long enough, and while he tended to avoid the overcrowded, commoditised London equivalent of this in Leicester Square, it was there if he ever needed it. But it did feel odd to believe that, depending on how things were going for Anya in the building over there, this kind of scene might feel a lot more familiar in a year's time.

So far that day, he had walked around the south side of Central Park, looked in at FAO Schwarz to see the piano from *Big*, then taken the subway to Greenwich Village to wander around the music venues that had hosted early Bob Dylan gigs, trying to imagine what life might've looked like back then, around there. He'd also looked in the guitar shops, wondering if one of them might give him a job – if everything turned out in the unlikely way it might.

It was part tourism, part research and part aimless meandering. All a reminder that he wasn't all that brilliant on his own with these things, with no one to talk to about what he was seeing, or guide him from place to place.

She eventually appeared at quarter past. Noticeable for the long dark red overcoat she was wearing. She had worried about it being 'too much' that morning while she was getting dressed in the room the television channel had paid for. As soon as she saw Dan, her face broke into a smile, no doubt full of all the things she wanted to tell him about the day, the people she'd met, the excitement of the processes she'd been part of.

They embraced and kissed, then walked east on 42nd Street, towards Bryant Park and their hotel for the few days they had in the city.

'Well, then?' Dan said. And she was off, reciting a list of new names and the jobs they were attached to. She told him about the feeling of being in a writers' room in *that* building, for *that* company. He smiled and asked more questions, wondering if this might be the big adventure for them – if they would make a home in a city he'd never expected to even see when growing up in Newcastle. And wondered, if they did, would he ever feel like anything but a tourist here?

'Sorry. I'm going on, aren't I?' Anya said as they approached the park, still busy with friends walking together holding takeaway cups of coffee, street vendors, and a few people playing pétanque or table tennis on the municipal courts.

'No. It's amazing,' he said, taking her hand. 'And do you think… you know. Or did they say?'

They crossed the road to their hotel, where a waiting security guard pulled open a heavy door for them.

'They want to talk,' Anya said. 'Tomorrow, at breakfast. Sorry, I know it's the weekend and I said we could—'

'It's fine. We've got the afternoon, haven't we?'

'You don't mind?'

'Anya. This is the most elaborate job interview I've ever heard of. If they wanted you to turn up and start presenting on the telly I wouldn't be surprised.'

'I want to make a good impression.'

'Listen. If they didn't think you were good enough, they wouldn't have flown us out here.'

'I know that,' she said, calling the lift, which would take them fifteen floors up to a small room with a half-obscured view of the Empire State Building. 'It's the dynamics I'm worried about. Do they like me? Do I fit in?'

'Anya,' he said. 'If they didn't like you, would you be going for breakfast tomorrow?'

Dan stopped and faced her, outside the lift on the fifteenth floor. 'I don't want to presume,' he said. 'But I think they're going to offer you a job as a kids' TV writer in New York.'

'Don't.'

'My question is if you're going to take it?'

* * *

Anya froze for a second. Everything inside her wanted to say yes. But the idea of the upheaval gave her pause. Not least the difficulty of Dan being able to come with her. During lunch she had googled the entry requirements to America. Her work visa would see her through easily. Dan, on the other hand, would be a different matter.

She didn't want to tell him. Dan was too much of an optimist. He would convince himself that whatever the problem, it would be okay. Things were resolvable. But his 'see what happens' spirit had never come up against the bureaucratic might and emotional disinterest of American immigration authorities. Anya didn't fancy his chances.

'Seriously?' he said, as she turned away towards their room, taking the key card from her inside pocket and swiping it down the door handle.

'Dan.'

'This is *it*, Anya. If they offer it you can't say no.'

'There's a lot to think about.'

'Like what?'

'Like… everything. Living here. Moving out of London.'

'What's wrong with that? It's not as if either of us have got much there.'

'Your job.'

'I earn seventeen grand a year fixing guitars in a shop I live above. I can get another job. I had a look around today. There's a load of shops.'

This, if anything, made it worse. The idea that he'd become invested in the move, in her career, that he was already conducting early research for a life he probably wouldn't be able to live.

'It's more than that.'

'What?' Dan said, taking his jumper off and rooting around in their shared suitcase for the one shirt he'd brought with him in preparation for the one nice meal out they had planned.

Anya sighed. Then relented. 'You,' she said. 'What if you can't come?'

'What do you mean me? Of course I'll come. I just said—'

'Dan. That's not the point. I'm saying what if you *can't* come? Not what if you won't. I looked it up,' she said, hastily, before he could leap in. 'You can't get a work visa if you don't have a job here. We're not married so you don't qualify as a spouse. So that means you're on a tourist one. And that's a hundred and eighty days. Max.'

'I can get a job.'

'And it still might not be enough. You'll get a year or something. Look, I don't want to have to choose between you and… this,' she said, vaguely gesturing with her arm to encompass the job, the career, New York City, and that life in general.

'Then don't,' he said, stood in front of her, topless, holding his only white shirt – the one with a yellowing neck from many years of occasional use – in the crook of his arm, alongside a Ramones T-shirt that she'd not seen since a high street fashion chain began selling facsimiles of it.

'What do you mean?' Anya said, dropping down onto the bed. He took a step towards her.

'You said I don't qualify as a spouse,' he said. 'And I'm saying, what if I did?'

Dan felt a little out of control in terms of where this was heading. Anya was blank-faced, confused, surprised. In fairness, he had only decided to suggest it thirty seconds ago, when she said the word 'spouse'. But he was still hoping for more than this.

'Well?'

'Sorry… Dan. Are you…?'

'I am,' he said, trying to recover the situation, not sure of which way she might fall. 'Yeah.'

'And have you got… like… a you know.'

'Ring?'

'Yeah.'

'No. Sorry. Bit spur of the moment, really. And your parents don't know either. So, well, that's two things going against it.'

'Right,' she said. 'Fuck.'

'Sorry. If you don't… Maybe I shouldn't have.'

'No. I'm… I don't know. Surprised, I suppose. But… do you mean it?'

'I do.'

'I mean, like, do you want to?'

'Yes.'

'Not just because—'

'No. Anya. I want to marry you.'

'Right,' she said, looking at him. 'Well, ask, then,' she added with a smile. 'Properly like.'

And Dan dropped to one knee, his clothes still on his arm, and looked up at Anya.

'Will you marry me?' he said.

'Yes,' she said, tears forming in her eyes.

And as the sky darkened outside, and Manhattan was lit by the windows of a million offices, hotel rooms, apartments and the residual light from Times Square, Dan and Anya kissed and fell onto the bed in their hotel room, in the city that soon they would both get to call home.

TEN YEARS AND EIGHT MONTHS AGO

Hampstead, London

The taxi carrying Anya, Nila and her dad, Colm, made slow progress up Rosslyn Hill. Outside, strollers and shoppers were meandering about their little enclave of North London, ducking in and out of shops and peering in restaurant windows. It was a nice day, bright, sunny and warm. Too warm for formalwear, so her dad had his suit jacket on his lap. He was anxious. Obviously worried about the speech he would have to deliver in a few hours' time, and unaccustomed to the heat in the first place.

For some reason, the driver had gone down through Highgate, then across the bottom of the Heath, instead of over the top, which was always quicker. So they were in danger of being more than the ten minutes late the venue allowed them. 'We understand you brides like to make an entrance,' the events organiser had told her. 'But we do like to keep to a schedule.'

She looked at the clock above the meter. Two o'clock. By rights, she should be walking down the aisle now. Instead, there they were at the bottom of the hill, in a slow-moving queue of cars, buses and bikes edging towards the top.

'For fuck's sake,' she muttered to herself, looking out at a couple chasing after a child on a scooter, who was rapidly rolling down towards Belsize Park.

'Come on now,' her dad said, softly, putting a hand on hers.

Anya gestured at the clock, the traffic, the driver. She was thinking about the guests all sitting there and waiting for her. About the close friends she knew would be running a book on how late she would be (quid in, winner takes all). And about her mum, checking her watch every fifteen seconds, wondering if and when she should send a message to her husband to find out what the hold-up might be. While her brother, Darragh, told her to put the phone away, to stop with all the stressing.

They'd chosen to have a smallish wedding. Just fifty people. Although it was striking how quickly they hit that number when shortlisting the All Dayers, Evening Onlys and Maybe Depending on Numbers – some of whom had eventually been invited, but weren't top-tier guaranteed bums on seats.

Then, as the driver pulled the handbrake on, she thought of Dan. He would be jittery and uncertain, for sure. But every time someone asked him how he was, he'd say 'fine' or 'great' or 'grand'. He'd be wearing his lightish grey suit, a white shirt and a black tie in a nod to Newcastle United. Underneath all that would be one of his band T-shirts to fit the occasion. If she had to guess, The Wedding Present. Unless he had managed to procure the Billy Idol 'White Wedding' rarity she'd seen him searching for every now and then.

George would be stood next to him, offering the occasional encouraging remark or comforting smile. Unlike her dad, he would be looking forward to his speech, relishing the chance to play at being a stand-up in front of a crowd that was more or less contractually obliged to laugh at his jokes.

The unspoken truth between them – and between everyone really – was that George was stood in another man's place.

The best man would have – should have – been Eddie. If it weren't for the news that came a month after she and Dan had returned from New York. The news that had nixed their plans to move to America, and instead kept them in London, above the flat, with Dan now the owner of String Theory.

'Here we go, then,' Colm said, as the 414 bus hissed and moved forwards in front of them.

'Don't get your hopes up,' the cabbie said bluntly, perhaps forgetting for a moment that he was carrying a bride towards her wedding.

'Fucking hell,' Anya said, frustrated, brushing a hair off her white dress (nothing too big or flouncy, something that in any other colour would've been a regular but nice cocktail dress).

'It'll be fine. I'm sure he'll wait for you,' Colm said.

'It's not the point. I don't want him to get nervous.'

'Bloody wants to be,' the cabbie interrupted. Everyone ignored him.

'Listen. If the lad isn't nervous then something's missing,' Colm said, tapping his head.

The traffic moved again and they progressed up the hill. Without warning, the driver flicked the indicator and swung right, down a side street full of well-to-do three-storey red-brick houses, in front of which were parked a row of Land Rovers, Mercs and those Porsche jeeps that Anya felt were exclusively driven by complete arseholes.

'Two minutes,' the driver said, with another flick of the indicator and a sharp left, sending them all lurching right as he carried on up the hill. Until they arrived at the pristine green gardens and wrought-iron gates of Burgh House.

Immediately, the nerves that the minor annoyance of lateness had suppressed made themselves known. In Anya's stomach, on her palms, and across the back of her neck. Colm got out of the cab and held out his hand for his daughter, who picked up her small bouquet of wild flowers and followed him, overhearing a little exchange with the driver as her dad paid.

'Good luck, then,' he said, taking a twenty-pound note and a ten.

'Married, are ye?'

'Divorced,' the driver said.

'I got that impression.'

Then her dad turned back and offered the crook of his

arm to his daughter, and the two of them walked towards her wedding.

* * *

Colm had just finished his speech. Mostly little amusing anecdotes about Anya as a girl. An overwrought statement about his pride in her career and his surprise that the daughter of a builder and a community nurse might become a scriptwriter. Topped off with a few little digs at Dan because he had proposed without 'doing the decent thing and asking me first, not that I'd have said no', and because the wedding was in London rather than Cork (conveniently ignoring the fact that Dan could be said to be from a lot of places – Norwich where he was born, Lincoln where he spent his earliest years, Newcastle where he grew up – but London was not one of them).

The guests cheered and whooped as he wrapped up, the odd tear creeping through his stout emotional defences, and passed the microphone down the line of top-table guests to Dan. He felt even less prepared for the speech now than he had last night, when at one in the morning, he still had barely anything to say and was making notes on the pad he used for work, in the half-light of George's living room.

He took the mic and stood up to more cheers and applause. Looking around the room didn't make things any better.

The circle of friends he had linked on to through Anya were all of a type. Educated, smart, witty. There were lawyers here, like Matt, who Dan was almost sure was in love with Anya and who hated him as a result. A couple of English teachers as well, who would readily spot the points where he'd used bigger words to make himself sound smarter. Some were even writers, and there was one actor – that Kelvin bloke who was making a name for himself in Anya's world of children's television.

Most of them would likely have felt fine in his position. A few would've relished it. He felt out of place, unnatural with a microphone, too attached to his script.

Fucking hell, he thought, opening the tightly folded piece of paper that would be his crutch for the next five minutes.

'Hi,' he began, and cleared his throat. 'Thank you to Colm for that lovely speech. I'm not sure how many times I'll have to apologise about proposing off the cuff like that. But I'm glad we got here in the end.'

A few laughs. Polite more than anything. What he had said wasn't funny. None of it would be funny, really. He looked down at Anya, who smiled back at him in that comforting, reassuring way he'd seen so much over the past year. The smile that had got him through – got *them* through.

The next few paragraphs were notes of thanks to bridesmaids, Anya's parents, his grandmother, and the best man, George, with the standard note of warning about the veracity of his speech that would come next. Then came the bit he had been dreading, but knew was important to say here, today. He had to acknowledge what had happened since he proposed in that New York hotel room.

'Now, Anya,' he said, looking at her again, then away quickly. He'd found a spot to focus on at the back of the room. A window ledge. It meant that he would be looking over the heads of everybody. But that was preferable to speaking through the little voice-staunching sobs and quavers that had plagued his rehearsal so far.

'When we decided to get married, things looked a little different for us. We'd decided to move to New York. You had an amazing job lined up.'

Deep breath, he told himself.

'But life doesn't always turn out the way we plan it. As you all know, my great friend, my boss, the man who gave me a chance when I moved to London, Eddie Webb, sadly passed away about a month after we got back from America.'

He looked across the room, knowing that every one of them would be aware of the circumstances around Eddie's death. How he had been on tour in Australia with a reasonably well-known band as their head roadie. And how the crash that killed Eddie also took the guitarist of the band, relegating his old friend to a footnote in the articles about the tragedy, caused by a drunk driver swerving across lanes and sending the taxi Eddie was in into a central reservation.

Dan, meanwhile, briefly remembered the phone call he had received to tell him the news. It had come from Eddie's sister, Janice, who he barely saw or knew any more. She thought she was delivering the news only to the bloke who ran the shop when her brother wasn't around and that would be that. Janice had no idea of the bond between her brother and the shocked, broken man on the phone. Or that their bond meant she wouldn't be getting the inheritance she had been expecting.

'And a couple of months after that, we discovered that I had become the owner of a guitar shop and a flat in North London. Something I'm still struggling to get my head round today,' Dan said to a few polite laughs. His distaste for admin and discomfort with the idea of being a business owner was well known among their friends and family.

'By that point, Anya had a job lined up, we were looking at areas we might move to. And then, we couldn't. Instead we spent months dealing with lawyers and legal bollocks,' he said, with a look at Matt. 'Anya helped me stay strong when it seemed easier to go against Eddie's wishes and give up the shop. And, of course, she's helped me figure out how to run the place, which neither of us thought we'd be doing.'

Anya then reached up to take his hand. Maybe she could see it shaking. Almost certainly, she could sense his discomfort.

He squeezed. She squeezed back. The little gesture was almost as symbolic as the rings they'd given each other a few hours ago.

'Now, I don't want to go into all the details of that time. But just to say, again, that without Anya's selflessness, support and kindness I'd never have got through it. And while we may not be living in New York, I hope the life we're building now makes up for it.'

A few cheers rang around the room. Dan saw glasses raised

and kind smiles. Then he looked down at Anya, who mouthed a silent, 'Thank you.'

Immediately, he relaxed. The hard part of the speech was done with. All that was left were a few jokes about his own ineptitude, a few notes of thanks to the people who had helped them organise the day, and he was out.

He cleared his throat and brought the microphone back up once more.

* * *

It was around 10:30 when the first guests began to leave and the evening started its slow fade away. They had rented a function room and part of the garden of a pub that led on to the Heath for the evening. There hadn't been much dancing, many of their guests a little shy or hesitant, what with the regular patrons of the pub half looking on and hampering their ability to go for it 'like no one's watching'. But there had been a lot of reminiscing with friends, standing outside on a warm summer's evening, talking over drinks, catching up with people they saw all too infrequently and swearing to change that.

What they'd missed was time to themselves. Until Matt and one of Anya's cousins left together to get a round before last orders. And she and Dan found themselves alone under a pagoda that was busy with the pinks, reds and whites of crawling clematis.

'Hello, then,' Dan said, taking his wife by the hand.

'All right,' she said, sipping gingerly from the top of a gin and tonic. Already a few down, Anya knew that one more might be enough to push her into the next stage of drunkenness, where unsteady feet and maybe even vomit would be waiting. While she wasn't sure there'd necessarily be sex on their wedding night, she didn't want to firmly rule it out by ending the day with her head down the toilet.

'It's gone fast, hasn't it?'

'Sort of,' she said. 'I'm struggling to believe that it was

only a few hours ago that I was getting ready for all this at home.'

'I know what you mean.'

They sat down at a pub garden bench, the wood of it split by rain, and bleached by the sun. A few hours ago, Anya wouldn't have sat anywhere there was so obviously dirt and bird shit. But she felt a lot more free now she didn't have to worry about getting anything on the bloody dress.

'Does it feel any different to you?' she said, as Dan lit a cigarette.

'I don't know. Probably not. I mean, it might one day, I suppose. But there's no, like, immediate change, is there?'

'No. I suppose not.'

* * *

Dan smiled at her. What he said was true in a way. But also, he wasn't quite telling her everything about how he felt.

That all of these occasions, these milestones in his life felt that bit more enormous because of where he'd come from and how he had expected things to turn out. The sheer unlikelihood of it all never failed to register, and some part of him always worried that one day the genie's spell would run out and he would be back up in Newcastle, living with his grandmother, working in the petrol station, his life unmoving – as it had been for a year or two before he decided to leave it and get a train to London to see if there might be anything better out there.

Anya had always marvelled about how and why he turned up in a strange city with hardly any money and no job. But the answer was simple enough. He had little to risk by it. The slim chance of success made the larger risk of failure easier to reckon with. Tonight was proof.

'It's good, though, isn't it?' Dan said, taking her hand.

'It is,' Anya said.

NOW

Friends had always told her about the warning signs they'd spotted in their marriages. Little tells that, in retrospect, showed things were doomed from the outset. In the endless round of divorce war stories that followed her news that she and Dan were separating, Anya had heard them all.

'Of course, I should've known then,' Nila said, suggesting that Luke's fussiness over not sharing chips on their third date was the reveal moment for the controlling behaviour that would eventually end their eight years together.

'*Those* were her true colours,' her workmate Christian offered over a drink one evening. Anya nodded along, but couldn't for the life of her understand why an argument about holidaying in Cornwall or France suggested his now ex-wife Mel would one day leave him for the twenty-four-year-old labourer who'd been working on their kitchen extension.

And 'I wouldn't have gone through with it if it weren't for the money' came from Tania, who wore her lavish, sixty-thousand-pound (by Dan's back-of-a-fag-packet fiscal analysis) wedding like a millstone. And had a litany of minor disagreements (Granny Smith or Pink Lady apples, his family at Christmas or hers, grass lawn or Astroturf) that foreshadowed her awful divorce with Carl.

When it came her turn to share, Anya could never think

of anything like that with her and Dan. Even now, at the end and looking back, she couldn't point to any historic event that might serve as an augur for this. No minor crack that revealed a major fissure. They were… good.

Sure, it wasn't always – or ever – fireworks and thrills. Their story didn't involve midnight walks through a city, declarations of love screamed up to a balcony, or mad dash to an airport. It was steady and comforting. Drinks on date one, a kiss on date two, sex on date five, decent sex on date seven. All over a couple of months of building excitement, and the sense from both of them that maybe this one could work.

They'd laid the foundations. The trouble was they'd let the building run into disrepair.

Anya dialled Nila. No answer. But a second later, a WhatsApp message arrived.

Nila: In a meeting. What's up? x

Anya: Question. Did you ever feel unsure when you and Luke were getting divorced? x

And then the phone rang.

'Hey. Sorry,' Anya said. 'You don't have to call.'

'*Uncertain?*' Nila said in a hushed voice, the sound of a door closing behind her.

'Honestly. You don't have to.'

'It's a finance meeting. I told them it was the kids' school.'

'*Nila.*'

'Uncertain, Anya?' she said, stern, like a disappointed headmaster.

'It's probably nothing,' she said, shuffling away from the family a few steps down who had turned to look at her. 'Buyer's remorse or something. But the opposite. Seller's.'

She could hear her friend sigh. Or seethe, maybe.

'No,' Nila said. 'To answer your question. There was

nothing. No regret. It wasn't easy, but it was right. There was nothing left there.'

'Right.'

Then came an unmistakable flutter in Anya's stomach, and her breathing felt a little tighter than normal. These were familiar enough feelings. They had come in the minutes before she slept with Kelvin for the second time (the first time sober). On her wedding day, when she was travelling up Rosslyn Hill in a black cab, pretending to care about the traffic. And, most memorably, when she called Janey Wiseman in New York to tell her that she wouldn't be taking that job, after all, that something had come up and she would have to stay in London for the foreseeable.

The flutter was a signifier. A way of her body telling her that she was in the process of making a very big decision, and that fucking it up one way or the other would have huge, long-lasting consequences. Sadly, that was where the usefulness of the flutter began and ended. It didn't also tell her what decision to make, or provide sufficient context and detail about the decision to help her make the right one.

'Tell me what's wrong.'

'You'll hate me.'

'Tell me.'

Anya drew breath and said quickly, 'I'm not sure we're doing the right thing.'

'For fuck's sake,' Nila said. Anya had been expecting maybe a moment of silence, of rumination. But no. 'Anya. You both had affairs. You were in separate rooms for months. By the end you couldn't talk for twenty seconds without arguing.'

'I know.'

'The marriage broke down, Anya. Jesus, I know it's hard to – hang on,' Nila said, going silent. Then returning seconds later. 'Sorry, boss's PA. Where was I?'

'You were telling me how my marriage had broken down.'

'Right. It had.'

'And that you knew this was hard.'

'Oh yeah. Look, it's hard to admit it, right? Divorce can feel like failure. But what if it isn't? What if the pair of you just ran your course? That was how long you had. Now you move on, you stay nice. Maybe you'll have another run with someone else.'

'Hmm.'

'What?'

'If I tell you, you won't judge me?'

'Of course I'll fucking judge you.'

'Fine,' Anya said. She stood up with her bag and climbed down the steps in front of the cathedral. It felt wrong to discuss it on God's porch. 'We… well… look… we had another run,' she said. 'If you get me.'

Anya had expected another reaction. Anger. Expletives. Disappointment. Instead all she heard was the quiet closing of a door, then Nila's whispered, 'You have got to be joking.'

'Last night. My train back was cancelled. So we—'

'Uber. Taxi. Fuck, hire a bike.'

'I was going to get a hotel. But Dan said there was no need. I could stay at the flat. And—'

'And what, he waited until you were half-drunk and half-asleep then put the moves on for old time's sake?'

'No! Listen,' she said, brushing some raindrops off of a bench with a useless brown Pret napkin and sitting down. 'It was me. I was in bed, thinking about what a nice, normal evening we'd had—'

'Is that all it takes these days? A nice, normal evening. A fish finger sandwich and an episode of *University Challenge* and that's it. Whoosh. Off come the knickers.'

'Nila. Fuck. Come on. In the context. We'd spent a day pulling apart our marriage, our house, talking about what happened. Then we had a couple of pints and a curry and… I don't know. It was like we were who we used to be.'

Again, nothing for a few seconds. Nila had always liked Dan. But when they separated, she and her new partner Joe had fallen firmly on Anya's side.

Luke, she knew, had been in touch with Dan, offering the non-specific and un-timestamped 'we should go for a beer' that men say in all potentially emotional and fractious WhatsApp conversations. Showing the willingness to talk, while knowing the offer was highly unlikely to be taken up, and even if it was, they'd find a pub showing the football so they could look at the screen rather than each other.

'And what?' Nila said, finally. 'If you are then…'

'I don't know. Maybe… fuck, I can't believe I'm saying it… maybe it's a mistake. Like, what if it was all salvageable? Maybe if we'd been better at talking about it… I don't know.'

'And what about if you're not the people you used to be? What if last night was the mistake?'

'Then… I still don't know.'

The two of them let things settle for a moment. Anya hadn't really got what she wanted from the call. Her gut was telling her something. She didn't know if she could believe it.

Before either of them spoke, Anya's phone started to buzz again.

'Shit, sorry,' she said. 'Mum. Probably the kids. Look, I'll call you later.'

Anya stood up from the bench, checked her watch and began the walk back to the office as she hung up one call and answered another.

'Anya,' her mum said.

'Hey. Look, sorry, I'm on my way back to the—'

'Hang on now, dear,' she said, and Anya immediately noticed the panic in her voice. 'Now, it's nothing to worry about. But…'

* * *

The lunch break was almost up. The collected frustrated employees of Melrose and White would be back at their desks now, assuming the fire warning hadn't been genuine. Matt would be in front of his computer, tearing at a Pret baguette while clicking through his emails. Margot would be in the little room, Serenity, waiting for her clients to come back to put in place some terms that would get them through the next couple of years of co-parenting, then to agree to bring their marriage to an end.

Of course, a judge would still have a say. And it would be a few months before the decree nisi arrived. But this was it. No going back now, Dan thought, as he finished his second pint at the same small table he'd sat at yesterday in Ye Old Mitre, with Anya opposite him.

He'd been here for almost an hour. When he lost sight of her on Holborn, he decided to head back to the pub, just in case she decided to turn up again – to find him. He was a Guinness down before accepting that wouldn't happen. She wasn't coming.

The last two days had felt like untangling a set of head-phones that had lived in the bottom of a rucksack for months. One little knot after another. Endlessly complex. Always frustrating. Not totally clear that it's worth the bother.

Dan tipped the remnants of his bag of Mini Cheddars down his throat and took his empties over to the bar. An old boy in the corner smiled at him over the top of his copy of *The Times*, and Dan pushed the heavy door open and stepped out into the rain.

He was almost back on to Hatton Garden when his phone began to vibrate in his trouser pocket.

Anya.

'Hello?'

'Where are you?' she said, sounding panicked.

'Hatton Garden. I'll be back in a minute. Just tell—'

'Don't go back. Go to King's Cross.'

'Anya—'

'It's Martha. My mum just called. She's hurt. They're taking her to hospital.'

'Fuck. Anya, what—'

'I'll tell you when I see you,' she said. 'Just get to the station. I'm in a cab now.'

Immediately, all thoughts of the rest of the day, the little room, Matt and Margot waiting for them there, disappeared. Dan ran to Holborn and stuck out an arm for a taxi to take him to the station.

* * *

They arranged to meet on the platform at St Albans station, having found themselves in different carriages of the same train and unable to locate each other during three frustrating phone calls.

Dan would usually pass a train journey with a book, a crossword or some mindless scrolling on his phone. But the worry about Martha made all of those distractions unavailable to him. He wondered what it was like for people taking long flights home after a death in the family. Would they be able to watch the films? Or was the entire flight spent in a sort of quiet, petrified contemplation?

'All right,' Anya said, finding him as a few commuters returning home early pushed past. The train doors hissed and closed shut behind them, carrying the remaining passengers further away from London, into the suburbs.

'Have you heard any more?'

'She's okay. On the children's ward.'

'But she's like…'

'Like what?' Anya said, walking away towards the barriers. Dan jogged a little to catch up.

'Like, you know, conscious?'

'Yes. Jesus. I wouldn't be standing here chatting if she wasn't conscious.'

'Right.'

'What, you think we shouldn't have come?'

'No!'

'We'll get back on the train, shall we? Pick up where we left off?'

'Christ. Anya, no. I was just asking. Don't be ridiculous.'

Anya held her phone against the sensor on the barrier, instantly parting with eighteen pounds.

'Sorry,' she said, as Dan followed her through. 'I'm just… you know. I could've done without it?'

* * *

She wondered if this was a bad thing to say, given that earlier that day they had been discussing the division of their children's lives.

If he was recording this then how would it look if they went back and he played Margot, Matt and Charlotte a recording of her saying that she 'could've done without' her daughter potentially suffering a concussion? Could've done without being called away to visit a strange hospital midway through an intensely laborious administrative process?

In fairness, the timing of her mother's call had been terrible. Not that she was close to any resolution about her marriage. But the way Martha immediately threw a cloak over everything else certainly put that resolution a little further away.

'This one,' she said, pointing to a black Audi that had just driven into the car park. The minicab she'd ordered from the train.

As Anya climbed in, she felt her phone buzz in her coat pocket.

Nila: Don't do anything rash x

She ignored it as they left the car park and emerged into the growing mid-afternoon school traffic.

They had been going for a few minutes before Dan coughed to get her attention and said, 'Puts it into perspective, doesn't it?'

'What?'

'I mean, like, Martha.'

'Right.'

'It puts it into perspective.'

'Puts what into perspective?' Anya said, as they slowed for another set of traffic lights. They seemed to be on a never-ending red wave. The delays were making her anxious.

'You know. The thing,' Dan said, trying to be suggestive with his facial expressions, not wanting to say too much in front of the cab driver, as though they were trying to keep a lid on an argument at a dinner party.

'Dan.'

'I'm just saying.'

'Well, don't say it now.'

They rumbled on a little further. Outside, the streets were quiet, the cold and the rain encouraging people indoors.

Anya tried to focus on anything but the time and distance. Every minute felt like it lasted five. Every metre travelled was a mile. She just needed to see Martha. No amount of being told she was okay would make this feel any better.

She felt Dan's hand on her shoulder. It was comforting. Somehow the only person who could make her feel that way. And there it was again. The little ripple running through her body. The voice telling her that they might actually, after all, despite everything, be better together.

'I only meant—'

'Seriously?' she said, brushing him away like an irritating gnat.

'I didn't—'

'You really want to have this conversation here, do you? Now? In the back of a taxi?'

The driver shifted in his seat, making it known that he was uncomfortable in their company and felt too exposed to the inner workings of their relationship. This was something Dan had seen a few times over the past few years. In friends, teachers at parents' evening, family members and various waiters and shop assistants.

'No,' he said. 'But, look. I can tell that you're thinking about this, too, Anya. I know it.'

She didn't reply, hating the fact that he knew her well enough to be able to discern her thinking and moods from otherwise imperceptible body language.

Instead, she pulled out her phone. Dan's vibrated a few seconds later.

Anya: Please stop! For fuck's sake.

Dan: Sorry.

Dan: I just think we need to talk about this.

He watched the three dots that signalled Anya typing a message, attention fixed to the screen.

Dan: Well?

Anya: Not now.

Dan: Fine. I know not now.

Anya: So why are we having a text message argument in the back of a taxi?

Dan: I wouldn't call it an argument.

'Fucking hell,' Anya said through her teeth, and threw her phone back into her bag. Only to pull it out again seconds later.

Anya: Enough.

Dan: Later?

Anya: Maybe.

Dan: I don't think last night was a mistake.

Anya: 😬 😬 😬 😬

Before Dan could reply again, they had arrived at the hospital.

* * *

He had seen one of his kids in a hospital bed before. Two years ago, Edie had a bad dose of scarlet fever and ended up in children's A & E. And not long after, Martha fell on a school trip and suffered a light fracture of her wrist. But no amount of experience could allay the initial shock of it. There was something unnatural about seeing a small child on a hospital bed.

And there she was. Lying down and propped up from the waist. Wearing her *Frozen* sweater and a pair of light blue leggings decorated with pink stars. Her trainers were on the floor beside the bed, and the bottoms of her socks were dirty, no doubt from wandering around the hospital. She smiled when she saw her parents and they smiled back. Although neither was looking at her face, or the broad, hopeful grin that revealed a gap where a front tooth had been until a week ago. Instead, they were drawn to her head, where blonde hair was obscured by a thick white bandage.

Anya's parents got up from the chairs flanking the bed. Edie put down her carton of orange juice.

'Oh, Anya,' Angela said, rushing over to hug her. 'I'm so, so sorry. And to you, Dan,' she said, grasping his hand as if nothing else was happening in their lives. 'The one minute she was up on that climbing frame. You know the one in the park down the road? The next there's all these people running over and she's there on the floor.'

The thought of it stunned Dan. He felt nauseous. Occasional catastrophising about accidents happening to his kids would keep him up at night. Although in those two-in-the-morning imagined disasters, he was in charge (another parental anxiety he put down to having no critical grounding in fatherhood – no example to base what he did on).

'So what… you know… what happened?' he asked.

'Someone called nine nine nine. Before I could even find my phone.'

'Why? Was she…?'

'She didn't move. For a minute. But she was up soon enough.'

'Oh, Mum,' Anya said, embracing her as Dan went over to Martha and kissed the top of her head.

'You should've seen them all. Taking over the situation. Thinking me and your father were a pair of daft old fools who couldn't cope with the kids.'

Anya knew exactly the kind of people they were talking about. Well-meaning, but ultimately interfering middle-class parents. The kind who were always ready with a look of disapproval when she placated one of them with a snack lacking in organic provenance, or forgot to make sure they were both wearing woolly hats on a winter's day.

'We went in an ambulance,' Martha said cheerfully, the enthusiasm children have for blue-light services undimmed by actually having to experience one of them.

'I know,' Dan said. 'I'm sorry, darling.'

'It's all right. It was fun,' she said, turning to Colm. 'Wasn't it, Grandad?'

'Oh. Well, you know… I'm not sure I'd say fun, now.'

He and Dan almost made eye contact. In spite of the circumstances, Dan couldn't ignore the strangeness of all this. It was unlikely that either man had expected to be so close to the other again. These past two days, the reason Colm was looking after Martha in the first place, was meant to be their definitive parting. But as well as his soon-to-be ex-father-in-law, Dan also now saw a man he knew was very unwell, and whose illness was influencing the decision that would soon take his kids away to Ireland.

The closer you got to someone, the more you had to untie. The longer you stayed, the harder that became.

'You all right, Colm?' Dan said.

'Been better, son,' he said, with a smile that told Dan the old man was thinking along the same lines.

Dan smiled thinly as he kissed Martha on the cheek and stepped away to let Anya, who was comforting a worried-looking Edie, closer.

'You must be the parents?' a new voice said. A doctor. Young, Asian. Wearing a teal roll-neck, white coat and carrying an iPad. 'I'm Doctor Sahota.'

'Dan.'

'Anya.'

'Well,' she continued. 'You'll be pleased to know that there's no signs of concussion. Or anything untoward. I think she just suffered a nasty bump on the head,' she said, with a smile at Martha. 'I'd like to keep her here a little longer, if that's okay? Just to make sure. But I see no reason you won't be able to take her home very soon.'

'Right,' Dan said. 'Thanks. And is there any, like, medicine, or… I don't know… advice?'

'Paracetamol if her head hurts. Should only be a couple of days. And don't let her climb anything for a while. Or at least don't let her jump off,' the doctor said, somewhat sarcastically.

As Doctor Sahota left them, Dan and Anya looked at each other across the bed, each holding one of Martha's hands.

Angela and Colm had gone to the hospital canteen for a tea and something to eat. So for the first time in months, it was just the four of them, together. Not handing over kids at a service station and sharing a few strained but polite briefing notes about homework to do, possible illnesses and recent fads. Not trying to keep a bitter argument about something trivial away from Martha and Edie, both of whom were far more perceptive than Dan and Anya gave them credit for.

No. They were just sitting and caring. A family. A

flawed one, for sure. One full of fractures, dents and some considerable cracks. But maybe one that could be patched up, Dan was starting to believe, in a way they had tried before, but failed. Perhaps because neither of them really knew what was at stake until they were so close to losing it forever.

Dan thought back to that little room in the plush Highgate garden where they'd gone for marriage counselling. Of the uncomfortable leather chairs that made his back sweat in the summer months. And the way the counsellor, Danielle, prodded and provoked, asked them to offer up the most lurid details of their infidelities, and admit to the darkest thoughts they'd had about one another ('I once thought if you died it'd be easier,' Anya said in their third session, they didn't talk for three days afterwards).

Afterwards things had improved organically. Initially, it seemed like the move worked. They were happy with each other and around each other. They had a house-warming party to mark their new start. And it was good.

But they were not ready to truly get past their problems back then, and sure enough, the rot set in again.

Now, it had to be different.

'We should talk soon,' he said quietly, while Martha watched *Minions* on Angela's iPad and Edie played a game on his phone.

'Not yet.'

'Soon, though. They'll be wondering.'

Anya showed him her phone. Six messages from Matt.

Hope all's okay. Let me know when we should recommence.

Take it you're not coming back?

Anya. If you could just confirm? Margot asking.

Shall I ask Dan?

Are you coming back? I'd really rather this not run into Monday.

This is really not on, Anya. I know we're friends and all. But come on now.

Dan checked his. One message from Charlotte.

Hope you're all okay. Let me know how you want to proceed. Or if x

He was going to reply. But then realised she'd be getting ready to go to *Hamilton* or whatever it was tonight.

'We have to tell them something,' Dan said.

'Do we?'

'Anya.'

'Fine. Look, when Mum and Dad get back we can get a coffee or something, okay?'

'Sure,' Dan said, with a smile.

EIGHT MONTHS AGO

Westleton, Suffolk

'Martha! Smile!' George called. Dan tapped her on the shoulder and pointed to where his friend was crouched down on their driveway, holding his big, professional-looking digital camera.

'Is that it?' Edie asked.

'Stay with me,' George called.

'Look, can we just get on with it?' Anya said. 'Darling,' she added, looking directly at Edie. 'Keep looking at George. Two seconds.'

More rapid bursts of clicks. He was making a bit of a meal of it. All they wanted was the four of them outside the front door as a memento. An iPhone probably would've done. But true to the manner of a man who rarely got to use his expensive toy, George had jumped at the opportunity to commemorate the Moorcrofts' house-warming party as though it was a paid gig.

'Done now?' Dan said.

'Two ticks.'

'We're done,' he said, and Martha ran off, Edie following on as soon as she realised they could go.

'The light was a bit iffy,' George said grumpily.

'I'm sure they'll come out fine.'

'I only needed a minute,' he said, packing his camera away. 'I'll send them this week. Just got to tidy them up a bit.'

'Cheers. And tell me what we owe you.'

'Hilarious.'

The three of them walked back towards the house, footsteps crunching on the gravel. Inside, a few old friends and new neighbours were mingling in the lounge over plastic flutes of Prosecco and slices of supermarket cakes Dan had bought from Marks & Spencer that morning. Anya went off to find Nila, who had come on her own after a row with her new boyfriend Joe and was potentially a bit volatile if left for too long with strangers and a ready supply of fizzy wine.

'It's looking all right,' George said.

'Cheers,' Dan said, closing the front door behind him. 'I don't know if it'll ever feel finished. You should've seen it when we moved in.'

'Bad?'

'Dated. The bloke before had been here for decades.'

'Chintz and textured wallpaper?'

'A bit of that. It's more that we had a lot to do to make it look like our house. When a family's there for that long you can't just paint over it, if you know what I mean?' he said, knowing that George didn't know what he meant. Fortune saw to it that George had married the daughter of an immensely wealthy architect, and his home was built new to his family's specific tastes and requirements on a patch of land in the Chiltern Hills. Anya referred to it as *Grand Designs* porn. All angular shapes, bold lighting and living spaces that could just as well be office spaces. George's wife Cat had documented the entire thing on a dedicated Instagram account (@GandCforeverhome), which both Anya and Dan followed to mock and envy.

As far as their own renovations went, work on the Westleton cottage had started the day after they moved in. So far they'd redone the hallway, lounge, three of the four bedrooms and the kitchen, sharing the place with a revolving door of builders, plasterers, carpet fitters and electricians. After a week, Anya had bought a set of plain white china workmen's mugs, and a huge value pack of chocolate digestive biscuits, causing Dan to feel a little part of himself die every time he passed over a mug of tea or coffee, knowing that the recipient was firmly aware they were being kept away from the best crockery.

And there was no Instagram account to mark their progress.

'Well, it's yours now. It'll feel like it soon,' George said, as the two of them ambled past the piles of kids' shoes, wellies, scooters and bike helmets, towards the kitchen, where Dan had left a keg of beer from a small nearby brewery.

'I know.'

'And this is it, then, is it? You're done after this one. Not moving again.'

'That's the plan.'

'And you're not missing London?'

In all the chaos and stress of moving, Dan hadn't really thought about it much. His general transience had instilled the idea that he would never really miss a place. Nowhere was home. Not the north-east or Lincoln, where he had formed his earliest memories. Not London, where he had met Anya, got married, become a father and built a life.

Unlike Anya, he had never been one of those people who had the confidence and friendliness to know café owners, shopkeepers and publicans by name. Once, a case of mistaken identity led to a florist at a nearby market refer to him as Chris, and he'd never been able to correct him, which Anya found hilarious. Yet there were people around Queen's Park he'd come to know by face, if not name. Uprooting had necessarily meant leaving all that behind. At the same time, moving to a small village like this would make his world smaller, with fewer of those familiar strangers in it. Or more intimate, depending on which way you looked at things.

'I don't think so,' Dan said. 'Anya might. But she goes back there often enough for work.'

He turned the tap on the keg and poured pints for himself and George.

'And what about that bit, then? The two of you.'

'It's all right,' Dan said between sips.

'Good.'

'Actually. It feels better than all right at the moment,' Dan said, looking away. He was usually more comfortable talking about this kind of thing over WhatsApp or text. When there would be no need for eye contact and all that sort of thing. 'I don't know,' he continued. 'It's been so fucking long since things were okay between us that I've forgotten what it feels like. But, you know, we're happy. We're getting along.'

'Sex?'

'Fucking hell, George.'

'What?'

'What kind of question is that?'

'I'm just saying. If things are going well, back on track and all that. Well, then you might be… a bit more.'

Dan had taken a deliberately big glug of beer while George was talking. Time to plan his answer. He could lie, of course, and say that they were healthily regular. Even though he wasn't sure what that was, numbers-wise (once a week? Twice? More?). The truth was trickier, in that it was infrequent and, when it did happen, was a bit awkward and stilted. Dan hoped they were like a sportsperson coming out of retirement and struggling to find their rhythm and form, while knowing that the class was still there. But he worried that now that part of their lives would always be lacking.

Still, every marriage's sex life dies at some point, doesn't it? They probably only had ten or so good years left as it was.

'Don't you worry about that,' Dan said with half a smile. 'Things are good. We're good.'

They tapped glasses again.

* * *

The next morning, Anya and Nila were up early collecting bottles and cans while Dan washed every glass and mug they'd ever owned. The girls were on the couch with a few friends who'd stayed over, picking at toast and watching the television, with Martha showing the others photos Rhys had sent her of him in his uniform.

The party had wound down in the early evening.

The neighbours were the first to go, deciding that a Saturday night with a pizza and a game show was better than one with the extended circle of a family they hardly knew. Then most of their friends who had travelled up for the do had made their excuses to get on the road back to London, or to the B&Bs and hotels they had rented for a night without their kids.

That had left a small group that kept things going to the early hours. George and Cat. Nila. Tania and her boyfriend Seb. Jenna, Anya's oldest work friend, and her partner Kate.

They sat in the conservatory with the double doors open so Seb and Jenna could smoke. At one point, George mooted the idea of buying some weed, until he was reminded that they were in a quiet Suffolk village, and procuring drugs would be about as easy as finding an Uber or ordering Deliveroo.

Anya felt relieved. It had been years since she'd touched anything stronger than a Negroni, and while she didn't want to be a spoilsport, the idea of being stoned and then having to deal with life again in the morning was too much.

In the end, she and Dan finally went to bed at three, once they'd drunk through all the wine, most of the beer, and made a decent dent on their small cupboard of mostly ignored spirits, settling on a bottle of peach schnapps Anya's parents had gifted them after a holiday in Austria. They had come close to having sex, but their eyes drooped before their underwear could come off. Eventually, they passed out and got fewer than five hours of fretful sleep, mouths dried out by booze and talking, before they were up again.

'Jesus. It's the bending down,' Anya said, reaching for a

Birra Moretti can underneath a coffee table, and throwing it into a recycling box.

'Don't. I can't do this any more,' Nila said. 'I don't know why I stayed up. About eleven I was fine. You know, about right. I should've called it a night then. I don't even like schnapps.'

'No one likes schnapps. Unless they're a sixteen-year-old girl or on a skiing holiday.' Anya sat down heavily on the wooden armchair in the conservatory and put her face in her hands. 'Fucking hell,' she said. 'I feel *awful*.'

'I'm telling you. It was the schnapps. When was the last time you drank anything like that?'

'Uni. I was an Archers-and-lemonade girl in my first year. And it's not the schnapps. It's because we're almost forty and tired,' Anya said. 'Ah, Jesus! Who leaves a half-full can?' she said, toppling a BrewDog and watching it spill across their laminate floor.

'It was good, though,' Nila said, crouching down to soak it up with kitchen roll. 'Everyone had fun.'

'Well, that's something, then.'

'And you?'

'What?'

'Have fun?'

'Yeah,' Anya said. 'I did.'

'I know you didn't want to have the party.'

'Dan said it would be a good idea. A proper new start or whatever.'

'He was right.'

'About the party maybe,' Anya said, shielding her face as the sunlight beamed in through the window next to her.

'Which means?'

'Nothing,' she said with a smile. 'Joke.'

'I'm just saying that you seem happier. I always said that you can't ignore the… you know.'

'Sex with other people?'

Anya's saying it made her friend wince. Like she'd been slagging someone off who was standing just behind her.

'If you must. Anyway. I thought that you can't put that behind you and move on. Like, once it's done it's done.'

'Trust me, it very much is done.'

'But,' Nila continued, gamely ignoring Anya's attempts to derail her, 'maybe you're the ones who can get past it? Keep going for the greater good.'

'Nila,' Anya said, audibly exhausted. 'I appreciate it. But I'm not really up for a talk right now. I can only focus on one thing and that is making this house less of a shithole.'

'Fine. I'm just saying. It looks like things are good.'

Anya looked over at her friend and smiled. 'They're better,' she said. 'A lot better.'

'See?' she said with a smile. 'You never needed the counselling. Just a new house and a big party.'

The mention of it reminded her of the three sessions they had made it to, before he refused to show up for one (which she then used for an hour-long vent-cum-character-assassination). The realisation that talking about their problems was only making them worse.

'Maybe,' Anya said. 'We could've saved that five hundred quid.'

* * *

Nila left the Moorcrofts alone shortly after lunch, heading back to London in her rented car, with half a cake and a platter of sausage rolls for company. As they stood on their doorstep to wave her off, Dan put his hand around Anya's waist and pulled her close. She looked round and kissed his cheek, as Edie and Martha turned away to go back into the house and recommence their argument about whose half-hour it was with the iPad.

'That was good,' Dan said, looking up into the bright, clear sky.

'It was.'

He kissed her again. 'You're good.'

'So are you,' she said.

Neither of them dared say it, but both were thinking the same thing.

We're good.

And neither of them knew that it would be the last time the statement was true.

NOW

They were sat at a small Formica table on uncomfortable hard plastic chairs, attached by a pair of chipped, black-painted metal arms, ensuring they stayed at a fixed distance from each other. Two cups of black coffee sat between them, as well as a blueberry muffin that looked a little sweaty inside a plastic wrapper branded with *The Happy Cake Co.*, amidst the leftover crumbs and granules of sugar from whoever had been sitting there before.

The hospital café was quiet, even though it was dinner time. Maybe the friends and relatives of patients were off at the nearest McDonald's, or the kebab shop across the road that Dan supposed did a roaring trade with new fathers, tired staff and the friends of drunkards who'd ended their Saturday nights in the A & E rather than the nightclub.

They had managed to escape when Colm and Angela returned with teas and Kit Kats. Edie was still on the iPad, engrossed in a subtitled episode of an internet TV show Anya was sure (but not certain) was too old for her. Martha was rereading the third Harry Potter book, now on her second lap around that particular track. The grandparents, perhaps sensing something, offered to watch them.

'Who wants to go first, then?' Dan said, opening the muffin. 'About us, I mean.'

'Thanks for clarifying,' Anya said, pulling off a lump of the cloying blueberry cake, immediately sure that one between two wasn't going to be enough.

'Only if you're okay to talk about it now, I mean. I know you weren't so keen on—'

'The cab.'

'No.'

'While I was worrying about our daughter in hospital.'

'Sure. No. I mean, I understand why you didn't want to—'

'With the driver sitting right there.'

'Fine. Look, Anya, I was just saying. I get it.'

She took another bit of muffin and tried the coffee – still far too hot to drink.

'So. I'll go first, then,' he said. 'If you want?'

'Okay,' she said. And as she did, Anya felt that flutter again.

'Well… look. I don't think either of us are sure about it, are we?' Dan said, looking up as she looked down. Would this whole thing happen without eye contact, he wondered. As if they were nervous teenagers negotiating the terms of a first kiss at a school disco.

'I mean. If we're going to go through with it. Like, actually do it. Well, we should be sure, shouldn't we? Because there's not a lot of going back when we sign the papers.'

'Tell me why you're not sure,' Anya said.

Dan thought for a moment, uncertain about how easy it would be to specify his feelings.

'Well…' he began. He would never have been any good at job interviews for just this reason. A difficult question with the expectation of an immediate answer was always likely to wrong-foot him. 'Well, I suppose you know why. I still love you. And I don't want this.'

'But you already said that. Outside at the office.'

'Because it's true.'

'But love was never the problem, was it? I look at you,' she said, and for a moment their eyes locked, before Dan

279

tilted his head back to drink some coffee, which set Anya off thinking that his was cooler than hers.

'You look at me, what?'

'Sorry. I was saying that I look at you and I know I still love you. I absolutely know that. Like, I'd be devastated if you died.'

'And that's how you quantify love, is it?'

'Well, how else do you quantify it? To the fucking moon and back?'

'Fine. So love isn't the problem.'

'No. And, you know, I admit that the past two days have made me wonder if we're making a fucking terrible decision. Particularly because of… you know.'

'Last night?'

'Dan,' she said firmly.

'Because it was good, wasn't it? Like old times.'

'Fine. Yes. But…'

'But what?'

Anya hesitated. The analogy had come to her earlier. Now she wasn't sure if it was too cruel. Too on the nose.

'Have you… Have you ever heard of this thing, right, where people who are about to die have, like, one last moment when they're lucid and okay? One last glimmer and everyone thinks they're going to be okay. And then the next day they're gone?'

'No.'

'Well, it happens,' she said, trying the coffee again. 'Apparently. And… well, what if that was us?'

'That we're dying anyway.'

'You know what I mean.'

'Lovely.'

'Come on, Dan. You take the point.'

'That last night was the last wag of the dog's tail before the vet puts the needle in?'

'I suppose. If you want to put it like that. What I mean is that, yes, fine, the love and all that. But we loved each other when we were arguing all the time. I loved you when I was with Kelvin. You loved me when you were screwing that Eleanor woman. The love was never in doubt. It was everything else.'

Dan didn't respond. Maybe, she thought, it was the mention of Eleanor and Kelvin. Those two spectres that continued to hover above them.

'I mean, we became those people, didn't we?' Anya said. 'The ones who paid too much attention to the kids. To the dog. To what to have for dinner. To bloody box sets. But not enough to each other. And who's to say that two months from now we don't do that again?'

'I know what you mean,' Dan said. He sounded pleading rather than as if he was trying to convince her. 'But I still don't think last night was a mistake. I think *that* was right. And maybe everything else is wrong,' he said. 'Sidebar, do you fancy another muffin?'

'That's not how it works. The sidebar has to be an observation. Not asking a question.'

'Shit,' he said with a smile that she returned, looking at the last mouthful being picked away at crumb by crumb, wondering if she should just go for it. 'Anyway. I mean, if it wasn't for Martha we might not even be having this conversation. Maybe—'

'If you even so much as dare say it was a sign I'll leave right now.'

'I wasn't!'

'Good.'

Dan and Anya picked up their drinks, as a man carrying the shell-shocked, hangdog look of a new father ambled in and picked up two teas and a cling-film-wrapped cheese roll that could well have been there since the hospital was built. The taps of cups being placed down on the table felt as loud as sirens.

'I just wish I could be as certain as you are,' Anya said.

'Jesus, Anya. I'm anything but certain. We've just done

two days of divorce mediation. We got as close as anyone does to ending a marriage. And now we're sitting here talking about trying again.'

The words were shocking and sobering to them both.

Trying again.

It was the first time either of them had said it out loud and admitted the purpose of this conversation.

Of course they had tried again. A few times. After each of their infidelities, they had tried again, promising to air out their problems, before stuffing so many of them under the rug it became impossible to walk across it. They'd tried again when things were so bad they could barely live together and committed to counselling sessions that neither were comfortable with. They'd tried when they moved out of London, mistakenly thinking that a change of scene would bring with it a change in attitude and temperament.

At their wedding, George had read Seamus Heaney's poem 'Scaffolding'. With more foresight, she'd have swapped it for some words by another Irish writer:

Ever tried. Ever failed. No matter. Try again. Fail again. Fail better.

Anya had once thought about getting it mocked up like other people have *LiveLoveLaugh*. It certainly represented their family life more than anything motivational.

But this was surely a different flavour of trying again.

'Do you think it'd be any different?' Anya said, knowing that this was the closest she'd got so far to admitting she had the same desires and the same worries as Dan. On one shoulder was her hope to have her partner back. On the other, wisdom and experience telling her exactly why she should let him go.

'I don't know. I hope so,' he said. 'Look. What I do know is that if we end this… as in… we decide that maybe last night was… whatever. My point is if we do that, then I don't think we'll be happier than we could be if we gave it another go. I don't think there's anyone… I don't know… better out there for us.'

'That's the big speech, then, is it?' she said. '"There's

nothing better coming along so you might as well stick with what you've got". It's hardly Richard Curtis, Dan.'

'You know I don't mean that.'

'I do,' she said. 'But even if you did, you've got a point.'

'What?'

'Fucking hell, Dan,' she said, attracting the glare of an elderly couple, both still in their winter coats despite the boiling hospital temperature. 'I'm forty. I don't want to find someone new. The thought of another first date kills me.'

'A new set of parents.'

'Don't. Can you imagine? You'd need a cargo plane for all the baggage.'

As Dan laughed, Anya looked around the room. How had they ended up having this conversation here? In a drab little hospital café, surrounded by posters about the signs of a stroke and domestic violence, and office-printed notices asking people to use the correct bins for the recycling.

'So,' Dan said, finishing his coffee. 'What are you thinking?'

Anya looked up. Her stomach was churning. More than it had been when they decided to get the divorce in the first place.

'I'll tell you what I was thinking on my way here,' she said. 'On the train.'

'That you want to move to St Albans?'

'Not quite. I was thinking that this, marriage – people say that it's a marathon, not a sprint, right? But it's not, is it? Sometimes it's a… a… a fucking trudge or something. It's slow and it's difficult and, you know, a lot of the time it's quite annoying.'

'Right.'

'And the last two days. Well, I suppose they've taught me that maybe I'm not done trudging yet,' she said.

And suddenly all the exterior noise was blocked out. The hiss of the milk frother on the coffee machine silenced, the quiet chatter hushed, the television muted. And it was just the two of them, there in the hospital canteen, a scrap of blueberry muffin, some crumbs and two empty coffee cups between them.

'So what are you saying?'

'I'm saying, I suppose, that I'm still here. Still in it, if you like,' she said, looking up at Dan. 'If you are.'

Dan didn't say anything, at first. Instead, he just reached across the table, and took her hand. In response, she squeezed his, as if to shake on the deal.

'You're saying you want to trudge on?' Dan then said, unwilling – unable – to let go.

'I mean, hopefully we might be running again some day. But for now I'm all right to trudge.'

'Trudging it is, then,' he said.

They didn't kiss. Or embrace. They both smiled a little, perhaps accepting that this wasn't a victory as such. More the narrow avoidance of defeat. A last-minute equaliser to save blushes.

Dan looked up above her head to the clock by the café. Well into the evening now. Almost the weekend.

'Can I ask something?'

'I'll warn you, I don't have many details to explain my decision. Jesus, Matt'll be livid.'

'Fuck Matt.'

'Sure,' she said, struggling to hide a grin. 'What do you want to know?'

'What changed your mind? Like, earlier today—'

'There was always doubt. A bit anyway. But if you must know, it's because I thought that one day I could look at you and say, nah, not any more. But every night I still go to bed and I miss you being next to me, and wish we'd made a better job of things. I always told myself that soon I'd be over it. I'd be fine. I'd move on. But that day never seems to fucking come. And that tells me that we're still worth something.'

'I know what you mean,' Dan said quietly.

'But if we do this, y'know… try,' she said. 'We've got to be better about it. Give each other space. Let ourselves make mistakes.'

'Sure.'

'And there's a lot to work out now. Houses and money. And where we want to live.'

'Ireland's fine for me.'

'Is it?'

'As long as you're there.'

'Fuck off,' she said, rolling her eyes. 'We'll have to tell the girls.'

'I'm sure they'll be all right with it.'

'Look. What I'm saying is that it's not going to be easy, necessarily.'

'I know.'

'We're not easy.'

'I know.'

'But we are… well, we're probably right for each other. As luck would have it.'

'I know,' Dan said, and squeezed her hand again. 'Good job we decided that before it was too late.'

'I know,' she said. 'You know I love you, don't you?'

'I do. And you.'

Anya smiled and nodded. Relieved. Almost happy. Still a little bit uncertain. But the flutter had gone for a moment. Which was a good sign, she supposed.

And that, seemingly, was it.

No romance. No celebrations. No glory in their saved marriage and family. Just acceptance that this was right, or at least better than the alternative. Instead, they stood up from the table and, hand in hand, went back to the ward where Martha was up from her bed, ready to be discharged.

Then the four of them – Dan, Anya, Martha and Edie, with her parents in tow – found their way back through the corridors of the hospital. They walked through the reception and out the sliding double doors into the cool February evening, ready to go back home.

ACKNOWLEDGEMENTS

Getting a book to publication relies on the help, support and guidance of a lot of people. I'd like to thank the following for their work on The Brink.

Firstly, my agent Charlie Campbell and everyone at Greyhound Literary for their dedication to my writing and books. And my editor Cari Rosen, along with the team at Legend Press, for taking The Brink on, turning a manuscript into a book, and their collective effort to get it to readers.

I'd like to thank the many reviewers and booksellers who have been a part of my career so far. Most notably Nina Pottell, Keeba Roy, Matt at Waterstones in Berkhamsted, and Ben and the good folk at the tremendous Our Bookshop in Tring. As well as the editors who have commissioned work from me over the years.

As ever, I want to thank my pals and colleagues at Octopus Group, the wonderful network of supportive friends around me, and my family – particularly my parents – for their unwavering support.

Finally, I want to thank and dedicate this book to my boys, Rufus and Wilf, and my brilliant wife, Alice.

Thank you all.

Follow Legend Press on Twitter
@legend_times_

Follow Legend Press on Instagram
@legend_times